Baroness Orczy was born i
of Baron Felix Orczy, a l
composer and conductor. O.... ....
Budapest to Brussels and Paris, where she was educated. She
studied art in London and exhibited work in the Royal
Academy.

Orczy married Montagu Barstow and together they worked
as illustrators and jointly published an edition of Hungarian
folk tales. Orczy became famous in 1905 with the publication
of *The Scarlet Pimpernel* (originally a play co-written with her
husband). Its background of the French Revolution and
swashbuckling hero, Sir Percy Blakeney, was to prove
immensely popular. Sequel books followed and film and TV
versions were later made. Orczy also wrote detective stories.

She died in 1947.

BY THE SAME AUTHOR
ALL PUBLISHED BY HOUSE OF STRATUS

SIR PERCY
HITS BACK

Baroness Orczy

HOUSE OF
STRATUS

This edition published in 2008 by House of Stratus, an imprint of Stratus Books Ltd., Lisandra House, Fore Street, Looe, Cornwall, PL13 1AD, U.K..

www.houseofstratus.com

Typeset, printed and bound by House of Stratus.

A catalogue record for this book is available from the British Library and the Library of Congress.

ISBN 0-7551-1667-4

One

On the spot where the Hotel Moderne now rears its more ambitious head, there stood at that time a cottage with sloping red-tiled roof and whitewashed walls. It was owned by one Baptiste Portal, an old peasant of the Dauphiné, who dispensed refreshments to travellers and passers-by, as his father and grandfather had done before him, in the shape of somewhat thin *vin du pays* and an occasional glass of *eau-de-vie*, while he spent his slack time chiefly in grumbling at the fact that the new posting-inn on the high road had taken all his trade away. He did not see the necessity of the posting-inn, did not old Baptiste, nor for a matter of that of the high road or the post-chaise. Before all these new notions had come into the heads of the government people up in Paris, travellers had been content to come squelching through the mud on the back of a good horse, or come ploughing through inches of dust in the old *cocith*. So why not now? And was not the old wine of Les Amandiers as good and better than the vinegar dispensed at the more pretentious posting-inn? The place was called Les Amandiers because at the back of the house there were two anaemic almond trees with gaunt, twisted arms which covered themselves in the spring with sickly blooms, and in the summer with dust. In front of the house, up against the whitewashed wall, there was a wooden bench on which Baptiste's privileged customers were wont to sit on fine evenings, to drink their *vin du pays* and join the old man in his wholesale condemnation of the government "up in Paris" and its new-fangled ways. From this vantage-point a glorious view was obtained over the valley of the Buëche, and beyond Laragne as far as the peaks of Pelvoux: whilst to the right towered in the distance the grand old citadel of Sisteron with its turrets and fortifications dating from the fourteenth century, and the stately church of Notre Dame. But views and winding rivers, snowy peaks and mediaeval fortresses did not interest Baptiste Portal's customers nearly as much as the price of almonds or the alarming increase in the cost of living.

Now on this particular afternoon in May the mistral was blowing mercilessly across the valley from over the snows of Pelvoux, and the cold and the dust had driven all the good Portal's customers indoors. The low-raftered room, decorated with strings of onions which hung from the ceiling together with a bunch or two of garlic, of basil and other pot-herbs, and perfumed also with the aroma of the *pot-au-feu* simmering in the kitchen, had acquired just that right atmosphere, cosy, warm and odorous, beloved of every true man born in Dauphiné. It was a memorable afternoon, remembered long afterwards and retold by the gossips of Sisteron and Laragne in all its dramatic details. But at this hour, nothing more dramatic had occurred than the arrival of a detachment of soldiers, under the command of an under-officer, who had come up from Orange, so they said, in order to fetch away the young men who were wanted for the army. They had demanded supper and shelter for the night.

Of course soldiers, as soldiers, were very much disapproved of by those worthies of Sisteron who frequented Les Amandiers, more especially now when what they did was to fetch away the young men for cannon-fodder, to fight the English and prolong this awful war which caused food to be so dear and hands for harvesting so scarce. But on the other hand, soldiers as company were welcome. They brought news of the outside world, most of it bad, it is true – nothing good did happen anywhere these days – but news nevertheless. And though at the recital of what went on in Paris, in Lyons or even as near as Orange, the guillotine, the tumbrils, the wholesale slaughter of tyrants and aristos, one shuddered with horror and apprehension, there were always the lively tales of barrack-life to follow, the laughter, the ribald song, and something of life seemed to filtrate into this sleepy half-dead corner of old Dauphiné.

The soldiers – there were a score of them – occupied the best place in the room, as was only fitting; they sat, squeezed tightly against one another like dried figs in a box, on the two benches on either side of the centre trestle-table. Old Baptiste Portal sat with them beside the officer. Some kind of lieutenant this man appeared to be, or other subaltern; but oh dear me! these days one could hardly tell an officer from the rag-tag and bobtail of the army, save for the fact that he wore epaulettes. Now this man – but there! what was the use of comparing these ruffians with the splendid officers of the King's armies in the past?

This one certainly was not proud. He sat with his men, joked, drank with them, and presently he convened friend Portal to a glass of wine: "À la santé," he added, "de la République, and of Citizen Robespierre, the great and incorruptible master of France!"

Baptiste, wagging his old head, had not liked to refuse, because soldiers were soldiers and these had been at great pains to explain to him that the reason why the guillotine was kept so busy was because Frenchmen had not yet learned to be good Republicans.

"We've cut off the head of Louis Capet and of the widow Capet too," the officer had added with grim significance, "but there are still Frenchmen who are bad patriots and hanker after the return of the tyrants."

Now Baptiste, like all his like in the Dauphiné, had learned in childhood to worship God and honour the King. The crime of regicide appeared to him unforgivable, like that mysterious sin against the Holy Ghost, which M. le Curé used vaguely to

3

hint at, and which no one understood. In addition to that Baptiste greatly resented His late Majesty King Louis XVI and his august Queen being irreverently referred to as Louis Capet and the widow Capet. But he kept his own counsel and silently drank his wine. What his thoughts were at the moment was nobody's business.

After that, talk drifted to the neighbourhood: the aristos who still clung to the land which by right belonged to the people. Neither Baptiste nor his customers – old peasants from the district – were a match for the lieutenant and his corporals in such discussions. They did not dare argue, only shook their heads and sighed at the coarse jests which the soldiers uttered against people and families whom everyone in the Dauphiné knew and esteemed.

The Frontenacs for instance.

The talk and the jests had turned on the Frontenacs: people who had owned the land for as long as the oldest inhabitant could remember and God only knows how long before that. Well! it appeared that in the eyes of these soldiers of the Republic the Frontenacs were bad patriots, tyrants and traitors. Didn't Citizen Portal know that?

No! Portal did not – he had never been called "citizen" before, and didn't like it: he was just Baptiste to those who knew him, quoi? – Nor would he admit that the Frontenacs were traitors. There was Monsieur, who knew more about cattle and almonds than any man for leagues around. How could he be a bad patriot? And Madame, who was very good and pious, and Mademoiselle who was so ill and delicate. But on this there followed an altercation – stern rebuke of Baptiste from the officer for talking of "Monsieur", of "Madame" and "Mademoiselle". Bah! there were no aristos left these days. "Aren't we all citizens of France?" the lieutenant concluded grandiloquently.

Silence and submission on the part of all the groundlings which followed on the lieutenant's rebuke, somewhat mollified the latter's aggressive patriotism. He condescended to relate how he had been deputed to make a perquisition in the house of the Frontenacs, and if anything was found the least compromising, then the devil help the whole brood: their lives would not be worth an hour's purchase. In fact, in the lieutenant's opinion – and who better qualified to hold one? – the Frontenacs were already judged, condemned, and as good as guillotined. He held with the "law of the suspect," lately enacted by the National Assembly, did Lieutenant Godet.

Again much wagging of heads! "The Committees in all Sections," Godet now goes on airily, and proceeds to pick his teeth after that excellently stewed scrag-end of mutton, "the Committees in all Sections are ordered in future to arrest all persons who are suspect."

No one knows what is a Committee, nor yet a Section: but they are evidently fearsome things. But no matter about them: the thing is who are the "suspect" who are thus arrestable?

"The Frontenacs are suspect," the lieutenant explains whilst sucking his tooth-pick, "and so are all persons who by their actions – or – their writings have become – er – suspect."

Not very illuminating perhaps, but distinctly productive of awe. The worthies of Sisteron, those who are privileged to sit close to the centre table and actually to put in a word with the soldiers, sip their wine in silence. Just below the tiny window at the end of the room two charcoal-burners, or wood-cutters – I know not what they are – are lending an attentive ear. They dare not join in the conversation because they are comparative strangers, vagabonds really, come to pick up a few sous by doing menial work too lowering for a local peasant to do. One of them is small and slender, but looks vigorous; the other, much older, with stooping shoulders, and grey, lank hair that falls over a wrinkled forehead. He is harassed by a constant, tearing cough which he strives in vain to suppress out of respect for the company.

"But," the worthy Portal puts in tentatively, "how does one know Monsieur le – I mean citizen officer, that a person is in verity suspect?"

The lieutenant explains with a sweeping gesture of the tooth-pick: "If you are a good patriot, Citizen Portal, you are able to recognize a Suspect in the street, you can seize him by the collar then and there, and you may drag him off before the Committee, who will promptly clap him in prison. And remember," he added significantly, "that there are forty-four thousand Committees in France today."

"Forty-four thousand?" somebody exclaims.

"And twenty-three," Godet replies, gloating over his knowledge of this trifling detail. "Forty-four thousand and twenty-three," he reiterates and claps the table with the palm of his hand.

"One in Sisteron?" someone murmurs.

"Three!" the lieutenant replies.

"And the Frontenacs are suspect, you say?"

"I shall know that tomorrow," rejoins the other, "and so will you."

The way he said those three last words caused everyone to shudder. Over at the far end of the room, the charcoal-burner, or whatever he was, had a tearing fit of coughing.

" 'Tis little Fleurette who will weep her eyes out," good old Baptiste said with a doleful shake of the head, "if anything happens to Mad – to the citizens up at the château."

"Fleurette?" the lieutenant asked.

"She is Armand's daughter – Citizen Armand you know – why?"

He might well stare, for the officer, for some unaccountable reason, had burst into a loud guffaw.

"Citizen Armand's daughter did you say?" he queried at last, his eyes still streaming with the effort of laughing.

"Yes, of course. As pretty a wench as you can see in Dauphiné. Why shouldn't Armand have a daughter, I'd like to know."

"Do tigers have daughters?" the lieutenant retorted significantly.

Somehow the conversation languished after that.

The fate which so obviously awaited the Frontenacs, who were known and loved, cast a gloom over the most buoyant spirits. Not even the salacious stories of barrack-life, on which the men now embarked with much gusto, found responsive laughter.

It was getting late too. Past eight o'clock, and tallow was dear these days. There was a cart-shed at the back of the house, with plenty of clean straw: some of the soldiers declared themselves ready for a stretch there: even the voluble officer was yawning. The regular customers of Les Amandiers took the hint. They emptied their mugs, paid over their sous, and trooped out one by one.

The wind had gone down. There was not a cloud in the sky, which was a deep and intense sapphire blue, studded with stars. The waning moon was not yet up, and the atmosphere was redolent of the perfume of almond-blossom. Altogether a lovely night. Nature in her kindest, most gentle mood. Spring in the air and life stirring in the entrails of the earth in travail. Some of the soldiers made their way to the shed, whilst others stretched out on the floor, or the benches of the room, there to dream perhaps of the perquisition to be made tomorrow and of the tragedy which would enter like a sudden devastating gust of wind into the peaceful home of the Frontenacs.

Nature was kind and gentle: and men were cruel and evil and vengeful. The Law of the Suspect! No more cruel, more tyrannical law was ever enacted within the memory of civilization. Forty-four thousand and twenty-three Committees to mow down the flower of the children of France. A harvest of innocents! And lest the harvesters prove slack, the National Convention has just decreed that a perambulating army shall march up and down the country, to ferret out the Suspect and to feed the guillotine. Lest the harvesters prove slack, men like Lieutenant Godet with a score of out-at-elbows, down-at-heels brigands, are ordered to scour the country, to seize and strike. To feed the guillotine in fact, and to purge the Soil of Liberty.

Is this not the most glorious revolution the world has ever known? Is it not the era of Liberty and of the Brotherhood of Man?

Two

The perambulating army had now gone to rest: some in the cart-shed, some along the benches and tables or floor of the inn. The lieutenant in a bed. Is he not the officer commanding this score of ardent patriots? Therefore must he lie in a bed – old Portal's bed – whilst old Portal himself and his wife, older and more decrepit than he, can lie on the floor, or in the dog's kennel for aught Lieutenant Godet cares.

The two wood-cutters – or shall we call them charcoal-burners? – were among the last to leave. They had petitioned for work among the worthies here present: but money was very scarce these days and each man did what work he could for himself, and did not pay another to do it for him. But Papa Tronchet, who was a carpenter by trade and owned a little bit of woodland just by the bridge, close to Armand's cottage, he promised one of the men – not both – a couple of hours' work tomorrow: wood-cutting at the rate of two sous an hour, and then he thought it dear.

And so the company had dispersed: each man to his home. The two vagabonds – wood-cutters or charcoal-burners, they were anyhow vagabonds – found their way into the town. Wearily they trudged, for one of them was very old and the other lame, till they reached a narrow lane at right angles to the riverbank. The lane was made up of stone houses that had overhanging eaves, between which the sun could never penetrate. It was invariably either as damp as the bottom of a well, or as dry and wind-swept as an iron stove-pipe. Tonight it was dry and hot: broken-down shutters, innocent of paint, creaked upon rusty hinges. A smell of boiled cabbage, of stale water and garlic hung beneath the eaves; it came in great gusts down pitch-dark stairways, under narrow doors, oozing with sticky moisture.

The two vagabonds turned into one of these doors and by instinct seemingly, for it was pitch dark, they mounted the stone stairs that squelched with grease and dirt underneath their feet. They did not speak a word until they came to the top of the house, when one of them with a kick of his boot threw open a door; it groaned and creaked under the blow. It gave on an attic-room with sloping ceiling, black with the dirt of ages, and with dormer window masked by a tattered rag that had once been a curtain. There was a wooden table in the centre of the room, and three chairs, with broken backs and ragged rush-seats, dotted about. On the table a couple of tallow candles guttered in pewter sconces.

One of the chairs was drawn close up to the table and on it sat a young man dressed in a well-worn travelling coat with heavy boots on his feet, and a shabby tricorne hat on the top of his head. His arms were stretched out over the table and his face was buried in them. He had obviously been asleep when the door was so unceremoniously thrown open. At the sound he raised his head and blinked drowsily in the dim light at the newcomers.

Then he stretched out his arms, yawned and gave himself a shake like a sleepy dog, and finally exclaimed in English: "Ah! at last!"

One of the vagabonds – the one namely who at Les Amandiers had appeared with bent shoulders and a hacking cough, now straightened out what proved to be a magnificent athletic figure, and gave a pleasant laugh.

"Tony, you lazy dog!" he said, "I've a mind to throw you downstairs. What say you, Ffoulkes? While you and I have been breaking our backs and poisoning our lungs with the scent of garlic, I verily believe that this villain Tony has been fast asleep."

"By all means let's throw him downstairs," assented the second vagabond, now no longer lame, whom his friend had addressed as Ffoulkes.

"What would you have me do but sleep?" Tony broke in with a laugh. "I was told to wait, and so I waited. I'd far rather have been with you."

"No, you wouldn't," Ffoulkes demurred, "for then you would have been dirtier than I, and almost as filthy as Blakeney. Look at him; did you ever see such a disgusting object?"

"By Gad!" rejoined Blakeney surveying his own slender hands coated with coal-dust, grease and grime, "I don't know when I have been quite so dirty. Soap and water!" he commanded with a lofty gesture, "or I perish."

But Tony gave a rueful shrug.

"I have a bit of soap in my pocket," he said, and diving into the capacious pocket of his coat he produced an infinitesimal remnant of soap which he threw upon the table. "As for water, I can't offer you any. The only tap in the house is in the back kitchen which Madame, our worthy landlady, has locked up for the night. She won't have anything wasted, she tells me, not even water."

"Fine, thrifty people, your Dauphinois," commented Blakeney, wisely shaking his head. "But did you try bribery?"

"Yes! But Madame – I beg your pardon, Citizeness Marlot – immediately called me a cursed aristo, and threatened me with some committee or other. I couldn't argue with her, she reeked of garlic."

"And you, Tony, are an arrant coward," Blakeney rejoined, "where garlic is concerned."

"I am," Tony was willing to admit. "That's why I am so terrified of you both at this moment."

They all laughed, and since water was not obtainable, Sir Percy Blakeney, one of the most exquisite dandies of his time, and his friend Sir Andrew Ffoulkes, sat down on rickety chairs, in clothes sticky with dirt, their faces and hands masked by a thick coating of grime. Down the four walls of the small, attic-room fillets of greasy moisture trickled and mingled with the filth that lay in cakes upon the floor.

"I can't bear to look at Tony," Blakeney said with a mock sigh, "he is too demned clean."

"We'll soon remedy that," was Ffoulkes' dry comment.

And behold Sir Andrew Ffoulkes at close grips with Lord Antony Dewhurst, and this in silence for fear of disturbing the rest of the house, and bringing attention on themselves. It was a sparring match in the best style, Blakeney acting as referee, its object – to transfer some of the grime that coated the clothes and hands of Sir Andrew onto the immaculate Lord Tony. They were only boys after all, these men, who even now were risking their lives in order to rescue the innocent from the clutches of a bloody tyranny. They were boys in their love of adventure, and in their hero worship, and men in the light-hearted way in which they were prepared for the supreme sacrifice, should luck turn against them.

The sparring match ended in a call for mercy on the part of Lord Tony. His face was plastered with grime, his hands as dirty as those of his friends.

"Tony," Blakeney said finally when he called a halt, "if her ladyship were to see you now she would divorce you."

Vent having been given to unconquerable animal spirits, there was a quick return to the serious business of the day.

"What is the latest?" Lord Tony asked.

"Just this," Sir Percy replied: "That those hell-hounds have sent out detachments of soldiers all over the country to ferret out what they are pleased to call treason. We all know what that means. Since their iniquitous 'Law of the Suspect', no man, woman or child is safe from denunciation: now with this perambulating army, summary arrests occur by the thousand. It seems that at any moment any of those brigands can seize you by the coat-collar and drag you before one of their precious committees, who promptly sends you to the nearest guillotine."

"And you came across a detachment of those brigands, I suppose."

"We have; Ffoulkes and I spent a couple of hours in their company, in the midst of fumes of garlic that would have reduced you, Tony, to a drivelling coward. I vow the smell of it has even infested my hair."

"Anything to be done?" Tony asked simply. He knew his chief well enough to perceive the vein of grim earnestness through all this flippancy.

"Yes!" Blakeney replied. "The squad of brigands who are scouring this part of France are principally after a family named Frontenac, which consists of father, mother and an invalid daughter. I had already found out something about them in the course of the day, whilst I carted some manure for a farmer close by. Beastly stuff manure, by the way! I tried to get into touch with Monsieur, who is a stubborn optimist, and does not believe that any man could mean harm to him or to his family. I went to him in the guise of a royalist agent, supposed to have inside information of impending arrests. He simply refused to believe me. Well! we've met that type of man before. He will have a terrible awakening tomorrow."

Sir Percy paused for a moment or two, a deep frown between his brows. His keen intellect, alive to all those swift tragedies which he had devoted his life to countermine was already at work envisaging the immediate future, the personages of the coming drama, husband, wife, invalid daughter; then the perquisition, the arrest, summary condemnation and slaughter of three helpless innocents.

"I can't help being sorry for the man," he said after awhile, "though he is an obstinate fool! but it is the wife and daughter whom we cannot allow those savage beasts to capture and to kill. I caught sight of them. The girl is pathetic, frail and crippled. I couldn't bear – "

He broke off abruptly. No need to say more, of course; they understood one another these men who had braved death so often together for love of humanity and for love of sport. Blakeney silent, one firm, slender hand clutched upon the table, was working out a problem of how to rescue three helpless people from that certain death-trap which was already laid for them. The other two waited in equal silence for orders. The League of the Scarlet Pimpernel! pledged to help the innocent and to save the helpless! One to command, nineteen to obey: the two who were here in this filthy, dark attic-room, were the chief's most trusted officers; but the others were not far away!

Seventeen others! scattered about the countryside, disguised, doing menial work in order to keep in touch with the population, spying, hiding in woods or huts; all of them under orders from their chiefs, and prepared for the call from him.

"Tony," Blakeney said at last, "you'd better find Hastings and Stowmaries at once and they must pass the word round to the others. I want three of them – they can draw lots for that – to go to the Four Oaks and there to remain until I can send Ffoulkes to them with full instructions. When you've done that, I want you and Ffoulkes to spend the night in and about Les Amandiers, and gather what you can of the projects of those brigands by keeping your ears open. I'll keep in touch with you from time to time."

"You think," Ffoulkes put in, "that we'll have trouble with the Frontenacs?"

"Not with the ladies, of course," Blakeney replied. "We'll get them safely out of the way before the perambulating army of jackals arrives. With God's help we ought to have time enough to gather a few valuables together. The trouble will be with that obstinate, tiresome man. I feel sure he won't move until the soldiers are hammering at his door. Anyway, I shall know my way in and about the château by tomorrow morning, and will then get into touch with you both at Les Amandiers."

He rose: a tall, straight figure on whom the filthy clothes of a vagabond wood-cutter sat with strange incongruity. But even in this strange garb, which was grotesque as well as degrading, there was an extraordinary dignity in the carriage of the head, the broad shoulders, the firm, long Anglo-Saxon limbs, but above all in the flash of the eyes beneath their heavy lids and in the quiet, low-toned voice so obviously accustomed to be heard and obeyed. The two others were ready on the instant to act according to instructions; to act without argument or question. The fire of excitement was in their eyes: the spirit of adventure, of sport for sport's sake had them in its grip.

"Do I go with you now, Blakeney?" Ffoulkes asked, as his chief had remained for a moment standing, as if following a train of thought.

"Yes," Blakeney replied. "And by the way, Ffoulkes, and you too, Tony, while you are at Les Amandiers try and find out about this girl Fleurette the old innkeeper spoke about. He said that the girl would cry her eyes out if anything happened to the Frontenacs. You remember?"

"I do. He also said that she was as pretty a wench as could be found in Dauphiné," Ffoulkes put in with a smile.

"Her father is named Armand," Blakeney rejoined.

"And the lieutenant called him a tiger, rather enigmatically I thought."

"This Fleurette sounds an engaging young person," Lord Tony commented with a smile.

"And should be a useful one in our adventure," Blakeney concluded. "Find out what you can about her."

He was the last to leave the room. Ffoulkes and Lord Tony had already gone down the stone staircase, feeling their way through the darkness. But Sir Percy Blakeney stood for a minute or two longer, erect, silent, motionless. Not Sir Percy Blakeney, that is, the elegant courtier, the fastidious fop, the spoilt child of

London society, but the daring adventurer, ready, now as so often before, to throw his life in the balance to save three innocent people from death. Would he succeed? Nay! that he did not doubt. Not for a moment. He would save the Frontenacs as he had saved scores of helpless men, women and children before, or leave his bones to moulder in this fair land where his name had become anathema to the tigers that fed on the blood of their kindred. The true adventurer! Reckless of risks and dangers, with only the one goal in view: Success.

Sport? Of course it was sport! grand, glorious, maddening sport! Sport that made him forget every other joy in life, every comfort, every beatitude. Everything except the exquisite wife who in far-off England waited patiently, with deadly anxiety gnawing at her heart, for news of the man she worshipped. She, perhaps, the greatest heroine of them all.

With a quick sigh, half of impatience, half of longing, Sir Percy Blakeney finally blew out the tallow lights and made his way out into the open.

Three

The house where Fleurette was born and where she spent the first eighteen years of her life, still stands about half-way down the road between Sisteron and Serres and close to Laragne, which was then only a village nestling in the valley of the Buëche. To get to it you must first go cautiously down the slope at the head of the old stone bridge, and then climb up another slope to the front door beside the turbulent little mill stream, the soft gurgle of which had lulled Fleurette to sleep ever since her tiny ears had wakened to earthly sounds.

The house is a tumbledown ruin now, only partly roofed in: doors and shutters are half off their hinges: the outside staircase is worm-eaten and unsafe, the whitewashed walls are cracked and denuded of plaster; the little shrine above the door has long been bereft of its quaint, rudely painted statue of St Anthony of Padua with the Divine Child in his arms. But the wild vine still clings to the old walls, and in the gnarled branches of the old walnut tree, a venturesome pair of blackbirds will sometimes build their nest.

A certain atmosphere of mystery and romance still lingers in the tiny dell, and when we fly along the road in our twentieth-century motor car, we are conscious of this romantic feeling, and we exclaim: "Oh! how picturesque!" and ask the chauffeur to halt upon the bridge, and then get our Kodaks to work.

Perhaps when the plate is developed and we look upon the print, we fail to recapture that sense of a picturesque by-gone age, and wonder why we wasted a precious film on what is nothing but a tumbledown old cottage, and why so many tumbledown old cottages are left to crumble away and disfigure the lovely face of France. But a century and a half ago, when Fleurette was born, there was an almond tree beside the front door, which in the early spring looked as if covered with pink snow. In those days the shutters and the doors and the outside staircase were painted a beautiful green, the walls were resplendent with fresh whitewash every year. In those days too the wild vine turned to a brilliant crimson in the autumn, and in June the climbing rose was just a mass of bloom. Then in May the nightingale often sang in the old walnut tree, and later on, when Fleurette was tall enough, she always kept a bunch of forget-me-nots in a glass, in the recess above the front door, at the foot of the statue of St Antoine de Padoue, because, as is well known, he is the saint to appeal to in case one has lost anything one values. One just made the sign of the cross and said fervently: "St Antoine de Padoue priez pour nous!" and lo! the kindly saint would aid in the search and more often than not the lost treasure would be found.

All this was, of course, anterior to the horrible events which in a few days transformed the genial, kindly people of France into a herd of wild beasts thirsting for each other's blood, and before legalized cruelty, murder and regicide had arraigned that fair land at the bar of history, and tarnished her fair fame for ever. Fleurette was just eighteen when the terrible events came to pass that threatened to wreck her young life, and through which she learned not only how cruel and evil man could be, but also to what height of self-abnegation and heroism they could at times ascend.

Fleurette's birthday was in May, and that day was always for her the gladdest day of the year. For one thing she could reckon on Bibi being home – Bibi being the name by which she had called her father ever since she had learned to babble. Fleurette had no mother, and she and Bibi just worshipped each other. And of course Bibi had come home for her eighteenth birthday, and had stayed three whole days, and he had brought her a lovely shawl, one that was so soft and fleecy that when you rubbed your cheek against it, it felt just like a caress from a butterfly's wing.

Old Louise – who had looked after the house and watched over Fleurette ever since Fleurette's mother had gone up to Heaven to be with the *bon Dieu* and all the Saints – old Louise had cooked a delicious dinner, which was a very difficult thing to do these days when food was scarce and dear, and eggs, butter and sugar only for the very rich who could bribe M'sieu' Colombe, the *épicier* of the Rue Haute, to let them have what they wanted. But no matter! Old Louise was a veritable genius where a dinner was concerned, and M'sieu' Colombe, the grocer, and M'sieu' Duflos the butcher, had allowed her to have all she asked for: a luscious piece of meat, three eggs, a piece of butter, and this without any extra bribe. Then there were still half a dozen bottles of that excellent red wine which Bibi had bought in the happy olden days; and he had opened one of the bottles, and Fleurette had drunk some wine and felt very elated and altogether happy – but for this there was another reason of which more anon.

Of course the latter part of the day had been tinged with sadness, again for that one reason which will appear presently: but not only because of that, but because of Bibi's departure, which, it seems, could not be postponed, although Fleurette begged and begged that he should remain at least until tomorrow so as not to spoil this most perfect day. *Le bon Dieu* alone knew when Fleurette would see Bibi again, his absences from home had of late become more frequent and more prolonged.

Mais voilà! on one's eighteenth birthday one is not going to think of troubles until the very last minute when it is actually on the doorstep. And the day had been entirely glorious. Not a cloud: the sky of such a vivid blue that the forget-me-nots that grew in such profusion beside the stream looked pale and colourless beneath it. The crimson peonies behind the house were in full bloom, and the buds of the climbing rose on the point of bursting.

And now dinner was over. Louise was busy in the kitchen washing up the plates and dishes, and Fleurette was carefully putting away the beautiful silver forks and spoons which had been brought out for the occasion. She was putting them away in the fine leather case with the molleton lining, which set off the glistening silver to perfection, and little Fleurette felt happy and very contented. She worked away in silence because Bibi had leaned his darling old head against the back of his chair, and closed his eyes. Fleurette thought that he had dropped to sleep.

He looked thin and pale, the poor dear, and there were lines of anxiety and discontent around his thin lips: his hair too had of late been plentifully sprinkled with grey. Oh! how Fleurette longed to have him here at Lou Mas. Always and always. It was the only home she had ever known; dear, beautiful, fragrant Lou Mas. Here she would tend him and care for him until all those lines of care upon his face had vanished. And what more likely to bring a smile to his lips than dear old Lou Mas with its white-washed walls and red-tiled roofs, with its green shutters and little mill stream beside which, for nine months in the year, flowers grew in such profusion; violets, forget-me-nots, and lilies of the valley in the spring, and meadowsweet throughout the summer until an early frost cut them down?

As for this room, Fleurette knew that there could not be in the whole of France, anything more beautiful or more cosy. There was the beautiful walnut sideboard, polished until it shone like a mirror, there were the chairs covered in crimson rep, rather faded, it is true, but none the worse for that, and there was Bibi's special armchair adorned with that strip of tapestry which Fleurette had worked in cross-stitch, expressly for his birthday the year of her first communion. Never had there been such chairs anywhere. And that beautiful paper on the walls, the red and yellow roses that looked as if you could pick them off their lovely chocolate-coloured ground, and the chandelier with the crystal drops, and the blue vases with the gold handles that adorned the mantelpiece, not to mention the print curtains and the pink and blue check cloth upon the table. Oh, Fleurette loved all these things, they had been the playthings of her childhood and now they were her pride. If only Bibi would smile again, she felt that the whole world would be like Heaven.

And then all at once everything went wrong. Fleurette had got her beautiful new shawl out of its wrappings and draped it round her shoulders and rubbed her cheek against it. Then she had said quite innocently: "It is so lovely, Bibi, and the wool is so soft and fine. I am sure that it came from England." And it was from that moment that everything went wrong. To begin with, and quite by accident, of course, Bibi broke the stem of the glass out of which he had been drinking, and a quantity of very precious wine was spilt over the beautiful tablecloth.

Whereupon, unaccountably, because of course the tablecloth could be washed, Bibi pushed his plate aside quite roughly and suddenly looked ten years older; so wan and pale and shrivelled and old. Fleurette longed to put her arms round him – as she used to do in the happy olden days – and ask him to tell her what was amiss. She was grown up now – eighteen years old today – quite old enough to understand. And if Bibi loved her as she thought he did, he would be comforted.

But there it was! There was something in the expression on Bibi's face that checked Fleurette's impulse. She went on quietly – very quietly, like a little mouse – with her work, and for awhile there was silence in the cosy room with the beautiful roses on the wall that looked as if you could pick them off their chocolate ground: a silence that was unaccountably full of sadness.

Four

Bibi was the first to hear the sound of footsteps coming up to the door. He gave a start, just as if he were waking from a dream.

"It's M'sieu' Colombe," Fleurette said.

At once Bibi reproved her, a thing he hardly ever did: "Citizen Colombe," he said sternly.

Fleurette shrugged her plump shoulders: "Ah well – !" she exclaimed.

"You must learn, Fleurette," Bibi insisted still with unwonted severity. "You are old enough to learn."

She said nothing more; only kissed the top of his head, the smooth brown hair, of late so plentifully tinged with grey, and promised that she would learn. She stood by the sideboard intent on putting the silver away, with her back turned to Bibi so that he should not see the soft tone of pink that had crept into her cheeks, as soon as she had perceived that two pairs of feet were treading the path outside the door.

Now there was a vigorous knock against the door, and a cheery, raucous voice called out loudly: "May one enter?"

Fleurette ran to the door and opened it.

"But certainly, certainly," she said, and then added, seemingly very astonished: "Ah! and M'sieu' Amédé too?" From which the casual observer would perhaps infer that the pink colour in her cheeks had been due to the arrival of M'sieu' Colombe, the *épicier* of the Rue Haute, rather than to that of his son Amédé.

It was no doubt also the worthy *épicier* with his round florid face, dark, twinkling eyes, and general air of ferocious kindliness that caused the pink colour to spread from Fleurette's cheeks down to her neck and the little bit of throat that peeped out above her kerchief.

The good Colombe had already stalked into the room and with a familiar: "Eh bien! Eh bien! We did contrive to come and drink Fleurette's health after all?" had slapped Bibi vigorously over the lean shoulders. But Amédé had come to a halt on the mat in which he was mechanically wiping his boots as if his very life depended on their cleanliness. Between his fingers he was twirling an immense posy of bright pink peonies, but his eyes were fixed on Fleurette, and on his broad, plain face, which shone with perspiration and good temper, there was a half-shy, wholly adoring look.

He gulped hard once or twice before he murmured, hoarse with emotion:

"Mam'zelle Fleurette!"

And Fleurette wiped her hot little hand against her apron before she whispered in shy response:

"M'sieu' Amédé!"

Not for these two the new fangled "citoyen" and "citoyenne" decreed in far-off Paris. To their unsophisticated ears the clamour of a trumpet-tongued revolution only came as an unreal and distant echo.

Amédé appeared to have finished cleaning his boots, and Fleurette was able to close the door behind him before she held out her hand for the flowers which he was too bewildered to offer.

"Are these beautiful flowers for me, M'sieu' Amédé?" she asked.

"If you will deign to accept them, Mam'zelle Fleurette," he replied.

She was eighteen and he was just twenty. Neither of them had ever been away more than a few hours from their remote little village of Dauphiné where they were born – she in the little house with the green shutters, and he in the Rue Haute above the shop where his father Hector Colombe had sold tallow candles and sugar, flour and salt, and lard and eggs to the neighbours, ever since he had been old enough to help *his* father in the business. And when Amédé was four, and Fleurette two, they had made mud pies together in the village street with water from the fountain, and Amédé had warded Fleurette against the many powerful enemies that sometimes threatened her and caused her to scream with terror, such as M'sieu' Duflos the butcher's dog, or Achille the garde-champêtre with his ferocious scowl, or M'ame Amélie's geese.

They had sat together – not side by side you understand, but the boys on the right of the room and the girls on the left – in the little classroom in the presbytery, where M. le Curé taught them their alphabet and subsequently the catechism; and also that two and two make four. They had knelt side by side in the little primitive church at Laragne, their little souls overburdened with emotion and religious fervour, when they made their first communion: Fleurette in a beautiful white dress, with a wreath of white roses on her fair hair, and a long tulle veil that descended right down to her feet; and Amédé in an exquisite cloth coat with brass buttons, a silk waistcoat, buckled shoes and a white ribbon sash on his left arm.

And when Amédé had been old enough to be entrusted with his father's errands over at Serres, a couple of leagues away, Fleurette had climbed behind him on the saddle, and with her arms round his waist, so as to keep herself steady, they had ridden together along the winding road white with dust, Ginette, the good old mare, ambling very leisurely as if she knew that her riders were in no hurry to get anywhere that day.

And now Fleurette was eighteen and Amédé twenty and her hair was like ripe corn, and her eyes as blue as the sky on a midsummer morn, whilst her mouth was dewy and fragrant as a rose in June. No wonder that poor Amédé felt as if his feet were of lead and his neck too big for his cravat, and when presently she asked him to fill a vase with water out of the carafe so that she could place the beautiful flowers in it, is it a wonder that he spilt the water all over the floor, seeing that his clumsy hands met her dainty fingers around the neck of the carafe?

The good Hector pretended to be very angry with his son for his clumsiness.

"Voyez-moi cet imbécile!" he said with that gruff voice of his which had become a habit with him, because he had to use it all day in order to ward off the naughty village urchins who tried to steal the apples out of his shop.

"Mam'zelle Fleurette, why don't you box his ears?"

Which, of course, was a very funny proposition that caused Fleurette and Amédé to laugh immoderately first and then to whisper and to chaff whilst they mopped the water off the tiled floor. And the good Hector turned once more to Bibi, and shaking his powerful fist at nothing in particular, he brought it down with a crash upon the table.

"And now those gredins, those limbs of Satan are taking him away for cannon-fodder. Ah! the devils! the pigs! the pig-devils!"

Bibi looked up inquiringly.

"Taking him away, are they?" he asked drily. Then he added with an indifferent shrug of the shoulders: "Amédé is twenty, isn't he?"

"What's that to do with their dragging him away from me, when I want him to help in the shop?" Hector retorted with what he felt was unanswerable logic.

"What would be the good of keeping shop, my good Hector," Bibi rejoined simply, "if France was invaded by foreigners as she is already ruined by traitors?"

"Well! And isn't she ruined now by all those devils up in Paris who can think of nothing better than war or murder?" growled

Hector Colombe, heedless of the quick gesture of warning which Bibi had given him.

Adèle, the girl from the village who gave old Louise a hand about the house when Bibi was at home, had just come in from the kitchen with a pile of plates and dishes which she proceeded to range upon the dresser. Hector shrugged his big shoulders. Whoever would think of taking notice of Adèle? A wench who got five sous a day for scrubbing floors! An undersized, plain-faced creature with flat feet and red elbows. Bah!

But Bibi still put up a warning finger:

"Little pitchers have long ears," he said in a whisper.

"Oh! I know, I know," Hector rejoined gruffly. "It is the fashion these days for us all to spy on one another. A pretty pass they have brought us to," he added, "your friends in Paris."

To this Bibi made no reply. No doubt he knew that it was impossible to argue with Hector, once the worthy *épicier* was in one of his moods. Adèle had finished her task and glided out of the room, silent, noiseless, furtive as a little rat, which she vaguely resembled with small, keen eyes, and pointed nose and chin. In a corner of the room, by the window, still busy with those flowers which seemingly would not set primly in the vase, Fleurette and Amédé were talking under their breath.

"I'm going away, Mam'zelle Fleurette," said he.

"Going away, M'sieu' Amédé? Whither? When?"

"They want me in the army."

"What for?" she asked naïvely.

"To fight against the English."

"But you won't go, will you, M'sieu' Amédé?"

"I must, Mam'zelle Fleurette."

"Oh, but what shall I – I mean what will M'sieu' Colombe do? You must remain here, to help him in the shop." And fight against it as she would, there was an uncomfortable little lump in her throat when she pictured how terribly lost M'sieu' Colombe would be without his son.

"Father is very angry," Amédé said rather hoarsely, because he too had an uncomfortable lump in his throat now. "But it seems there's nothing to be done. I have to go."

"When?" Fleurette murmured, so softly, so softly, that only a lover's ears could possibly have caught the whisper.

"I have to present myself tomorrow," Amédé replied, "before M'sieu' le Commissaire de police at Serres."

"Tomorrow? And I have been so happy today!"

The cry came from an overburdened little heart, brought face to face with its first sorrow. Fleurette no longer attempted to keep back her tears, and Amédé, not quite sure whether he should cry because he was going away, or dance with joy because it was his going that was making Fleurette cry, put in time by wiping his face which was streaming with perspiration and tears.

"I wish I could at least have seen those children wedded," the worthy *épicier* muttered in the interval of blowing his nose with a noise like a cloud-burst. "At least," he added with the good round oath which he reserved for occasions such as these, "before they take my Amédé away."

Bibi on the other hand appeared to be more philosophical.

"We must wait for better times," he said, "and anyhow Fleurette is too young to marry."

Five

Parting is not such sweet sorrow as the greatest of all poets
would have us believe. At any rate Fleurette did not find it at all
sweet, on this her eighteenth birthday, which should have been
a very happy one.

It was bad enough saying "adieu" to Bibi. But Fleurette was
accustomed to that. Of late Bibi had been so often and so long
absent from home; sometimes weeks – nay! months – would
elapse and there would be no Bibi to fondle Fleurette and bring
life and animation within those whitewashed walls that held all
that was dearest to her in the world. It was undoubtedly heart-
rending to bid Bidi adieu: but in a way, one knew that the
darling would come back to Lou Mas as soon as he was able,
come for one of those surprise visits that made Fleurette as gay
as a linnet all the while they lasted. But to say goodbye to
Amédé was a different matter. He was going into the army.
He was going to fight the English. *Le bon Dieu* alone knew if
Amédé would ever come back. Perhaps he would be killed.
Perhaps – oh! perhaps –

Never in her life had Fleurette been so sad.

And now the last goodbyes had been said. Bibi, accompanied
by M'sieu' Colombe and Amédé, had walked away in the
direction of the village, where he would pick up his horse,
and start along the main road that led to Serres and thence
to Paris.

Fleurette remained on the bridge for some time, shading her eyes against the sun, because they ached so from all the tears which she had shed. The three men had become mere specks, 'way down the road: old Louise had gone back to her kitchen with Adèle, only Fleurette remained standing on the bridge alone. Tears were still running down her cheeks, whilst with aching eyes she strove to catch a last sight of Bibi as he and his two companions disappeared round the bend of the road. Or was it Amédé she was trying to see?

The afternoon sun had spread a mantle of gold over the snowy crests of Pelvoux: on the sapphire sky myriads of tiny clouds seemed to hold hearts of living flame in their fleecy bosoms. The wavy ribbon of the Buëche was like a giant mirror that reflected a whole gamut of glowing tints, blue and gold and purple, whilst on the winding road the infinitesimal atoms of dust seemed like low-lying clouds of powdered topaz. Suddenly in the direction of Sisteron those clouds rose, more dense: something more solid than powdered topaz animated the distance: grew gradually more tangible and then became definite. Fleurette now could easily distinguish ten or a dozen men coming this way. They all wore red caps on their heads. Ahead of them came a man on horseback. He wore a tricorne hat, adorned with a tricolour cockade, and the sun drew sparks of flame from the steel bit in his horse's mouth and from the brass bosses and buckles on the harness.

Now Fleurette could hear the dull stamping of hoofs on the dusty road, and the tramping of heavy, weary footsteps: and she watched, fascinated, these men coming along.

All at once the rider put his horse to a trot, and the next moment he reined in on the bridge. He put out his hand and cried a sharp: "Halte!" whereupon the other men all came to a halt. Fleurette stood there wondering what all this meant. Vaguely she guessed that these men must be soldiers, though, of a truth, with the exception of the one on horseback, and who appeared to be their officer, there was very little that was soldierly about them. Their red caps were of worsted, and adorned with what had once been a tricolour cockade, but was now so covered with dust that the colours were wellnigh undistinguishable. The men's coats too, once blue in colour and fitted with brass buttons, were torn and faded, with several buttons missing: their breeches were stained with mud, they had no stockings inside their shoes, and it would have been impossible to say definitely whether their shirts had been of a drabby grey when they were new, or whether they had become so under stress of wear and dirt. Fleurette's recollection flew back to the smart soldiers she used to see when she was a tiny tot and Bibi took her to Serres or Sisteron on fête days when the military band would march past in their beautiful clothes all glittering with brass buttons, and their boots polished up so that you could almost see yourself in them.

But there! everyone knew that these were terribly hard times and that new clothes were very, very dear: so Fleurette supposed that the poor soldiers had to wear out their old ones just like everybody else. And her sensitive little heart gave an extra throb or two, for she had suddenly remembered that M'sieu' Amédé would also be a soldier very soon, wearing a shabby coat, and perhaps no stockings inside his shoes. Still thinking of M'sieu' Amédé, she was very polite to the man on horseback, although he was unnecessarily abrupt with her, asking her gruffly whether Citizen Armand was within.

Fleurette said "No!" quite gently, and then, choosing to ignore the coarse manner in which the man uttered a very ugly oath, she went on: "Father has been gone a quarter of an hour and more, and if you – "

"Citizen Armand, I asked for," the officer broke in roughly, "not your father."

"Father's name is Armand," Fleurette said, still speaking very politely. "I thought you were asking for him."

The horseman, she thought, realizing his mistake, should have excused himself for speaking so rudely: but he did nothing

31

of the sort. He just shrugged his shoulders and said in a very curious way, which sounded almost like a sneer:

"Oh! is that how it is? You are Citizen Armand's daughter, are you?"

"Yes! M'sieu' l'officier."

"Call me citizen lieutenant," the man retorted roughly. "Hasn't your father taught you to speak like a good patriot?"

Fleurette would not have admitted for the world that she was half afraid of this unkempt, unshaved officer with the gruff voice, but she felt intimidated, shy, ill at ease. She would have given worlds to have someone friendly beside her, old Louise, for instance, or even Adèle.

"Shall I call M'ame Louise," she suggested, "to speak with you?"

"No," the man replied curtly, "what's the use if your father isn't there? Which way did he go?"

"To the village first, M'sieu' – I mean citizen, to pick up his horse which he always leaves at M'sieu' Colombe's stables. He is going to Paris afterwards."

"How far is it to the village?"

"Less than a quarter of a league – er – citizen."

"And the house," the officer asked again, "where the ci-devant Frontenacs live, is that far?"

"About half a league by the road from here," Fleurette replied, "the other side of the village. There is a short cut behind this house, past the mill, but – "

The man, however, was no longer listening to what she said. He muttered something that sounded very much like an oath, and then turned to the soldiers: "Allons! Marche!" he commanded sharply. The men appeared terribly dusty and tired and hardly made a movement to obey: at the first call of "Halte," some of them had thrown themselves down by the edge of the road and stretched out full length on the heaps of hard stones piled up there; others had wandered down the slope by the bridge, and lying flat on the ground were slaking their thirst in the cool, clear water of the stream. Fleurette was very sorry for them.

"May they wait a moment, M'sieu' le – I mean citizen lieutenant," she pleaded, "I'll get them something to drink. We haven't much, but I know Louise won't – "

But the officer took no further notice either of her or of the men. Having given his order to march, he had readjusted the reins in his hands, and struck his spurs somewhat viciously into his horse's flanks. The horse reared and plunged for a moment, then started off at a sharp trot, clouds of dust flying out from under its hoofs.

The men made an effort to rise. Fleurette put up a finger and smiled at them all.

"Wait one minute," she said, and ran quickly back into the house.

There was the best part of a bottle left of that good red wine: Bibi had not touched it again after he broke the stem of his glass. Fleurette had picked up the bottle and taken a tin mug from the dresser and was about to start out again before Louise thought of asking her what she was up to.

"There are some poor, tired soldiers outside on the bridge," Fleurette replied, "I want to take them something to drink. There's not much of it, and twelve of them to share it, but it will be better than nothing, and perhaps *le bon Dieu* will make a miracle and make it be enough. They seemed so thirsty, poor dears."

"Let Adèle go," Louise said curtly, "I don't like you speaking with those vagabonds."

And while Adèle ran out, as she was bid, with mug and bottle, Louise continued to mutter half under her breath:

"I can't abide those sansculottes. Brigands the lot of them. What are they doing in the neighbourhood, I'd like to know. Up to no good you may depend. Let Adèle talk to them. It is not fit for a well-brought-up wench like you to be seen in such company."

Fleurette did not pay much attention to old Louise's mutterings. There was plenty to do in the house with washing up and tidying things away. And it was Louise's habit to grumble at anything that was in any way unusual: a wet day in August, or a mild one in December, a *calèche* on the road, a horseman, a soldier, or a letter for Bibi. She was always called "old Louise," although, in truth, she had scarce reached middle age; but her skin was dry and rough like the soil of her native Dauphiné, her face and hands were prematurely wrinkled and her voice had become harsh of late, probably for want of use, like a piece of mechanism that has stood still, and begun to grind for want of a lubricant. In Armand's house, when he was absent, she ruled supreme. Fleurette never dreamed of disobeying, and Armand's only peremptory orders to Louise were never to mention politics or current events to the child.

Louise had nursed Fleurette at her breast when Fleurette's mother died in child-bed, and she had left her own baby in the care of her sister, already a widow and childless. Considerations of money had prompted her at the time, for Monsieur Armand, as he was then, had made her liberal offers: afterwards it was too late to regret. Her own daughter, Adèle, born of an unknown father who loved and rode away, had been brought up to a life of drudgery by her aunt, who sent the girl out to earn her own living as soon as she could toddle, whilst Fleurette was brought up to have everything she wanted: petted and idolized by a father plentifully supplied with money. Fleurette and Adèle were foster-sisters, but with destinies as wide apart as the peaks of Pelvoux.

But Louise never spoke one bitter word, when she saw Adèle with toil-worn hands scrubbing the kitchen floor on which Fleurette trod with dainty, high-heeled shoes. Perhaps she loved her foster-child more than she did her own: perhaps it was only the same considerations of money that already guided her conduct before, which prompted her later to indulgence toward the rich man's daughter, whilst reserving her pent-up acrimony for the household drudge. No one knew what Louise's feelings were towards Adèle – Adèle herself least of all. The girl was silent, reserved, self-contained, very conscientious in her work, but not very responsive to the many kindnesses shown her by M'sieu' Armand or Mam'zelle Fleurette. She still lived with her aunt who had brought her up, and she appeared to lay no claim on her mother's affection: she had earned her own living ever since she was ten years of age, and now, at eighteen, she looked more like a woman than a girl: her little face was all pinched up, the lips thin, the eyes either sharp as needles or expressionless like those of a rodent. She hardly ever spoke and no one had ever seen her smile.

Old Louise's mutterings presently turned to Adèle's prolonged absence:

"What is the girl about now, I should like to know? She is not a gossip as a rule."

She went on with her washing up for a moment or two longer and then said sharply:

"Run along, Fleurette, and see what the wench is doing. Lazy baggage, with all the work there's still to do."

Fleurette ran out at once. She too wondered why Adèle was such a long time. And there, sure enough, standing on the bridge was Adèle talking to the soldiers. The officer was already out of sight. Adèle talking! and Fleurette even thought that she heard her giggle. Incredible! The soldiers were all laughing and one of them was in the act of drinking the last drop out of the tin mug.

Fleurette stood for a moment on the doorstep, vaguely wondering what in the world had come over Adèle, when a rather curious incident occurred: the soldiers were all laughing, jesting apparently with the girl, and one of them, with head tilted back, was draining the last drop out of the tin mug. Fleurette was on the point of calling to Adèle when her attention was arrested by the appearance of an old man carrying what looked like a load of faggots tied up in a coarse sacking.

He seemed to have climbed the slopes on the opposite side of the road; at any rate there he was, all of a sudden, immediately behind the group of soldiers.

He appeared to be drunk, for he staggered as he walked and leaned heavily on a stout gnarled stick. Fleurette could not have told you exactly how it all happened, but all of a sudden Adèle's giggling and the soldiers' jests were interrupted by the old faggot-carrier tumbling down clumsily, right between them all.

Adèle screamed. The soldiers swore, and one of them went to the length of giving the old man a savage kick, whilst two others incontinently picked him up between them and flung him over the parapet of the bridge. Fleurette gave a cry of dismay and ran to the poor man's assistance. She felt hot with indignation at such wanton brutality. How right, she thought as she ran, had old Louise's estimate been of these soldiers – little better than brigands they were, and cruel to boot. The poor faggot-carrier, for such he seemed to be, was lying half in and half out of the stream: the grass and sloping ground had somewhat broken his fall but nevertheless there he lay, motionless and groaning piteously. Fleurette called peremptorily to Adèle to come and help her hoist up the poor man on his legs again. He was very dirty, dressed in nothing but rags, his feet swathed in coarse bass matting; he was stockingless, shirtless and hatless; but he appeared to be powerfully built and Fleurette marvelled how he could have allowed himself to be thus maltreated without a struggle. No doubt he was drunk or crippled with rheumatism.

Up on the bridge the soldiers were preparing to start once more on their way. They took no more notice of their unfortunate victim nor of Adèle; but Fleurette looking up felt that their last glance was for her; some of them were regarding her with a leer, others with more pronounced malevolence. She distinctly saw one man nudge his neighbour and point a finger at her: whereat both of them gave a mocking laugh.

She felt hurt and indignant: in her sheltered life she had never met with malevolence before. However for the moment, her first care was for the poor faggot-carrier. Adèle had come to her assistance, and together the two girls succeeded in getting the old man on his legs again. He appeared more scared than hurt, and with his big, toil-stained hands, he felt himself all over to see, perhaps, if any bones were broken; and all the while he kept on murmuring rather pathetically: "Nom de nom, de nom de Dieu!" as if surprised that such a tragic adventure should have happened to him.

Fleurette asked him if he were hurt, and he replied: "No, Mam'zelle – that is citizeness," and he added: "Ah, I shall never get used to these new ways. I am too old."

"Can you get on your way now?" Fleurette asked.

"Yes! yes, Mam'zelle, that is citizeness. But," he went on piteously, "I am so hungry. I come from over Mison way and I have not had a bite since seven o'clock this morning."

This naturally stirred Fleurette's kind, compassionate heart. She told Adèle to run into the house and ask Louise for a hunk of bread. Adèle, silent and self-contained once more, obeyed without comment. The incident was closed as far as Fleurette was concerned. Her thoughts flew back to Amédé and to his last day and evening which he would be spending in his cosy home. She wished she had been bold enough to ask him to come and bid her a last adieu tomorrow morning before he went away to fight the English.

And while she stood there gazing out over the valley where the metal cross on the church steeple of Laragne glistened like gold in the sunlight, a strange voice – soft yet firm – suddenly struck her ear from somewhere close behind her.

"Papers and valuables are behind the panel in Madame's room."

She swung round terrified, so terrified that the cry she was about to utter died away in her throat. She looked about her, scared, shivering with that nameless dread which assails every mortal in face of the supernatural. And yet everything seemed as peaceful as before: the little mill stream splashed and gurgled with its soft, persistent sound; in the old walnut tree a thrush was calling to its mate and the old faggot-carrier was busy tying up his faggots into the sacking again. Fleurette's eyes rested for an instant anxiously upon him. She expected to see him raise his head, to look about him, to appear scared as she was herself; but he gave no sign of having heard anything of that mysterious voice, fresh and compelling like a command from heaven. Oh no! Fleurette could not have screamed. She was too panic-stricken just at first to utter a sound.

And yet nothing had really happened to alarm the most timorous. Only those few words spoken by an unseen tongue. What did they mean? What could they mean? They were simple and commonplace enough: Fleurette repeated them to herself mechanically:

"Papers and valuables are behind the panel in Madame's room."

What did it mean? What papers? what valuables? and why should the mysterious speaker have wished her to know that they were behind the panel in Madame's room? Madame was, of course, Madame de Frontenac over at the château, and all of a sudden Fleurette remembered that the mounted soldier had asked her the way to the château. Gradually she was feeling less scared. Less scared but more excited. She looked round at the statue of St Antoine, at whose feet she had this morning placed a fresh bunch of forget-me-nots. Somehow she associated the mysterious voice with St Antoine. Perhaps Madame had lost some valuable papers, and the kind saint had chosen this means of letting her know where her treasure was. Fleurette made the sign of the cross on her bosom; she remembered the story of Jeanne d'Arc which M. le Curé used to tell her, of how the humble shepherdess of Domrémy had been compelled by heavenly voices to go forth and deliver France from her enemies and never rest until she had seen the King crowned in his cathedral of Rheims.

Fleurette felt something of that same fervour which had animated Jeanne d'Arc. She felt that she must go forth and tell Madame about the valuables and the papers. The evening was warm and she would not need her shawl. She could go just as she was as far as the château and be back before the twilight had faded into night. Adèle in the meanwhile appeared at the front door, she had her shawl over her head, and a hunk of bread in her hand. Then only did Fleurette remember the old faggot-carrier. She turned to him in order to bid him "God-speed." He stood there quite motionless, leaning upon his stick bending under the weight of his load of faggots which he had hoisted upon his back. His lank hair hung over his wrinkled forehead and half concealed his eyes. But, suddenly through the veil of lank grey hair Fleurette met the man's glance fixed upon her; and her heart gave a queer jump. Those were not the eyes of a decrepit old man; they were young and clear and bright: of a luminous grey-blue, with heavy lids that could not wholly conceal the humorous twinkle in the eyes, nor yet the kindly, searching glance which was fixed on Fleurette.

This was the moment when she really would have screamed. The sense of something ununderstandable and unreal was more than she could bear, she would have screamed, but those twinkling, searching eyes held her, and at the same time seemed to reassure her, to tell her not to be afraid. She felt as if she were in a dream: unable to do anything, only to stare and stare at the old faggot-carrier, while gradually all her terrors seemed to fall away from her, and she was filled with a sense of courage and of determination. The whole incident, the voice, the glance, her terror and reassurance had lasted less than five seconds. Already Adèle was close by. She was bringing the bread for the poor, half-starved man, and Fleurette now watched him, fascinated, as he took the bread with a humble: "Merci, Mam'zelle," and started at once on it, like a man who has not tasted food all day.

He was just a decrepit old man, bent with rheumatism, dirty, unkempt, insecure on his tottering limbs. He even raised his eyes once, and once more looked at her; but the glance was dim like that of an old man; there was no twinkle in the eyes, only the weariness of poverty and old age.

And Fleurette felt that she had dreamed it all: the voice, the glance, the message from St Antoine, just as her terrors had faded from her, so now her excitement vanished too. It must all have been a dream. It *was* a dream! Perhaps old Louise, who was versed in all kinds of dreamlore, would know of an explanation for the whole mysterious occurrence. Feeling very tired all of a sudden – for she felt the reaction after the tenseness of the last few moments – she went back into the house. In the doorway she turned to have a last look at the old faggot-carrier; leaning heavily upon his stick, he was making his way along the bank of the stream. The last she saw of him was his big bundle done up in sacking and his legs bending beneath the weight.

Adèle wrapped in her shawl had gone the other way. She was already up on the bridge. With a little sigh of disappointment Fleurette went into the house. It had been such an exciting dream!

But she did not speak about it to old Louise; she just went quietly about the house, doing one or two little bits of work that Adèle had left undone.

The slowly-sinking sun had turned the gold on Pelvoux' snowy crest to a brilliant rose, when Fleurette suddenly announced to Louise that she was going over to the château. She often went there, and at all hours of the day.

"So long as you are home before dark," was Louise's only remark. "I don't like those down-at-heel soldiers being about."

Fleurette promised that she would not be late. She picked up her beautiful new shawl and wrapped it round her shoulders. The château was not far; over by the mountain track, it was not more than a quarter of a league at most. Swiftly Fleurette ran out of the house and then along the edge of the stream – the

things, detached as far as he was able from the turmoil that was ruining his country and shaming her in the eyes of the world.

At all seasons of the year, and in all weathers, he could be seen out on his farm, directing the work in fields or stables, clad in rough boots and breeches, abrupt of speech, but kindly in deeds, beloved by some, envied by others, hated only by those few who see in every noble life a reproach to their own. His wife was the daughter of an Admiral in the late King's navy, who had thought it prudent to serve the Republic, as he had served his King, with commendable detachment from his country's politics. Though brought up in the midst of the gaieties and luxuries of Paris, Anne de Grandville had been quite content to follow the husband of her choice to the lonely farmhouse in Dauphiné, and to fall in with his bucolic ways: she donned a cotton kirtle and linen apron as readily as she had donned silken panniers in the past, and took as much pride in her cooking now as she had done once in her proficiency in the dance.

At one time Charles de Frontenac had sorely grieved because he had no son to whom he could bequeath his glorious name and fine inheritance, but now he was glad. With France handed over to the control of assassins, bandits, and regicides, the name of Frontenac might, he opined, just as well die out. What was the use of toiling to improve land which tomorrow might be wrested from its rightful owners: what was the use of saving money which would probably on the morrow fall into the hands of brigands? "Lay not up for yourselves treasures on this earth where rust and moth doth corrupt and where thieves break through and steal!" had never been so wise an admonition as it was today. All that Charles de Frontenac hoped to do was to put by a sufficient competence to keep his wife and invalid daughter in comfort once he was under the ground. That daughter was the apple of his eye. Bereft of position and most of his wealth, all his thoughts and hopes were centred on this delicate being who seemed like the one ray of sunshine amidst thunder-clouds of disappointment and treachery.

Rose de Frontenac had been a cripple from birth, and it was her delicacy and her helplessness that had so endeared her to her father. He was a man resplendent with vigour and of herculean strength: one of those bull-necked men who could have taken his place in an ox-team and not proved a weakling. His hands were rough, his fist as hard as a hammer. His clothes smelt of damp earth and of manure; the descendant of a long line of aristocrats, Charles de Frontenac, was above all a son of the soil. To him his pale-faced, fragile daughter seemed like a being from another world; he hardly dared touch her cheek with his thick, clumsy fingers, nor dared he approach her save after copious ablutions and sprays of scent. His heart was as big as his body. He adored his daughter, he loved his wife, he beamed with fondness for Fleurette: Fleurette who was as gay as a linnet, who could always bring a smile to the pale lips of his wan, white Rose: Fleurette, who could sing like a lark, prattle like a young sparrow and whose corn-coloured hair smelt of wild thyme and of youth.

Seven

Fleurette had walked very fast. She was still tremendously excited and would have run all the way, only that the road for the most part led sharply uphill and that her heart was beating and pumping wildly with agitation.

Strangely enough the gates of the park were wide open, which was very unusual, as they were always kept closed for fear of the foot-pads and vagabonds. Old Pierre, who was in charge of the gate, was nowhere to be seen. Fleurette ran along the sanded avenue which, bordered by bosquets of acacia and elder, led in sharp curves up to the house. Twilight was slowly fading into evening, but even through the gathering darkness Fleurette noticed that the avenue, usually so beautifully raked and tidy, was all trampled and knocked about as if by the weight of many heavy feet. A minute later the main block of the château stood out before her, like a solid mass silhouetted against a jade-coloured sky. Just above the pointed roof of the turret at the furthest angle of the façade, a star shone with a cold, silvery radiance.

The entrance into the main building was under a broad archway which intersected the façade and led into the great farmyard and to the sheds and farm buildings. Fleurette felt vaguely conscious that something unusual had occurred at the château; though the place looked peaceful enough, it appeared strangely deserted, at this hour, when usually men and maids were still about their work. She slipped quickly under the archway, and turning sharply to the left, she came to the great paved hall where servants and farm-hands sat at meals.

She found the place in a strange state of confusion: the men – they were all old men these days, as all the young ones had had to go and join the army and fight the English – the men were standing about in groups, talking and gesticulating with their arms, after the manner of the people of Dauphiné who are glib of speech and free with their gestures; the maids were gathered together in the dark corner of the room, holding their aprons to their eyes. The oil lamp which hung from the white-washed ceiling had not yet been lit: only one or two tallow candles on the table guttered in their pewter sconces.

Old Mathieu, who was the acknowledged father of the staff and who was affectionately called Papa by the maids, was the first to spy Fleurette, who stood disconcerted in the doorway.

"Ah! Mam'zelle Fleurette! Mam'zelle Fleurette!" he exclaimed and lifted his hands and cast up his eyes with an expression of woe: "Quel maiheur! Mon Dieu, quel malheur!"

He had on his bottle-green coat, his buckled shoes, and the white cotton gloves which he wore when he served the family at meals upstairs. They had just finished dinner, it seems, when the awful calamity occurred.

"But what is it, papa?" Fleurette asked, feeling quite ready to cry in sympathy. "What has happened?"

"The soldiers, Mam'zelle!" papa replied, and a fresh groan went the round of men and women alike, and one or two of the girls sobbed aloud.

Now as far as Fleurette was concerned, as recently as this very morning, the inner meaning of these words "the soldiers!" would not perhaps have had much significance. In her own little home, by Bibi's strict orders, politics and social questions were never discussed. Fleurette was not supposed to know anything of the conflicts that were raging in the great cities, in the name of liberty and of fraternity. The horrors of summary arrests, of perquisitions, of sentences without trial, of wholesale executions, of hatred and revenge and lust were supposed to be beyond her ken; and knowing Bibi's abhorrence of those subjects being broached, she kept her counsels and her knowledge to herself. But Fleurette was not brainless, and she had a large heart. With her brain she had noted many things which were wilfully kept away from her, and her kind heart had often been filled with pity at many of the tales which she had heard in the village, tales of suffering under this new kind of tyranny, wielded, it seems, in the name of liberty and of the brotherhood of man. She had heard many things and had forgotten nothing; but somehow until this morning these things had seemed remote, like the tales of ogres and demons which are told to frighten children. She had not disbelieved them, but vaguely she felt that nothing of the sort could possibly happen to people whom she knew and loved.

But since this morning many things had occurred which had widened her range of vision. Amédé, who did not want to go away, was being dragged from home in order to be made into a soldier and to fight the English. She had actually seen some of those soldiers, ragged, uncouth and unkempt, with their officer, like a great bully, speaking to her, as if she were a mere slut out of the streets. He had jeered when she told him that she was Citizen Armand's daughter, and the soldiers had nudged one another and seemed to mock her when she met their glance. Then again she had heard mysterious voices and seen something in the person of a decrepit old faggot-carrier that had thrilled and puzzled her. All these things had worked a subtle change in Fleurette. The tales of ogres and demons no longer appeared quite so remote. The fact that there were evil and sorrow in the world had in a vague kind of way been brought home to her, and also that the spectre of death and misery of which she had only heard was actually lurking in this peaceful corner of Dauphiné and had already knocked at this very door.

"The soldiers!" meant something to her now.

"What happened?" she asked, and a dozen tongues were ready to embark on the telling of the tragic event. It was just after dinner. Madame and Mademoiselle had retired to the boudoir, as usual, and Monsieur was sipping his wine in the dining-room, when the great bell at the gate clanged loudly. Pierre, who was still at work in the stables, ran to open the gate: he was almost knocked down by two men on horseback who, without a word or question, rode past him along the avenue up to the house followed by a dozen men or more in tattered uniforms and wearing dirty red caps on their heads. The sound of horses and of men stamping the ground brought some of the maids and farm-hands out into the yard. The soldiers had come to a halt under the archway, the two riders then dismounted and ordered André to take their horses round to the stables. André, of course, did not dare disobey. Then, as the entrance door was closed, one of the soldiers knocked loudly against it with the butt-end of his musket, whilst one of those who had been on horseback and who appeared to be in authority called out summarily:

"Open in the name of the Republic!"

Old Mathieu, who was upstairs clearing away the dinner things, terribly scared, ran down to open the door. Again without a word or question, the soldiers pushed past him until they came to the vestibule where they demanded to know where were the ci-devant Frontenacs. Old Mathieu here paused in his narrative and once more threw up his hands and cast up his eyes in horror.

"Ci-devant, Mam'zelle!" he exclaimed. "I ask you! Just as those devils up in Paris talked of our poor martyred King and Queen!"

Of course he tried to stop the brigands from going up to see Madame like that, in their dusty shoes and dirty clothes. But what could he do alone among so many? Ah! if only Baptiste and Jean, Achille and Henri had been there, as in the good old days, fine sturdy fellows of the Dauphiné: they would soon have

48

got the better of these down-at-heel bandits, and if it was a case of protecting Madame and Mademoiselle, why! there would have been some broken heads, and the soldiers of the Republic would have sung another song than they were singing now – the muckworms! But there! Henri and André and the lot of the young ones had all been taken for cannon-fodder, to fight against the English, and there were only a few fogies left now like he – Mathieu – and the women.

Anyway, poor old papa was helpless. All he could do was to precede those hell-hounds upstairs, so that he might at least warn Monsieur of what was coming. But even this they would not let him do; as soon as he had reached the upstairs landing, the same man who had ordered him to open the front door in the name of the Republic, and who wore a tricolour sash round his middle, this same man grabbed him by the shoulder and thrust him aside as if he were a bundle of faggots. And without more ado, he just walked into the dining-room where Monsieur was still quietly sipping his last glass of wine.

From seeing Monsieur sitting there, the beautiful long-stemmed wine-glass in his hand, his face quite serene, you would have thought that he had heard nothing of the turmoil on the stairs. But he had heard everything, the tramping of feet, the rough voices, the curt command to open in the name of the Republic. He knew what was coming. Perhaps he had expected it long ago. It was well to be prepared for anything these days. Anyway, there he sat, glass in hand, his elbow resting on the table, where Mathieu had but a few minutes ago been engaged in clearing away the dessert. At the rude entry made by all those ragamuffins into his beautifully ordered dining-room, he just turned his head and looked at the men.

"In the name of the Republic," the man with the sash said curtly.

Monsieur put his glass down and rose slowly to his feet:

"What is it you want?" he asked quietly.

"The rest of the family, first of all," the man with the sash replied. "I want you all here together."

"Madame de Frontenac and my daughter Rose are not at home," said Monsieur, still speaking very quietly.

"That's a lie," the other retorted. "They were at meal here with you."

And with careless finger he pointed to the serviettes and plates which still littered the table. Monsieur did not wince under the insult; nor was the saying of such a brigand an insult to so high-minded a gentleman as Monsieur. All he said was:

"That is so. Madame and Mlle de Frontenac were at dinner with me, until half an hour ago when they left the house together."

"Whither did they go?"

"That I do not know."

"Which is another lie."

"If I did know," Monsieur rejoined imperturbably, "I would not tell you."

"We'll soon see about that," the man with the sash said grimly. He then turned to the soldier who appeared to be in command over the others:

"Allons! citizen lieutenant," he said curtly, "the rest is your business. The two women have got to be found. That is the first thing, after that we shall see."

The officer then ordered two of his men to stand on guard over Monsieur, and since then the tramp, tramp of the soldiers' feet had resounded throughout the château. Upstairs they went, and downstairs; in Madame's room and in Mademoiselle's, in the kitchen, the stables, the offices. They interrogated the men, they bullied the women; they turned everything topsy-turvy; they raked about in the hay and the straw of the stables, they scoured the park, they glued their ugly, dirty noses to the sanded paths, to try and find the imprint of footsteps. But neither of Madame or of Mademoiselle had they yet found a trace. They were still at it, raking and scouring and searching. In the intervals they tried to browbeat Monsieur, threatening him with summary shooting one moment, which only made him laugh and shrug his shoulders, and promising him immunity for his women-folk if he would say where they could be found. But these promises only made Monsieur laugh and again shrug his shoulders.

"Immunity?" he said. "They have that already, thank God! for they are beyond your reach now. If they were not, do you think I would trust to your promises?"

Old Mathieu paused. The story had neared its end – this tale of woe and anxiety and horror, such as the worthy old man had never thought to see. The others had not much to say; the maids were still crying, with excitement rather than with grief, and the old men had stared open-mouthed, or sagely nodded their heads.

"Then," Fleurette put in at last, "Madame and Mademoiselle have gone. Really – really gone?"

Mathieu nodded with another sigh, half of perplexity, half of woe.

"But whither?" Fleurette insisted. "How? Why?"

"God alone knows, Mam'zelle," papa averred. "He has spirited Madame and Mademoiselle away to save them from these brigands."

"Did anybody see them go?"

Men and maids shook their heads. No one had seen Madame or Mademoiselle go. Old Mathieu was the last to have seen the ladies. He had just begun to clear the table, when they rose, and, as was their custom, went through to the boudoir. Mathieu had opened the door for them. And now he came to think of it, the ladies had each kissed Monsieur very tenderly before they went out of the room. Yes! the kiss had seemed like a farewell. Mathieu shook his head dolefully; he remembered it now, but hadn't thought anything about it at the moment. Monsieur certainly appeared more thoughtful. Usually, while he drank his last glass of wine and Mathieu was engaged in washing the silver in the large copper bowl which he always brought into the room for that purpose, Monsieur would chat with him, talk over the gossip of the day. But tonight he had been unusually silent. Yes! Mathieu now remembered quite distinctly about the kiss, and about Monsieur being so silent. But he certainly had noticed nothing else unusual, until the moment when those brigands banged at the door and demanded admittance in the name of their godless Republic.

Mathieu was on the stairs at that moment, so he did not know how Monsieur had looked when he heard all the tramping and the noise. But Madame and Mademoiselle were gone, of that there could be no doubt. The brigands had searched for them, like so many dogs digging for a bone, and not a trace was there of the two ladies, for the *bon Dieu*, no doubt, had made them invisible.

Of old Mathieu and the staff, the officer in command took no notice, after he had summarily ordered them to muster up in the hall; he counted up the indoor-servants and the farm-hands; those who had their homes outside the precincts of the château, he ordered roughly out of the place.

"Get back to your homes!" he had said to them, after he had inspected and questioned them; "and stay there quietly, if you value your lives."

So there were only half a dozen old men, the four girls and the staff's cook left in the château. All of them were scared, and as Mam'zelle Fleurette could see, they just stood about and talked and talked while the girls did nothing but cry. He – Mathieu – could do nothing with any of them. The work of the house ought to be carried on; none of them had had any supper yet. But there! young and old, they were, all of them, too much upset to work or to eat; and the tramp-tramp-tramp, upstairs and downstairs was nerve-shattering to everybody.

Fleurette listened to the amazing story until the end. As Mathieu said, there was the ceaseless tramping of feet still going on. They – those horrible soldiers of the Republic, unworthy to be called Frenchmen – were still searching for Madame and Mademoiselle in order to drag them to Orange where the awful guillotine had been at work these months past; or perhaps even to Paris – that den of horrors beside which the stories of demons and ogres were but trivial tales.

Madame and Mademoiselle! who never in their lives had done any harm to anyone: but rather spent every hour of the day planning and executing kind deeds! And Mademoiselle! so delicate and frail that even her father, who idolized her, hardly dared touch her. And now these men, these rough and uncouth soldiers, with their harsh voices and bullying ways, to think of their approaching Mademoiselle, pushing her, dragging her, it made Fleurette's blood boil even to think of such a possibility. No wonder that the *bon Dieu* had made them invisible to the eyes of all those bandits.

Tramp! tramp! tramp! and now a loud banging as if pieces of furniture, chairs, tables were being overturned and then a crash, as of broken china!

"Holy Virgin!" Papa Mathieu exclaimed with a loud groan; "to think of Madame's beautiful things! Those brigands are furious at not finding Madame and Mademoiselle, and are venting their wrath on inanimate things."

It was these words of old Mathieu that sent Fleurette's thoughts flying in another direction – back to the early afternoon of this memorable day – back to the first visit of these awful soldiers, and to the faggot-carrier with his bundle tied up in sacking. From thence to the voice! The mysterious voice that had told her where valuables and papers were to be found. It was such a flash of recollection that her whole face became transfigured; anxiety and superstitious awe gave place to that same fervour which had animated her when she met the eyes of the faggot-carrier: eyes that conveyed a message, which at last she was beginning to understand.

"Papa!" she cried impulsively.

"Yes, Mam'zelle?" Mathieu asked with another sigh.

"Did anything else happen? – I mean anything unusual? – Did Madame – or Monsieur – receive a letter? a message? or – or did any other stranger come to the château this afternoon?

"Oh think, Papa Mathieu, think," she implored with tears of agitation choking her voice. "I cannot tell you how important it is. Try to remember – was there anything? – anybody? – "

Papa persistently shook his head, until Pierre, who was the gate-keeper, reminded him that Monsieur had gone down the avenue as far as the gate, just ten minutes before dinner was served.

"There's nothing very unusual in that," Mathieu retorted. "Monsieur is often out just before dinner is served."

"Yes!" Pierre insisted. "But what did he do this evening? He walked straight to the gate, which I had closed half an hour before. I saw him. He walked straight to the gate, he did, and you know the old acacia tree just the other side? Well! Monsieur put his foot on a bar of the gate and reached over to the forked branch of the old tree. I saw him quite plainly, I tell you. And when he walked back to the house he had a piece of paper in his hand with some writing on it, which he was reading. And I think, papa," Pierre concluded triumphantly, "you'll have to admit that there was something unusual in that."

But Mathieu, with the obstinacy of old age and long service, would not admit it, even now.

"Monsieur," he said, "met the mail-carrier at the gate, he often comes at this hour. He gave Monsieur a letter. Monsieur often gets letters – "

But here André interposed. Old André – they were all of them old – worked in the stables, and it was he who had taken the two horses from the soldiers when ordered to do so, and walked them round to the stables. It was then that he noticed two beggars hanging about in the yard: a man and a woman. He had peremptorily ordered them off the premises.

"Beggars!" Fleurette exclaimed eagerly. "What were they like?"

André said that as the sun was in his eyes he couldn't see them very well. There was a man and a woman. He was busy with the horses and upset by the arrival of all these brigands. The woman he couldn't see at all because of the shawl which covered her head, but he recollected that the man was a big fellow, bent nearly double under a huge bundle tied up in sacking.

"When I spoke to him," André went on, "he mumbled something or other, but I just told him to clear out, he and his woman; we'd enough of vagabonds, I said, in the place with all these soldiers."

"And did he go?" Fleurette asked.

"Yes. I must admit that he went off quite quietly after that. I did not think he meant any evil, because when he first caught sight of me he did not attempt to hide or to run away."

"If he had," André went on after a moment or two, "I would have been after him pretty quickly, and wanted to know what was in that big bundle."

He paused, a look of perplexity and of shamefacedness came over his wrinkled old face while he thoughtfully scratched his head: "Now I think of it," he said, "I ought to have inspected that bundle. It looked mighty heavy for faggots or for rags. Perhaps he had been up to no good after all. And directly after I lost sight of him and his woman I saw a whole lot of faggots lying in a heap close by the stable door."

The other old men and the maids had gathered closer round André and Fleurette. This was the first they had heard of the old vagabond and his woman, and the bundle which appeared so heavy.

"You certainly ought to have inspected that bundle, André," Mathieu said sententiously. He felt that there was a chance of recapturing his dignity which seemed to have been slightly impaired through his argument with Pierre. He could reassert his authority at any rate by rebuking André. "It looks," he went on, "as if the old vagabond had brought a lot of faggots with him, then turned them out of the sacking and replaced them by God knows what valuables he may have stolen."

"I was so upset, you understand, papa!" André murmured ruefully.

"We were all of us upset, as you call it, André," papa rebuked sternly, "but that is no excuse for neglect of duty."

"Don't scold André, papa," Fleurette broke in excitedly. "My belief is that the old vagabond, as you call him, was a messenger from the Holy Virgin, sent on purpose to get Madame and Mademoiselle safely out of the way."

"Oh, Mam'zelle!"

"From the Holy Virgin!"

"Sainte Marie, mère de Dieu, priez pour nous!" came in chorus from the maids. Even the cook, an elderly woman, jealous of her own dignity, was unable to conceal her excitement. The old men shook their heads, looked wise and sceptical.

"What makes you say that, Mam'zelle Fleurette?" Mathieu asked in an awed whisper.

But Fleurette was silent now. Already she had repented of having said so much. Discretion would have been so much wiser. That was the worst of her: she always allowed her tongue to run away with her. She looked eagerly from one anxious face to the other: well she knew that the little she had said would be talked over and commented on and be made the subject of gossip until it reached the village and possibly even Serres and Sisteron; and God only knew what harm this might do to Madame and Mademoiselle. She bit the tip of her tongue hard just to punish it for having wagged too freely, and seized with a sudden impulse, which she found irresistible, she snatched up a candle from the table, and incontinently turned and fled out of the hall, leaving the others to gape and stare after her, to scratch their heads, and to conjecture.

Aye! and to gossip too.

Eight

Perquisitions in these days of Liberty, Fraternity and Equality were perhaps among the minor horrors that befell innocent and guilty alike, at the behest of tyrants more implacable than the Inquisitors of Mediaeval Spain, more cruel than the Borgias: but they were terrible nevertheless. A perquisition meant, in most cases, the destruction of every household treasure, every family relic cherished through generations, it meant the wanton smashing of furniture and mirrors, the ripping up of valuable tapestries and of mattresses, the defacement of priceless pictures, it meant prying, hostile eyes thrust into receptacles, however secret, into private papers and even letters.

Nothing was sacred to men deputed to insult and to offend, just as much as to search.

When Fleurette reached that part of the house which was occupied by the family, she was confronted by the wildest, the most heart-stirring confusion. The carpets had been torn off the floors, the furniture for the most part lay in broken heaps about the rooms, mirrors and pictures had been dragged off the walls, broken crockery and glass was scattered everywhere, intermingled with horsehair and other stuffing out of chairs and mattresses, whilst all the walls, the doors, the window-frames bore traces of rude handling with bayonet or the heel of a boot. Fleurette, wide-eyed and appalled, ran from room to room; the guttering tallow candle which she held threw flickering lights and grotesque shadows on the scattered objects about her, made

58

them seem more weird, like the appurtenances of an abode of ghosts. Here in the pretty boudoir Mademoiselle's embroidery-frame lay smashed to tinder-wood with threads of the work still hanging to it, bits of rags, pathetic in their look of abandonment and desolation. There in the withdrawing-room, the beautiful satinwood spinet with its painted panels and exquisite mar-queterie was lying on its side, its body gaping like a gigantic wound, the strings emitting a final vibration like the last song of a dying swan.

From the direction of the dining-room came the incessant murmur of voices, but throughout the rest of the apartments, in the midst of all the wreckage, a silence reigned as of the grave. The place now was completely deserted. It seemed almost as if some terrible tornado had swept through these living-rooms: some implacable forces of nature rather than the hatred and cupidity of men. An earthquake could not have been more devastating, a fire more destructive.

And now in the midst of it all Fleurette came to a standstill, candle in hand: her breath came and went in quick short gasps, and her heart was beating furiously. The silence in this semi-darkness with those long, ghost-like shadows seemed to oppress her; the broken bits of beautiful things which she had known and loved ever since she remembered anything, gave her an awful feeling of desolation and a kind of foreboding of things, still worse, to come. It was instinct which had brought her to a halt here in this one room amongst the others. It was always known as Madame's room, for here Madame would always sit when she gave her orders to various members of the household, here that she would look through the household accounts whilst Fleurette and Rose, when they were still children, would sit in a corner of the sofa by the huge hearth, hand in hand, with a picture-book on their knees, silent like a pair of tiny white mice, waiting until Madame had finished her accounts, because then they would all go into the garden to gather flowers for the rooms, and fruit for dessert, or perhaps go down into the kitchen and learn how to dress a chicken for the table, or how best to mix a salad.

And Fleurette stood for a moment or two quite still, holding the candle high above her head, contemplating this wreckage. Then, having found a safe place on which to deposit the candle, she carefully closed the door which gave, like several others, on a long corridor that led to the main staircase at one end and to the service stairs at the other. The time had come to cease contemplation, to drive away superstitious fears and to act. Closing her eyes, Fleurette strove first of all to recapture pictures of long ago, to recreate the scenes enacted in this room, before this awful calamity had fallen on these people whom she loved so dearly. Memory was not rebellious. She could see the whole picture just as it had impressed itself on the tablets of her mind when she used to sit here as a child. There by the window Madame's desk used to stand. It was lying on its side now, the drawers wrenched open, the handles broken, papers, pen and sand scattered about; the ink had run out of the glass container and stained the beautiful old Aubusson carpet. But there Madame used to sit. Fleurette could almost see her now, at the desk. Her big household books open before her. Writing, calculating, and putting her money by in a leather bag. And presently she would rise, pick up her bag and books and carry them across the room to a spot close to the wall, the other side of the hearth. Here she would come to a standstill, and putting her beautiful hand somewhere against the wall, she would turn to the two girls – they were mere children then – and smile at them in a mysterious way; and they would say solemnly: "Open Sesame!" just as they had heard in the tale of Ali Baba and the forty robbers, which Monsieur de Frontenac had often told them. As soon as they had said the magic words the wall would open like the entrance of the robber's cave in the tale of Ali Baba, disclosing a recess into which Madame would put her books and her bag of money. Then she would once more turn and give a sign to the children and they would say: "Close

Sesame!" and the mysterious door would swing to again and no trace be left of the recess which lay hidden somewhere behind the panelled wall.

The whole of this picture stood out before Fleurette's mental vision in every detail; the exact spot where Madame used to stand, the way she put out her hand and touched the panelled wall. Carefully picking her way through the maze of broken furniture, Fleurette came to a halt on the very spot where she had so often seen Madame standing, with her books and money-bag in her arms. She put out her hand and touched the panel as Madame had done: all over the carved panel she put her hand, touching and pressing each bit of carving in its turn. Her heart was still beating wildly, but not in any way with fear. In fact she was surprised at herself for not being afraid. It was just the excitement of this wonderful adventure! She, Fleurette, who had seen nothing of the world beyond her own village of Laragne and an occasional glimpse at Sisteron, suddenly found herself guiding the destinies of people whom she loved – the messenger sent by the *bon Dieu* to help them in their need. There is no young human creature living who would not respond, heart and soul, to such a call, and Fleurette was of the South, a child of that romantic land of Dauphiné which had given so many of her heroic sons to strive and work for France.

And suddenly, as Fleurette pressed her finger on every piece of carved relief, one by one, she felt the centre of a dog-rose yield to the pressure. Softly, noiselessly, the panel swung outwards, and there in the recess were the familiar household books and the money-bag. Beside them lay a leather wallet and a small casket fitted with a brass lock. Without any hesitation Fleurette took the bag, the wallet and the casket, leaving the books where they were. Never for a moment did the thought occur to her that she might be discovered in what would be a highly compromising position. She was too simple-minded, too innately honest to think that she might be suspected of theft.

Having stowed the wallet and the bag in the wide pockets of her kirtle and hidden the casket beneath her shawl, Fleurette picked her way back across the room. She left the mysterious recess open because she did not know how to close it, and did not want to waste any time in trying to find out. She found her way to the door and opened it, then she blew out the candle and finally peeped out into the corridor.

It was deserted. The lingering evening light, pale and ghost-like, came creeping in through the row of tall arched windows facing her. As everywhere else in the château, the corridor bore the melancholy traces of the soldiers' passage. It was the same devastation. The same wanton destruction was only too apparent in the torn carpet and the fragments of glass and broken sconces that littered the floor. Fleurette, turning her back on the direction of the main staircase, made her way to the back stairs which wound in a close spiral down to the service door.

Fleurette descended with quick, furtive steps, until, past the first curve of the spiral, the stairs were in total darkness. But she would have found her way all about the château blindfold, so well did she know its every nook and cranny. She came to the door and fumbled for the bolts. She had drawn one and taken off the chain, when she heard a measured tramp on the other side of the door. Steps were coming this way along the flagged path; a moment or two later they came to a halt close to the door. Fleurette hardly daring to breathe, listened. A voice said: "Did you go in there?"

"No, citizen," replied another, "not by this door. The bolts are fastened on the inside."

Something else was said which Fleurette did not catch, and the steps receded in the direction of the front of the house. She waited a minute or two longer, breathless and motionless, until she heard what she thought was the tramp of feet in the corridor above her. The soldiers had apparently been ordered to come round again, perhaps they would be coming down those stairs. To hesitate now might prove fatal. Fumbling once more in the gloom, Fleurette found the last bolt and drew it, and the next moment was out in the open. The back door gave on the yard. On the right were the stables, and facing the door, the riding-school and one or two sheds; on the left the kitchens and servants' quarters. In this direction too was the great archway and the main entrance into the house. Past the archway was the park and the avenue leading to the big gates.

After a moment's reflection Fleurette decided to avoid these main approaches: there was another way across the park, past the stable gate. Hugging the casket closely under her shawl, Fleurette set out in the direction of the stables. There was no one about and she felt comparatively safe. Night was now rapidly drawing in, and she fortunately had on a dark kirtle and dark worsted stockings. The air was very still and the waning moon not yet risen in the east. From far away came the sound of the bell of Laragne church. It struck eight. Fleurette felt a pang of anxiety. She had promised to be home before dark and Louise would be anxious and cross: and there was still something she wanted to do before she went home. Now she was past the stable door where, in a heap, just as old André had said, there lay a pile of faggots. The sight of them gave Fleurette a happy thrill. Was she not obeying the dictates of the mysterious voice which had spoken to her through the medium of the old faggot-carrier?

The next moment, a firm step resounded on the flagstones of the stables, and a second later a man appeared under the lintel of the door.

"Fleurette! what in God's name are you doing here?"

Smothering a startled cry, Fleurette turned and found herself face to face with her father. He was standing at the stable door; his hands were clasped behind his back, and he had a tricolour sash round his waist. Now women, young girls especially, those born and bred in outlying country districts, are credited with being stupid, silly in their fears, timorous like hens; and so no doubt would Fleurette have been in ordinary circumstances. She may not have been either clever or brave originally; she would perhaps have behaved in a silly, timorous fashion but for this one fact, that she knew that something terrible was happening to the Frontenacs whom she loved, and that she had been deputed by the *bon Dieu*, or merely by a human friend, to do something important for them. In order to do this she must keep her head; and trust any woman to keep her head if one she loves is in peril.

"What are you doing here, Fleurette?" Bibi reiterated rather sternly.

And Fleurette with a well-simulated nervous little laugh, retorted lightly:

"Why, Bibi chéri, I might retaliate. What are *you* doing here? I thought you were on your way to Paris."

"What are you doing here, Fleurette?" Bibi said once more, and Fleurette thought that his voice had never sounded so harsh before.

"But Bibi," Fleurette said simply, "I often come to see Madame and Mademoiselle. And after you left this afternoon I felt so lonely and sad, I thought I might seek Mademoiselle Rose for company."

"And have you seen her?"

"No. They told me Madame and Mademoiselle had gone."

"Who told you?"

"Papa Mathieu."

"What else did he tell you?"

"Only that there were soldiers come to the château; and that I'd better go home again – and so I'm going."

"He didn't tell you anything else?"

"No," Fleurette replied innocently. "Was there anything else to say?"

"No – er – no," Bibi rejoined. "Of course not. But Fleurette – "

"Yes, Bibi darling?"

"How often must I tell you that you must not talk of 'Madame' and 'Mademoiselle'? There are no Madames and Mademoiselles now; we are, all of us equally, citizens of France."

"Yes, Bibi," Fleurette rejoined demurely. "And I really, really am very careful when strangers are about. It doesn't matter what I say before you, does it, chéri Bibi?"

"No, no," Bibi muttered, seemingly without much conviction, and Fleurette then went on quickly:

"I must run home now, chéri Bibi, or Louise will be getting anxious. You are coming too, aren't you? Louise will get you such a lovely supper and then – "

"No, my little one," Bibi said. "I can't. Not tonight. I must be in Orange tomorrow."

"But Bibi – "

"Run along, child," Bibi broke in almost fiercely.

"It's a dark night, and there are always vagabonds about."

"Ah well then, good night, Bibi," Fleurette murmured meekly.

"Good night, little one."

And suddenly Bibi put out his hand and grasped Fleurette by the wrist.

"Are you not going to kiss me, Fleurette?" he asked with oh! such a tone of sadness now in his voice.

It was a terrible moment. What a mercy that the darling had seized her left wrist rather than her right, because with her right hand Fleurette was hugging the small casket under her shawl. There were also the wallet and the money-bag in the pocket of her kirtle: oh! if Bibi should knock against them! Fortunately it was dark, and he could not see the bulge under her shawl. But, of course, she could not part from Bibi chéri without giving him a farewell kiss. He seemed sad and unhappy, and there was

65

something about his whole manner that Fleurette did not understand.

At first, when he startled her by suddenly appearing at the stable door, she had not even tried to conjecture what he was doing here; she was too deeply absorbed in her own adventure for the moment to do more than vaguely wonder what part Bibi was playing in the tragic events that had wrought such desolation at the château. Bibi chéri, who worshipped his little Fleurette, who was always so kind, so gentle, a slave to every one of her whims; he must have been dragged into this horrible affair, was perhaps an innocent tool of those cruel people in Paris, who monopolized his time and kept him away from his home.

Indeed, she had no mistrust in him whatever; but her trust in him did not go the length of telling him about the casket, or the mysterious voice of the faggot-carrier; those were her own secrets, secrets too which concerned the Frontenacs for whom Bibi had never evinced a very great affection, and had even tried to dissuade Fleurette from having too much intercourse with them. It was in fact her love for Madame and Monsieur, and for Mademoiselle Rose, and Bibi's strange dislike of them, which had brought the only clouds in the sunshine of their affection.

But of this Fleurette was not thinking at the moment, her one thought was of her secret and how best to guard it. All the same she would not have denied Bibi chéri the kiss he asked for. She must take the risk, that was all, and once again trust to her wits. She allowed him to put his arms round her neck and held up her fresh young face for his kiss: she held the casket so carefully that he did not feel its sharp angles. All was well, for now she was free from his embrace, but still he had hold of her left hand, and drew her close to him.

"Fleurette, my little one," he said earnestly.

"Yes, Bibi."

"Do you know where the two Frontenac women have gone to?"

"No, Bibi, I do not," Fleurette was able to reply in all truthfulness, and looked her father straight in the eyes. "They were gone before I came."

"It is for their good that I ask you."

"I am sure it is, Bibi chéri, but really, really I do not know."

Bibi gave a quick, impatient sigh.

"Ah, well! goodbye, my Fleurette."

"Good night, Bibi."

At last she was free. With her left hand she blew a last kiss to Bibi, and then quickly sped across the yard. Her heart felt heavy, and there was an uncomfortable lump in her throat. For the first time she had been brought face to face with the realities of life. Hitherto she had lived in a kind of fairyland in which she was the carefully tended and guarded queen, and Bibi the acknowledged king as well as slave. Everything in the world was perfect, and lovely and wonderful; the men and women in it – not only Bibi, but Louise, and M. Duflos the butcher, and M. Colombe the grocer, and – and M. Amédé – they were all kind and generous and gentle. But now cruelty and spite had come within her ken. An ugly ghoul called "hatred" had passed by hand in hand with his ugly brother "mistrust" and the latter had whispered something in her ear just now, which had caused her to shrink within herself when Bibi had kissed her, and to turn from him and to run away with a strange sense of relief.

She did not look back as she sped across the yard, and when she came to the small postern gate she was thankful to find it on the latch, so that she could slip out unseen.

Nine

Fleurette was too young, too ignorant for self-analysis. She could not have told you what had made her act in the way she did, nor what had caused her so to mistrust Bibi as not to share her precious secret with him. All she knew was that she had had a wild desire to get away from him.

A cart-track led from the postern gate across a couple of fields where it joined the main road; one or two isolated farm buildings belonging to M. de Frontenac, and the open fields on both sides, made the track fairly safe from foot-pads. The main road too which led through the village would be safer after dark, than the short cut over the mountains. Fleurette hastened along, hugging her treasures, hoping that she would not fall in with the soldiers on their return from the château.

The weather had not fulfilled the promise made by the beauty of the sunset: heavy clouds hung over the sky; only one or two streaks of pale lemon-coloured light, like great gashes through the leaden clouds, still lingered in the West. Through the gloom farm sheds and isolated trees loomed out like great immobile giants, and, on the right, the dense mass of the avenue of acacias and elder and the great gates of the château.

Fleurette was already well on her way along the high road and in sight of the first house of the village, the cottage where Adèle lived with her aunt, the widow Tronchet, when she heard the all too familiar sound behind her of the heavy tramping of feet and of horses' hoofs raising the dust of the road. The night was so still that the sounds reached her ears distinctly. She heard the lieutenant's harsh voice giving a brief word of command: the creaking of the château gates, as they swung upon their hinges. Just then Roy, Monsieur's dog, set up a dismal howl, and from one of the tall poplar trees that bordered the road an owl gave a hoot and fluttered out into the night.

Fleurette broke out into a run. She knew that she could ask for shelter in the widow Tronchet's cottage and wait there until the soldiers had gone by. Perhaps Adèle would walk home with her after that. Fortunately she could already perceive the light glimmering in one of the tiny windows, and just at the moment Adèle came out of the front door, probably to see for herself what the unusual sounds were about.

She was mightily surprised to see Fleurette come running along.

"They are the same soldiers, Adèle," Fleurette explained breathlessly, as she followed her foster-sister into the cottage, "who were at Lou Mas this afternoon. Close the door, do, and I'll tell you all about them."

The widow Tronchet came out of her kitchen, and looked disapprovingly at Fleurette. She did not like the girl, and discouraged all intercourse between her and Adèle. She was a thrifty, hard-featured, hard-hearted peasant – older than her sister Louise by a couple of years – who had exacted every ounce of work and obedience from Adèle in payment for the shelter of her roof and for her daily bread. She had never forgiven her sister for leaving Adèle on her hands, though the girl had always worked her fingers to the bone, grudgingly no doubt, but diligently, in order to bring additional comfort into the cottage. But it was a poor, ill-furnished cottage, wherein food was none too plentiful, and beds hard, whereas Louise at Lou Mas lived in the lap of luxury; and envy had fostered dislike until it had almost become hatred.

She listened, with a frown on her hard wrinkled face, to Fleurette's breathless tale of what had happened at the château.

69

It would be the gossip of the village by tomorrow, that the soldiers of the Republic had arrested Monsieur, and that Madame and Mademoiselle had fled no one knew whither.

"Oh, Ma'ame Tronchet," Fleurette concluded, her fresh voice hoarse with sobs, "dear Ma'ame Tronchet, you don't think they're really going to harm Monsieur, do you?"

The widow Tronchet shrugged her shoulders and gave a short, harsh laugh.

"I'm not thinking about it at all one way or the other," she said drily. "What difference does it make to us poor people," she went on, grumbling, while she busied herself about the room, "what happens to all those aristos? They never cared what happened to us."

For the moment Fleurette could do no more than stare at the widow Tronchet, in horror. Never had she heard anyone say anything so wicked. She was quite ready to defend Monsieur and Madame against any accusation of hard-heartedness, and would have done so at risk of offending the disagreeable, ill-natured old woman, but for the moment her attention, as well as that of Adèle's, was riveted on the sounds outside. The soldiers had just come round the bend of the road; they were quite close to the cottage already, with the two horsemen walking their mounts in the van.

"They are going on to Serres," Fleurette whispered. In her heart she was wondering what Bibi was going to do. He was evidently not going to Orange, as he had said he would. Would he spend the night at Lou Mas after all? If he did, was there any danger of Fleurette's secret leaking out? Of Bibi chéri finding out something about the casket and the precious wallet? Fleurette was still hugging the casket, she could see the widow Tronchet's hard, steely eyes, gazing curiously at the bulge underneath her shawl, and then at the fullness in her kirtle where the wallet and the money-bag lay hidden in the pockets: Fleurette felt the blood rush up to her cheeks, and then had the mortification of seeing Adèle's pinched-up little face break into a smile. Of what were those two women thinking? Surely not that she, Fleurette, had been stealing. Their faces were so inscrutable: the older woman's hard and set, and Adèle's rat-like and furtive, as if determined to conceal her thoughts.

The next moment they all heard the horsemen go by. Adèle ran to the door and peered out into the night. Over her shoulder she said to Fleurette:

"There's your father riding with the soldiers. Shall I shout to him and tell him you are here?"

Instinctively Fleurette shook her head, and with that same inscrutable smile still on her face, Adèle deliberately closed the door again.

"They've got Monsieur walking between them," she commented drily.

"It would have been better," the widow said acidly to Fleurette, "for Citizen Armand to know that you are here. It won't be safe for women to be alone on the high road this night, I am thinking."

Then, as Fleurette remained silent, debating within herself what she had best do, the old woman went on curtly: "The sooner you get home now, my girl, the better. Adèle has got to put in an hour's work at Citizen Colombe's up at the village; it is miserable pay enough," she continued muttering to herself, "and a shame that one girl should have to work so hard, whilst another lives a pampered life of luxury. But anyway," she concluded abruptly, "I can't be wasting any lamp-oil on you."

"No – no – of course not, Ma'ame Tronchet," Fleurette stammered. But the widow, still muttering under her breath, was paying no more attention to her. She had climbed onto a chair, and reaching up to the lamp that hung from the ceiling, she turned out the light. The room was now in darkness except for the light that came in through the open kitchen door. The widow with a curt: "Don't be late, Adèle," went off into the kitchen, and a moment or two later could be heard busy with her pots and pans.

Adèle had picked up her shawl, and equally unceremoniously gone as far as the door, when Fleurette called her shyly back.

"Adèle!"

The girl turned without speaking, her hand on the door which she was holding open.

"If you are going to M'sieur Colombe, could you – " Fleurette stammered, "I mean, would you tell Monsieur Amédé, that – that I am here, and perhaps – "

"Why don't you come along with me?" Adèle retorted drily, "and tell him what you want."

Of course Fleurette could not tell her that she did not want Monsieur and Madame Colombe to know that she had something important to say to M'sieu' Amédé. So all she said was: "Oh, Adèle, please!"

Adèle retorted with a shrug of the shoulders and an ugly little sneer:

"You don't want his papa and mama to know, I suppose."

Fleurette whispered: "No!"

"Very well!" was all that Adèle said in reply. "I'll tell him."

And in her usual, furtive, noiseless way she went out of the house, closing the door behind her.

Ten

Fleurette remained in darkness, silent, motionless as a little mouse, listening for the well-known footstep which in a few minutes, she knew, would be at the door. It had perhaps been a rash thing thus to give herself away to Adèle, but the girl was uncommunicative and had never been known to gossip. Between two risks Fleurette had chosen the lesser one. If Bibi – as she feared – was going back to Lou Mas, there would be no chance whatever of keeping the secret of Madame's casket and valuables from him, and what Bibi's attitude would be towards them, Fleurette could not guess. It was the great Unknown. For Madame's sake and Mademoiselle's she would not risk it.

Like an inspiration the thought of M'sieur Amédé had occurred to her; of Amédé who, when she was a little girl and he a growing lad, would always take the blame on himself and know how to shield her when they had got into mischief together. She felt now, especially since this afternoon, that she could trust Amédé in a way that she had never trusted anyone else. Not even Bibi. Unfortunately Adèle had to be made a part confidant of the purpose: but after all what did Adèle know? She couldn't know anything about the casket and Madame's valuables: and if she did sneer, or even talk to her aunt about this message sent to M'sieu' Amédé through her, well! Fleurette was prepared to face the gossip – as long as her secret was safe.

She was counting the minutes – the seconds – Five minutes for Adèle to go to the Rue Haute: three and a half for Amédé to run along here – she did not doubt but that he would run. Then there would be the intervening time whilst Adèle sought for an opportunity to speak to him alone. But oh! how Time dragged on leaden-footed! Nearly fifteen minutes must have gone by since Adèle went away. The widow Tronchet was still busy in the kitchen, rattling her pots and pans: but any moment she might finish and perhaps come in here and find Fleurette still waiting. Then there would be more acrimonious remarks, questions, arguments. Had Fleurette known anything about nerves, she would have said that hers were irritated to snapping-point; but there was little talk of nerves in that year, 1794, and none in this remote corner of Dauphiné.

Fleurette found it very difficult even to sit still. Would Amédé never come! All sorts of possibilities occurred to her, bringing her to the point of screaming with impatience. Perhaps he was from home, or working in the shop under his father's eye. Perhaps the soldiers had called at the *épicerie* and taken him away, and Fleurette would never see her again – Oh! if only time would stand still until Amédé came!

Then at last, when she was on the point of bursting into tears with disappointment, she heard the quick, familiar step. Amédé!!! As noiselessly as possible she opened the door and slipped out. There, sure enough, was Amédé coming along. Though it was very dark now, Fleurette knew it was he because of the sound of his footsteps. Hearing hers, he came to a halt, and she ran up to him, breathless with excitement. All at once the enormity of what she had done struck terror in her heart. She, Fleurette, whose reputation had stood hitherto above all gossip, who for three years in succession had been crowned Queen of the month of May, an honour only accorded to girls of spotless character, she had actually given an assignation to a young man – at night – far from her home and his!

And with the horror of what she had done came an intense shyness. What would M'sieur Amédé himself think of her? Indeed, she had to evoke all her fondness for Madame and all her fears for Mademoiselle before she could summon enough courage to approach him, and to place a timid little hand upon his arm. She felt it trembling at her touch, and through the silence of the night came an answering timid sigh and whisper:

"Mam'zelle Fleurette! What can I do in your service?"

His timidity gave her courage. Gently she led him to the edge of the road where the tall poplar trees cast long, impenetrable shadows.

"M'sieur Amédé," Fleurette began, whispering low so that chance eavesdroppers might not hear: "I don't know what you'll think of me. I know I have done something which everyone in the village would call reprehensible. I sent for you in secret because – because, M'sieur Amédé, there is no one in the world I could trust, as I do trust you."

This time there came no sigh on the part of the young peasant, only a quick intaking of the breath, as if he had suddenly been dazzled by a wonderful light. His hard, rough hand crept up shyly and fastened over the soft, quivering one that lay upon his sleeve just like a frightened bird. But he was a man of few words, and therefore said nothing: and Fleurette, encouraged by the pressure of that rough hand, went on more glibly.

"It is about Monsieur, Madame and Mademoiselle," she said, "up at the château. Soldiers have visited the place and they have broken the furniture and torn the beautiful carpets and the curtains: why, I know not. They have also called Monsieur, Madame and Mademoiselle traitors and aristos, and they have seized Monsieur and dragged him away from his home. By a miracle, M'sieur Amédé, a miracle wrought by the *bon Dieu* himself, Madame and Mademoiselle were able to escape out of the château before those awful soldiers came. I know that they are safe, but – "

75

"How do you know that, Mam'zelle Fleurette?" Amédé asked also in a whisper.

"Because, M'sieur Amédé," she replied, "there is a mysterious personage working for the safety of Madame and Mademoiselle, under the direct guidance of the good God. I feel quite sure that Monsieur will also presently be saved through him."

"A mysterious personage, Mam'zelle Fleurette?"

"Yes, a direct messenger from Heaven. He has come down to earth in the guise of an old faggot-carrier. He looks old and decrepit and toil-worn, but when he speaks his voice is like that of an archangel, and if he looks at you his eyes give you the strength of giants and celestial joy."

"But, Mam'zelle Fleurette – "

"His voice spoke to me this afternoon, M'sieu' Amédé. All it said to me was that papers and valuables were behind the panel in Madame's room. At that time I knew nothing about the soldiers. I had seen them but did not know that they were going to the château to arrest Monsieur and Madame and Mademoiselle Rose. Nevertheless when that voice spoke to me, I felt I must go over to the château as quickly as may be."

"Why did you not send for me then, Mam'zelle Fleurette?"

"I seemed to be in a hurry, impelled to run along as fast as I could. So I went by the mountain track. When I arrived at the château, the soldiers had been there some time. They had turned the place topsy-turvy, scared the servants and smashed and torn up everything, leaving nothing but the walls intact. It seemed as if a great tempest had swept by and wrecked everything. Monsieur was under arrest and Madame and Mademoiselle had gone. No one knew whither. Then suddenly I remembered that mysterious voice: I found my way to Madame's room, and I found the panel, behind which Madame used to hide her household books and her money. I had often watched her doing this when I was a child. I tried to remember how to make the panel work and the good God helped me. And behind the panel I found Madame's papers and her money,

76

and a small box which, I am sure, has precious things in it, or it would not have been there."

"Then what did you do, Mam'zelle Fleurette?" Amédé gasped under his breath, his none too sharp wits slowly taking in the details of the amazing adventure.

"I just took the wallet, M'sieu' Amédé," she replied simply, "and the money-bag, and the box. And here they are."

She tapped the pockets of her kirtle and made him feel the bulge underneath her shawl.

"Oh, mon Dieu!" he exclaimed fervently.

And then she told him about Bibi, and how frightened she was lest when she returned to Lou Mas she should find him there. Bibi's sympathies seemed to be all with the soldiers, she explained, and he would for certain make her give up Madame's papers and valuables to the lieutenant.

"That is why," she concluded with a return to her first timidity, "I wished to speak with you, dear M'sieu' Amédé."

"The Eternal Eve!" It was the first time Fleurette had used an endearing word when speaking to Amédé. Born and bred in this remote corner of Dauphiné, unsophisticated, untutored in the ways of coquetry and cajolery, she knew nevertheless, true daughter of the first mother that she was, that after this he would be mere wax in her hands.

He was!

All that he wanted to know was what he could do for her. Had she asked him to throw himself into the Buëche, he would have done it: but all that she wanted was for him to put her treasures in a safe place, until such time as Madame required them.

"If Bibi knew what I was doing, M'sieu' Amédé," she pleaded, "he would order me to give up Madame's property. But I know that the *bon Dieu* meant me to take charge of it, or why," she argued naïvely, "should He have sent His messenger to me?"

Of course Amédé was only too ready to share the burden of this wonderful secret with Fleurette.

It was wonderful to share anything with this loveliest being in all the world; and the thought that she trusted him more even than her father, was sending him well-nigh crazy with joy.

"I'll tell you what I'll do, Mam'zelle Fleurette," he said: "There's an old tool-shed at the back of our house where all sorts of rubbish are kept. It is an absolute litter now, and the back of it has not been cleared or interfered with for years. But I know of a convenient hole in the flooring, hidden well away in a corner. I'll put these things there. They'll be quite safe – Mam'zelle Fleurette, you'll know where to find them after I've gone away, if you want them."

"After you've gone away?"

For the moment she had forgotten. Of course he was going! How could she forget? He was going to join the army – to fight the English – ! Perhaps he was never coming back – oh! How could she – how could she forget?

Amédé after the long speech which he had delivered in a whisper – his longest speech on record – had remained silent. The tone of anguish in Fleurette's voice, just now when he recalled the fact that he was going away, had given him an immense thrill of joy. Altogether poor Amédé felt so happy that he was almost ashamed. The night was so beautifully still: the wind had gone down, and slowly the great clouds that had obscured the sky since sunset were rolling away over the valley. Already overhead a patch of translucent indigo appeared, ever-widening, and revealing one by one the scintillating worlds that are beyond man's ken. Amédé did not want to speak; he wanted it less than he had ever done before. He just wanted to stand there beside this exquisite creature, wrapped in the silence of the night, feeling her nearness, hearing the gentle murmur of her breath come and go through her perfect mouth. She had extracted the casket from under her shawl and given it to him to hold, and she also gave him the wallet and the money-bag; and as she did this, her little hand, so soft and so warm, came in contact with his now and then – quite often – and poor Amédé was on the point of swooning with delight.

"I do trust you, M'sieu' Amédé," she whispered in the end: "and you'll do this for Madame's sake, will you not? and also Mademoiselle's. And also," she added softly, "for mine."

"Oh! Mam'zelle Fleurette," Amédé sighed. What he had wished to say was: "I would die for you, beloved of my heart: at a word from you I would lay down my life, or barter my soul." But Amédé had no command of words, and was now cursing himself for being a clumsy fool. He stowed away the wallet and the bag into the pockets of his breeches, and tucked the casket underneath his blouse.

"And now I must go home, dear Monsieur Amédé," Fleurette said. "As it is, I am afraid Bibi will be anxious."

Her hand was on his arm: and with a sudden impulse he stooped and pressed his lips against that exquisite little hand. Fortunately they were still standing in the shadows cast by the poplar trees, or Arnédé must have seen the blush that rose to Fleurette's cheeks when she felt the delicious thrill of that timid kiss. A soft breeze stirred the branches above their heads, and through the quivering leaves there came a sigh that was like an echo of their own. And above the crests of Pelvoux the waning moon suddenly rent the last clouds that veiled her mystery, and flooded the snowy immensities with a shower of gold. Slowly the shades of night yielded to the magic, and the high road glistened like a silvery ribbon winding, snake-like, toward Laragne.

Fleurette gave a sudden start of alarm.

"What is it, Mam'zelle Fleurette," Amédé asked.

"Someone," she said. "I saw someone move there – furtively – among the shadows."

He turned to look. A small figure wrapped in a shawl had just gone past on the other side of the road.

"It is only Adèle," he said carelessly. "She is going home."

Not altogether reassured, Fleurette peered into the shadows. She did not think that it was Adèle whom she had seen, or, if it was Adèle, there was someone else lurking in the shadows, she felt sure: and though she was not altogether frightened, she felt herself trembling, and her knees giving way under her.

No doubt it was in order to save herself from failing that she had leaned more heavily against Amédé's arm. Certain it is that he put that arm round her, only in order to support her; but the contact of that warm, quivering young body against his breast sent the last shred of his self-control flying away on the evening breeze.

The high road was bathed in honey-coloured light, but these two were standing in the deep shadows cast by the poplar trees; and the darkness wrapped them round as in a velvety, downy blanket. His arm tightened round her shoulders, pressed her closer and closer to his breast, held her there so closely that she could scarcely breathe.

It was only in order to get her breath that she raised her face to his; far be it from me to suggest that it was for any other motive; but this proved the final undoing of poor M'sieu' Amédé; for the next moment his lips were fastened hungrily on hers, and her sweet young soul went out to him, in a first, a most delicious kiss.

Eleven

It all seemed like a lovely dream after that: this walking together arm in arm down the high road with the waning moon throwing great patches of silvery light to guide them on their way.

They went through the village, not caring whom they met. They belonged to each other now; that wonderful kiss was a bond between them that only death could sever. That was how they felt; supremely, marvellously happy, thrilled with this new delight, this undreamed joy: and with it all a cloud of measureless sorrow at the impending farewell. The magic words had been spoken: "You love me, Fleurette?" The eternal question to which the only answer is a sigh. No, they did not care whom they met. They could laugh at gossip now: from this night they were tokened to one another, and only M. le Curé's blessing could make their happiness more complete.

As a matter of fact they met no one, for they avoided the main street of the village and made their way to Lou Mas along narrow by-paths that meandered through orchards of almond trees heavy with blossom. For the most part they were silent. Fleurette's little hand rested on Amédé's arm. Now and then he gave that hand a quick, excited squeeze and this relieved his feelings for the time being. Under his other arm he hugged the casket, the precious treasure that had been the mute but main spring of his happiness. It represented Fleurette's trust in him:

that priceless guerdon he would not have bartered for a kingdom.

"You will not part with Madame's valuables, will you, Amédé?" she had enjoined him most solemnly. "Not to anyone?"

"Never, Fleurette," he had replied solemnly. "On my soul!"

When they were within sight of Lou Mas, they decided that it would be best for him to turn back. She, Fleurette, was quite safe now, and of course old Louise would be waiting for her – and perhaps Bibi. She was not going to make a secret of her walk home with Amédé. Indeed she wished it proclaimed from the house-tops that they were tokened to one another, and that they would be married as soon as this horrible war was over. There was to be no secret about it, and Fleurette knew well enough that neither Bibi nor M'sieu' Colombe would object; but because of Madame's valuables, she did not want Amédé to come to Lou Mas until tomorrow. And so that first wonderful kiss found its successor in another – one that was perhaps even more delicious, because it was more poignant – the precursor of the last farewell. Fleurette found Louise anxiously waiting for her.

Bibi had not returned and the old woman knew nothing, of course, of the tragic events that had occurred at the château. Fleurette told her what had happened, and while she was speaking Bibi came in. He looked tired and anxious, but Fleurette thought it prudent not to appear to notice anything unusual about him. He made no reference to the events at Frontenac, and when nine o'clock came he kissed Fleurette as tenderly, as unconcernedly as usual. Nine o'clock! What a lifetime, as far as Fleurette was concerned, had been crowded into this past hour!

She went to bed as in a dream, partly made up of sorrow and partly of great joy: even the excitement of her adventure at the château was lost in the immensity of that joy. Fleurette fell asleep with her cheek against the hand on which Amédé had planted that first timid kiss.

When she came down in the early morning Bibi had already gone.

Twelve

The soldiers of the Republic together with their officer had spent half the night at Laragne in the tavern kept by the Père Gramme, drinking and jesting with the drabs of the village. Each man had a tale to tell of his own prowess at the château, and how but for him, the ci-devant Frontenac would have slipped through the fingers of justice as readily as the two women had done.

They were very proud of their prisoner, who sat lonely and silent in a corner of the low-raftered room, foul with the odour of sour wine and perspiring humanity. Monsieur de Frontenac – the ci-devant as he was curtly termed – was apparently taking his misfortune calmly; neither threats nor vain promises caused him to depart from his attitude of quiet philosophy. The soldiers had, of course, made up their minds that he knew well enough where his wife and daughter were in hiding, but they had also realized by now that it was not in their power to force him to divulge what he knew.

The lieutenant – a man who had begun life as a notary's clerk, and therefore had some education – was content to shrug his shoulders and to declare that the citizens of the nearest Committee of Public Safety, had plenty of means at their disposal for making an obdurate prisoner speak. He recalled that at the trial of the Widow Capet she had been forced into admissions which, before that, she would sooner have died than make. Mocking glances, jeers and insults were thereupon cast on the prisoner who remained as unconcerned, as serene as before.

The lieutenant had commandeered billets for his men in the better houses of the village, and just before midnight the party broke up. The prisoner was then conducted to the small, local *poste de gendarmerie* and there incarcerated in the cell usually occupied by vagabonds and cattle-thieves. Two or three of the soldiers remained at the *poste* to reinforce the local gendarmes, in case some hotheads in the village meditated a coup to wrest the traitor Frontenac from the clutches of justice. The lieutenant himself had selected the house of Citizen Colombe the grocer of the Rue Haute for his night-quarters. To say that the worthy *épicier* did not accord this representative of his country's army a warm welcome, would be to put it mildly. He was furious, and showed it as plainly as he dared; but there is in every French peasant a sound vein of common sense, and he knows – none better – when submission to the ruling powers is not only the best policy, but at the same time the most conducive to the preservation of his own dignity.

Ma'ame Colombe – or rather the citizeness – made the lieutenant comfortable and that was all; but at the bottom of her heart she felt that she must do unto him as she would wish her own son to be done by presently, when he too was a soldier in that army which she detested. She fell asleep thinking of Amédé tramping the high road as these men had done, stockingless, hatless, with unwashed shirt and a dirty worsted cap on his head; and she dreamed all night of him, deprived even of his weekly bath in the big tub, over in the wash-house. That is what she objected to mostly in these men: the dirt. It was wonderful, of course, their fighting for their country, now that all the other countries in the world were attacking France, but Ma'ame Colombe argued to herself that patriotism might just as well be allied to cleanliness. Even the lieutenant, who was after all an officer, and should be setting a good example to his men, would have looked much more imposing if he had washed his face and taken the dust of the road out of his hair.

Great, therefore, was Ma'ame Colombe's astonishment the next morning when she, along with several of her friends, being at the market, saw another detachment of soldiers marching into Laragne from the direction of Sisteron. Only eight of them there were, with one officer and a wagon drawn by two splendid horses; but *nom du ciel!* what a different set of men and horses these were. The men clean as new pins, magnificently dressed in blue coats with white facings and belts, white breeches – all spotless – and black gaiters that reached midway up their thighs. Beneath their elegant *chapeau-bras*, each adorned with a silk tricolour cockade, they wore their own hair, down to their shoulders, unfettered by the old, ridiculous *queue*, and each man had successfully cultivated a fierce and magnificent moustache. Everything about them glistened with cleanliness, their boots, their buckles, their muskets; as for the officer, never in all their lives had the good ladies of Laragne seen anyone so magnificent: tall, blond, with a moustache that he could easily have tucked behind his ears, and a little tuft of blond beard at the tip of his chin, he walked with drawn sword at the head of his squad, a superb tricolour sash further enhancing the glory of his attire.

Potatoes and eggs and butter were forgotten, while market-women and customers stood gaping, open-mouthed. Never had such beautiful specimens of manhood been seen in Laragne. By the time they reached the Rue Haute all the village had turned out to have a look at them, and heads appeared at every cottage window. The village urchins followed the little squad, intoning the "Marseillaise" and giving vent to their excitement by performing miracles of acrobatic evolutions. Even Ma'ame Colombe, who was at the moment selecting a piece of meat for Sunday's dinner, could not help but say to herself that she would not mind Amédé being in the army if he was going to look like that!

At that very moment one of the urchins paused in the midst of a magnificently sketched somersault in order to run down the street and back to the market-place, shouting excitedly:

"Ma'ame Colombe! Ma'ame Colombe! the soldiers are at the *épicerie*."

And so they were! Ma'ame Colombe hastily straightened her cap and snatching up her market basket, ran to the corner of the Rue Haute just in time to see the soldiers with their officer and wagon come to a halt outside her front door. The worthy Hector with his son Amédé, and the old man who helped in the shop, were busy taking down the shutters and displaying the sacks of various kinds of haricots and lentils in tempting array all along the shop front. Ma'ame Colombe heard the magnificent officer give a quick order: "Halte!" and "Attention!" and the next moment she saw him enter the shop followed by his men, the wagon remaining drawn up a little further down the street. The urchins and gaffers crowded round the doorstep open-mouthed, and Ma'ame Colombe had some difficulty in pushing her way through into her own house.

The officer began by asking Hector Colombe how many soldiers of the Republic were still sleeping under his roof.

"Only the lieutenant and two men, M'sieu' l'officier," Hector replied. Whereupon the officer broke in curtly:

"Call me citizen captain. This is the army of the Revolution and its soldiers are not aristos meseems."

Which remark boded no good to Ma'ame Colombe's ears. Clean or dirty they all appeared to be the same type of brigands; overbearing, exacting and merciless! Ah that poor dear Amédé!

The officer then demanded to see the lieutenant and the two soldiers. Amédé offered to call them, but was stopped by a brief command from the captain:

"No, not you," he said curtly, "I want you here, the citizeness can go."

Ma'ame Colombe, obedient and vaguely frightened, put down her basket and went upstairs to fetch the lieutenant and the two men, who were still in bed. But although she had only been gone a couple of minutes, her sense of fear took on a more tangible form when she came down again, for she found all the drawers of the counter open, and much of their contents scattered about the floor. Some of the soldiers were busy ferreting about, behind and under the counter. The officer stood in the middle of the shop talking with Hector, who looked both choleric and sullen; in the doorway, the crowd of gaffers were being kept back by two of the soldiers, who were using the butts of their muskets when some venturesome urchin tried to cross the threshold. But what filled poor Ma'ame Colombe's heart with dismay was the sight of Amédé sitting in the parlour behind the shop, with two other soldiers obviously on guard over him.

Her instinct prompted her to run first of all to her husband with a quick whispered: "Hector, what does this mean?"

But the magnificent officer brusquely thrust himself between her and Hector and said gruffly: "It means, citizeness, that not only treason, but also theft has been traced to this house, and that it is lucky for you that news of it reached the Committee of Sisteron in time, else," he added grimly, "it had been worse for you and your family."

"Treason and theft?" Ma'ame Colombe exclaimed in hot indignation. "You must take it from me, young man, citizen, captain, or whatever you may be, that I'll allow no one to – "

"Hold your tongue, woman," the officer broke in curtly; "you do yourself no good by these protests. Obedience is your wisest course."

"Good or no good," Ma'ame Colombe persisted heatedly, "I won't have the word theft used in connection with this house, and if – "

"Make your wife hold her tongue, citizen," the officer, now addressing Hector once more, broke in curtly, "or I shall have to send her to the *poste* for interfering with a soldier of the Republic in the execution of his duty."

Poor Hector Colombe, whose choler was shrinking in inverse ratio to that of his wife, did his best to pacify the worthy dame.

"It is all a mistake, Angélique," he said gently. "M'sieu' le Capitaine – pardon! the citizen captain thinks that Amédé has some papers and valuables belonging to Madame – I mean, to the Citizeness Frontenac – "

"Are they calling my Amédé a thief, then?" Ma'ame Colombe demanded hotly.

"No! No!" Hector replied, trying to be patient and conciliatory. "Have I not told you that it is all a mistake? Every- one knows there are no thieves in this house; but it seems the authorities think that Amédé may have hidden those valuables pour le bon motif."

"If he had," the mother retorted obstinately, "he would say so. Let me just ask him – "

Hector had hold of her hand, but she wrenched it free, and before any of the soldiers could bar the way, she had run into the back parlour, shouting:

"Amédé, my little one, have you told those soldiers that you know nothing of Madame's valuables? Why, nom de Dieu!" she went on, hands on hips, defiant and aggressive like the true female defending its young, "look at the innocent. Is that the face of a thief?"

She pointed at Amédé, who, however, remained strangely silent.

"Voyons, mon petit, tell them!" Angélique Colombe went on with perhaps a shade less assurance than she had displayed at first. The next moment, however, the captain had seized her unceremoniously by the arm, and dragged her back into the front shop. Here he gave her arm a good shake.

"Did I not order you to hold your tongue?" he demanded roughly.

Cowed, in spite of herself, not so much by the officer's tone of command as by Amédé's silence, Ma'ame Colombe did, in effect, hold her tongue. A sense of disaster as well as of shame had suddenly descended upon her. Her ample bosom heaving, she sank into a chair, and threw her apron over her head. She was not crying, but she felt the need of shutting out from her vision the picture of Amédé looking so confused and sullen, of Hector looking as perplexed as she was herself, as well as of that magnificent officer with his fine clothes and his tricolour sash. But chiefly she wanted for the moment to lose sight of that crowd of gaffers and urchins and neighbours, all staring at her, with that unexplainable feeling, not exactly of contentment for her misfortune, but which can only be expressed by that untranslatable word *Schadenfreude*. Thus shut out from the rest of her little world, the poor woman slowly rocked herself backwards and forwards, murmuring inaudible words under cover of her apron, until she heard the captain's voice saying abruptly:

"Were you the officer in charge of detachment number ninety-seven?"

Curiosity got the better of sorrow, and Ma'ame Colombe peeped round the edge of her apron. The picture which she saw made her drop her apron altogether. The lieutenant who, the night before, had been so overbearing and so hilarious, stood before his superior officer now, a humble, dejected figure, dreading reprimand, like a schoolboy fearing the cane.

"I am in charge of the detachment ninety-seven – yes, citizen captain," he replied haltingly.

What a contrast these two! Ma'ame Colombe, in spite of her anxiety, her indignation and what not, could not help but compare. Woman-like, she had an eye for the handsome male, and what more gorgeous than this captain of the Republican, or revolutionary army, as he apparently liked to style his men, with his braided jacket and superb tricolour sash, with his blond hair and fierce moustachios? He poked his tufted chin out at the bedraggled-looking lieutenant before him, looked down with obvious contempt at the latter's ragged coat and mud-stained breeches. But he made no remark on the want of cleanliness and decency, as Ma'ame Colombe expected him to do.

"Where do you come from?" he demanded.

"From Orange, citizen captain."

"What is your objective?"

"After this, Serres, citizen captain, and then Valence."

"And your orders are to arrest on the way every person suspected of treason against the Republic?"

"Yes, citizen."

"And how have you obeyed these orders, citizen lieutenant?" the captain demanded sternly.

"I have done my best, citizen captain," the other replied with an attempt at bluster; "at Vaison – "

"I am not talking of Vaison, which you know quite well, citizen lieutenant. I wish to know how you obeyed the orders given to you to arrest the ci-devant Frontenac, his wife and daughter?"

"Citizen – "

"Have you done it, citizen lieutenant?" the officer thundered, and all of the bluster went out of the subaltern as he stammered meekly:

"When we reached the house of the ci-devant Frontenac, the two women had gone."

"Gone?" and the captain's voice boomed through the low-raftered room like a distant roll of cannon. "Gone? Whither?"

"Gone, citizen captain," the lieutenant murmured under his breath: "spirited away. The devil alone knows how."

"Which means that there is a traitor among you."

"Citizen captain – " the other protested.

"A traitor I say. You had secret orders, and yet the women were warned!" And once more the officer's glance flashed down with scorn on his unfortunate subordinate. His blond hair seemed to bristle with wrath; his moustachios stood out like spikes: he looked a veritable god of vengeance and of wrath.

"Where," he thundered, "is the ci-devant Frontenac?"

"At the commissariat, citizen captain, guarded by our men," the lieutenant replied.

"And the rest of your detachment?"

"In billets in the village."

"And did you search this house when you entered it?"

"No – that is – no – I did not – that is – " stammered the wretched man.

"Or the other houses where you billeted your men?"

But this time the lieutenant only shook his head in dejected silence.

"Which means that you allowed soldiers of the Republic to sleep under strange roofs without ascertaining whether they were safe. Why, citizen lieutenant, this place might have been swarming with traitors."

"The people here, citizen, are – "

"Enough. You are relieved of your command, and you will proceed now with us to Sisteron where you will render an account of your conduct before the Committee of Public Safety."

Ma'ame Colombe, who had watched the two men closely during this exciting colloquy, saw an ashen hue spread over the lieutenant's face, beneath the thick coating of grime. Though they did not know much in this tucked-away corner of Dauphiné, of what went on in the great cities, they had vaguely heard how great officers of the army had been deprived of their rank and sent to the guillotine for not doing their duty by the army of the Republic. The crowd at the door had also listened in silence; many a cheek turned pale at sound of that thundering voice which held in its arrogant tone a menace of death.

And now the captain turned to the other two down-at-heel soldiers who stood skulking behind their lieutenant.

"Go," he commanded, "round the billets where your comrades are. Bring them hither. And one of you to the commissariat, and bring the ci-devant here too. And no delay, remember. No gossip on the way as you value your lives. I give you five minutes to have all the men and the prisoner here."

The men went immediately to execute the peremptory order, while the lieutenant remained in the shop looking the picture of humility and dejection. Ma'ame Colombe who had a kindly heart inside her ample bosom, felt almost sorry for the man, so miserable did he look. Indeed, it seemed as if this squad of elegantly clad soldiers sowed anguish and terror in their path.

But the worst was yet to come. Ma'ame Colombe thought that she had probed the last depths of humiliation when she heard that gorgeous officer call her Amédé a thief. To such a pass had this so-called revolution brought the respectable children of France, that they saw themselves bullied and insulted, and held up to shame before their neighbours. What was all that in comparison with the shame of seeing Amédé confronted with the proof that in very truth he was in possession of papers and valuables which were the property of Madame de Frontenac?

It all happened so quickly. Poor Ma'ame Colombe could scarce believe her eyes. All that she saw was two soldiers guided by their sumptuous captain go straight through the back parlour and out by the back door into the yard. What happened out there she did not know, but a minute or two later the three men were standing once more in the parlour, and the captain had in his hand a small box, a thick leather wallet and a bag which obviously contained money.

At sight of these Amédé – her Amédé – had jumped to his feet as if he had been stung; all the blood rushed to his face, and made it crimson with choler, and it looked for the moment as if he would hurl himself on the officer of the Republican army – which would have meant instant death for him, as the soldiers had already shouldered their muskets. Ma'ame Colombe gave a terrified shriek, whereat Amédé suddenly seemed to realize his position, the flush died out of his poor face, and with eyes downcast he resumed his former silent, constrained attitude.

The captain shrugged his shoulders and with a note of dry sarcasm in his voice he said:

"I see you make no attempt at denial. You are wise, citizen. Try and induce your mother not to shriek and you'll find that everything will turn out for the best."

He did not say this unkindly, and poor Ma'ame Colombe even thought that she detected an indulgent tone in his voice. She rose to her feet and put her podgy hands together, and when the captain re-entered the shop she looked up at him with tearful, entreating eyes.

"He did it with a good motive, M'sieu' le – I mean citizen captain. Look at the innocent. He is no thief. I swear he is no thief. I'd like," she went on, turning fiercely round and darting defiant glances on the crowd of gaffers on the doorstep, "I'd like to see the man who dared to say that my Amédé is a thief."

The officer had handed the *pièces de conviction* to one of his men, with orders to put them in the wagon. Then he commanded Amédé to stand up before him.

"Thief or no thief," he said drily, "you are guilty of having acted contrary to the interests of the Republic. You know what that means?"

Amédé made no reply, only hung his head, and twiddled his hot fingers together.

"It means," the officer continued, "that but for one thing, your life would have had to answer for this act of treason."

A groan went round the crowd on whose ears those words had fallen like the toll of a passing bell. But Ma'ame Colombe did not utter a sound. She clung to her Hector and the two old people stood there hand in hand, striving by this loving contact to conquer the icy fear that had gripped their hearts.

"The one thing that will probably save you," the officer resumed after a dramatic pause, "is that the Republic has need of you in her revolutionary army. The enemy is at the gates of France, you are young, healthy, vigorous; it is for you to show your mettle by defending your country. Thus you will redeem the past. For the moment it is my duty to take you before the Committee of Public Safety, whose final word will dispose of your fate."

He spoke loudly so that all the listeners might hear. Gaffers and urchins and market-women hardly dared to breathe. They felt awed, and could only gaze at one another, as if trying to read each other's thoughts. And while awed whispers still went the round, the down-at-heel soldiers, who had spent the night in the village, came skulking back in groups of two or threes. They pushed their way through the crowd into the shop. One of the last to arrive was M. de Frontenac, closely guarded by two of the men.

And there they all stood now in the shop, a dozen or so of them, beside the sacks of haricots and button-onions and split peas; all of them with the exception of the prisoner, looking dirty and bedraggled, with their worsted caps covered in dust, bits of hay and straw clinging to their coats and to their hair, barelegged and grimy-faced, the steel of their bayonets dull with sludge, their breeches mud-stained. Such a contrast to their superb officer and his splendidly attired squad. And they could hear the women drawing humiliating comparisons, tittering and pointing fingers of scorn at them, whilst even the drabs, with whom they had drunk and jested the night before, turned contemptuous shoulders upon them now.

And thus they were mustered before the magnificent captain; all soldiers together, shoulder to shoulder, the down-at-heel and the grandees – aristos one would have called them, only that they were of the revolutionary army, which set out to exterminate the very last of the aristocracy, the hated tyrants and dissolute brood. And while they stood there, under the eye of the officer, the crowd outside watched them, and instinctively something of the spirit that animated the rest of France, swept like a poisonous sirocco over these worthy villagers of Laragne; the same spirit that in the great cities sent old women knitting and gossiping at the foot of the guillotine and that prompted young girls to dip their kerchiefs in the blood of its victims. A poisonous wind like the breath of demons! Some of the men and women had been to Sisteron and heard the hymn of hate, the *Carmagnole!* "Ça ira! Ça ira! Les aristos à la lanterne!" One or two of them began to hum it, stamping their feet to its rhythm.

Gradually the song swelled, one after another they took up the tune, these village men and maids who, unbeknown even to themselves had absorbed some of the insidious poison of hatred and black envy.

"Right! Turn!" the captain commanded, and marking time with their feet, the little squad now over twenty strong, started on its way. Ma'ame Colombe, now loudly moaning, still clung to her boy. He was very brave and tried to reassure and to comfort her. Anyway, he would have had to go today, he argued, his orders were to report himself at Serres, to be drafted into the army. From the officer's attitude it certainly seemed as if nothing more terrifying was to happen to him. The boy was brave enough too not to let his mother know how doubly his heart ached, because he was saying goodbye to his home, and could not say goodbye to Fleurette. His heart was filled with the image of Fleurette, but he would not add to his mother's sorrow by speaking to her of his own. He was just an un-sophisticated village lad, knowing little, understanding less. His own life and comfort were nothing to him, beside the sorrow which his mother felt and which, he knew, would bring such countless tears in Fleurette's lovely blue eyes. The father too tried to be brave; the effort to keep back his tears brought the perspiration streaming down his round, kindly face. When the crowd – his friends and neighbours some of them – intoned the revolutionary song, his powerful fist was clenched, but he did not shake it at the singers. His sound common sense had come again to his rescue, and whispered to him that for Amédé's sake, quiet submission was the soundest policy.

While mother and son clung to one another in a last farewell, Hector contrived to approach M. de Frontenac who, alone in the midst of such excitement and such conflicting emotions, had remained perfectly calm. The casual observer, not knowing him, might have thought that the fate of his wife and daughter, his separation from them, and the blow that destiny had dealt to these worthy folk here, whom he had known all his life, had left him completely indifferent. He had spent the night in a prison cell, under the eye of men – the local gendarmes – whose welfare and whose families had been his care for years; but seemingly he had slept peacefully. At any rate his face showed no sign of fatigue, or his eyes of sleeplessness. He had dressed with scrupulous care; his well-worn clothes, the ones he was wearing at dinner when the soldiers made irruption into the château, were clean and tidily put on; his cravat neatly tied, his hair smooth. When Hector Colombe approached him, he gripped the worthy *épicier* warmly by the hand.

And now the crowd parted to allow the soldiers to pass. Some of the girls tried to ogle the handsome ones and to leer at the others, but no one attempted to do more than stare in awe and admiration at the magnificent officer. The two prisoners were ordered to mount into the wagon; one of the soldiers took the reins and the next moment the order, "Quick March!" was given.

The crowd broke into an excited "Hurrah!" and the little squad slowly moved off, officer *en tête*, and the wagon in the rear, in the direction of Sisteron.

Then one of the villagers once more struck up the *Carmagnole*, and the crowd took it up. "Ça ira! Ça ira!" they sang gaily, and the men took the girls by the waist and twirled them round in a gay rigadoon. Old men and young girls; for there were no young men in the villages of France these days, when the army claimed them all, they danced and twirled in the wake of the retreating squad, and around them barefooted urchins somersaulted along in the cloud of dust raised by the horses and wagon.

And that was the picture that Amédé Colombe and Charles de Frontenac, sitting side by side in the wagon, saw gradually receding before their eyes as they were driven away, prisoners from their homes.

Thirteen

But in Lou Mas nothing was known of the tragic events that were occurring at Laragne. Old Louise and Fleurette were busy with housework, and if Fleurette went about the house, silent and wistful, it was because presently she would have to say the inevitable farewell to Amédé.

It was Adèle who brought the news. Young Colombe had been arrested by soldiers of the revolutionary army, she said, and he and M'sieu' de Frontenac had been taken to Sisteron. A superior officer of the army had come in this morning and relieved the lieutenant of his command. There had been great excitement in Laragne owing to the arrival of this new detachment of soldiers who were as splendid as those of last night had been travel-stained and bedraggled. The whole of the squad, headed by that magnificent officer, had marched away in the direction of Sisteron, the two prisoners sitting in the wagon in the rear.

It was only bit by bit that old Louise succeeded in dragging all this news out of Adèle. The girl's habitual reticence was put to a severe test by all the the questions and cross-questions, whilst Fleurette stood by wide-eyed, distraught with the idea of these horrible complications in which her poor Amédé was being involved. But she would not show any emotion before Adèle; she felt vaguely that her foster-sister, never very expansive towards her, had suddenly become almost inimical. So she waited until Louise had extracted all the news she could out of the taciturn girl, and curtly ordered her back into the kitchen; then as the old woman was about to follow, Fleurette caught her by the hand.

"Louise," she said in a tone of almost desperate entreaty, "dear, kind Louise, I must go to Sisteron – at once."

"To Sisteron?" old Louise exclaimed, frowning. "Heavens alive, what is the child thinking of now?"

"Of M'sieu' Amédé, dear Louise," Fleurette replied. "You heard what Adèle said. They have taken him to Sisteron."

"And what of it?" Louise asked – but she asked for form's sake only, she knew quite well what was going on in Fleurette's head.

"Only this, dear Louise," the girl said with a little note of defiance piercing through her shyness. "We – that is Amédé and I – are tokened to one another."

"Tokened?" the old woman exclaimed with a gasp. "Since when?"

"Since last night."

"And without your father's consent? Well! of all the – "

"Chéri Bibi would approve," Fleurette asserted, "if he knew."

Old Louise shrugged her shoulders. She would not trust herself to speak because the child looked so sweet and so innocent, and her pretty blue eyes were so full of tears, that Louise felt an almost unconquerable desire to take hold of her and hug her to her breast. Which act of weakness would have seriously impaired her authority at this critical juncture. She was wondering what to say next – for in truth she more than suspected that the child was right, and that Citizen Armand would not object to those two young things being tokened to one another, when Fleurette broke in gently:

"So you see, dear, kind Louise, that I must go to Sisteron – now – at once."

"But Holy Virgin, what to do?"

"To see Amédé and comfort him."

"They won't let you see him, child."

"Then I will find chéri Bibi," Fleurette retorted calmly. "He has a great deal more authority than you and I credit him with, Louise. He can order whom he likes not only to let me see Amédé, but even to set him free."

"He would be very angry," Louise argued, "to see you wandering about the high roads alone, while all those soldiers and riff-raff are about."

Fleurette gave a quaint little smile.

"Bibi's anger against me never lasts very long," she said. "Anyway, I will risk it. Louise dear, will you come with me?"

"I?"

"Of course, you said that Bibi would be angry if I roamed about the high roads alone."

Louise stood squarely in front of Fleurette, looked straight into those blue eyes, which never before had held such a determined glance. Fleurette could not help smiling at the old woman's look of perplexity; she was the typical hen seeing her brood of ducklings take their first plunge in the pond.

"If you won't come with me, Louise dear," the girl said simply, "I shall have to go alone."

"Get along with ye, for an obstinate wench," Louise retorted gruffly. But the next moment she had already changed her tone. "Get on your thick woollen stockings, child," she said, "and your buckled shoes, and your brown cloak, while I put a few things in a basket for our dinner. If we don't hurry, we shan't be in Sisteron before nightfall."

"M'sieu' Duflos will lend us his cart or a horse," Fleurette rejoined gleefully, "but I won't be long, dear, kind Louise."

And swift as a young hare she ran out and then up the outside staircase to her room under the overhanging climbing rose.

A few minutes later the two women started on their way. Fleurette had on her dark kirtle, her thick stockings and buckled shoes; her fair hair was tucked away underneath her frilled mob-cap. She carried her own cloak and Louise's on her arm, whilst Louise tramped beside her, carrying a basket in which she had hastily packed a piece of bread, some cheese, and two hard-boiled eggs. If M'sieu' Duflos, the butcher, would lend them his cart, they would be in Sisteron by midday; but in any case they would be there before dark.

Fourteen

But M'sieu' Duflos had no cart to lend them – that is he had no horse. Didn't Mam'zelle Fleurette and Ma'ame Louise remember? Some of those brigands had been round the week before and requisitioned every horse they could lay their hands on all over the countryside; old nags, mares with foals, butchers' cobs, nothing came amiss to them, nothing was sacred. Oh those soldiers! Were they not the curse of the country? And what difference there was between the so-called revolutionary army and a pillaging band of pirates, M'sieu' Duflos, the butcher, really couldn't say.

All this he told the two women, to the accompaniment of wide gestures of his powerful arms and much shrugging of his broad shoulders. It was Fleurette who had put the question breathlessly to him, as soon as she had caught sight of him standing on the door of his shop, blocking it with his massive bulk.

"A horse? A cart? Alas! it was impossible! Ah! those brigands! those brigands!"

Fleurette could not conceal her disappointment at first; but she was so brave, so resolute; she was for making an immediate start so as to get to Sisteron before dark. Perhaps they would meet horse and cart belonging to some neighbour luckier than poor M'sieu' Duflos. But Louise, more prudent, saw an opportunity for putting the mad adventure off until the next day. A start in the early morning could then be made, she argued, and horse or no horse, Sisteron might be reached before the sun was low, A good project forsooth. Let Fleurette return with her quietly now to Lou Mas and sleep on it. That was it! sleep on it! If only Fleurette would do that she, Louise, felt quite sure that counsels of prudence would prevail.

M. Duflos sagely nodded his head. Sisteron? He could not conjecture why Mam'zelle Fleurette should wish to go to Sisteron. Without an escort! And on foot! What would Citizen Armand say to it, if he knew?

Up to this point, you perceive, not a word about the exciting events that had convulsed Laragne a little over two hours ago. M'sieu' Duflos, watching Fleurette, marvelled how much the girl knew. She on the other hand was longing to ask questions, whilst dreading to lose time in unnecessary gossip. She looked about her at the familiar objects: the pump, the shop fronts, the *poste de gendarmerie*, on the other side of the square, and in the corner of the Rue Haute where the soldiers must have stood this morning with Amédé, a prisoner amongst them.

Everything for the moment in Laragne appeared calm, not to say commonplace. The women had all gone home to cook the midday dinner; the men were at their work. Every moment she thought that she must see Amédé coming round the corner with his slow swinging step, looking for her! M'sieu' Duflos and Louise were talking together, not exactly in whispers, but under their breath; the way people talk when the subject is exciting and perhaps awe-inspiring. And suddenly M. Duflos exclaimed with a great, big sigh of compassion:

"If it is not a misery! Mon Dieu! Mon Dieu! those poor Colombes!"

His kindly glance turned to Fleurette, and he saw her big blue eyes fixed on him. And as he was a very worthy fellow this M. Duflos, with a daughter of his own, he could not somehow return that glance; there was something in it that reminded him of a young animal in pain. He guessed that she had heard the news about young Colombe, and he knew, as everyone did in

Laragne, that Fleurette, over at Lou Mas, and Amédé Colombe were fond of one another, and that they would be tokened as soon as the girl had turned eighteen. This love-romance had been part of the village life ever since the two children had made mud pies together in the market square with the dust of the road and the water from the fountain, and though Armand, over at Lou Mas had become very queer of late, and no one knew anything about the mysterious business which, of recent years, kept him away from home for months on end, everyone remembered the pretty Marseillaise whom nineteen years ago he had brought to Lou Mas as a blushing bride, and no one had forgotten the terrible tragedy of her death when she gave birth to Fleurette. With the kindliness, one might say the indifference, peculiar to the peasant, the neighbours put down Armand's growing moroseness after that terrible event, and his secretive ways, to grief over the death of his young wife; and then after a while, they ceased to trouble about him at all, and almost forgot him as it were. But Fleurette had grown up among them all, a true child of sunny Dauphiné, in spite of her fair hair and blue eyes. They all loved her because she was so pretty, and though M'sieu' Colombe, the prosperous grocer of the Rue Haute, might at one time have had more ambitious views for his son, he and Ma'ame Colombe soon fell victims to Fleurette's charm, her dainty ways, her quaint little airs, as if she were a lady strayed into this remote village from some great city, and, above all, being natives of the South, and children of France, they succumbed to the fascination of her wealth; for there was no doubt that Armand was rich, and no doubt that he had made a declaration both privately to his friend Colombe and officially before the notary at Sisteron, that he would give his only child a dowry of ten thousand livres tournois, the day she married with his consent.

And here was this child now, whom everyone knew and whom everyone loved, turning great, pleading eyes on M'sieu' Duflos until the worthy fellow felt so uncomfortable that he had to clear his throat very noisily and to expectorate on the sanded floor of his shop with a sound like the falling of a shower of hailstones on a tiled roof. He thought that Fleurette knew all the details of this morning's dramatic story.

"Voyons, Mam'zelle Fleurette," he said with a rough attempt at consolation. "They won't do anything to Amédé. Really. The boy meant no harm."

All then would have been well if that fool Aristide Sicard, who was M'sieu' Duflos' errand-man, had not put in a word.

"No one," he said, "is going to believe that Amédé Colombe is a thief."

"A thief?" and Fleurette gave a funny little gasp. "Why should they think that Amédé is a thief?"

M'sieu' Duflos, the butcher, had given his errand-man a vigorous kick, but the correction came too late. And now Fleurette wanted to know more.

"What is your meaning, M'sieu' Aristide?" she insisted with that funny little air of determination of hers, whilst a frown appeared between her brows.

As M'sieu' Duflos explained to the neighbours afterwards, Fleurette looked as if she might be capable of anything at that moment. He was quite frightened at the expression in her blue eyes. It was too late to undo the mischief that that fool Aristide had done, so the butcher took the matter into his own hands. He had a sound knowledge of human nature, had M'sieu' Duflos, and he prided himself on his tact.

"You see, Mam'zelle Fleurette," he began, "it's this way. Those scurvy knaves – I mean the soldiers of the Republic – were full of choler because they had not found enough to steal at the château when they arrested poor M'sieu' de Frontenac. At first, it seems, they thought that Madame and Mademoiselle had taken their valuables away with them when they ran away; but later on something must have aroused their suspicions, or else the same kind of fool as Aristide here must have got talking.

Anyway, they seem to have got the idea that Amédé Colombe had hidden Madame's valuables away somewhere and – "

"Madame's valuables!" Fleurette exclaimed, trying to hide something of the excitement which was causing her heart to thump furiously. "They thought that Amédé – ?"

"Why, yes!" M'sieu' Duflos replied to her half-formulated query. "And unfortunately – "

"Well! They found Madame's valuables – "

But the worthy butcher got no further with his story. Without another word and swift as lightning, Fleurette had turned on her heel, and the next moment she was speeding across the market-place in the direction of the Rue Haute, whilst M'sieu' Duflos was left gazing in ludicrous perplexity at old Louise.

"What's the matter with the child?" he queried, and thoughtfully passed his hand through his harsh, bristly hair. "I thought she knew."

Old Louise shrugged her shoulders.

"She only knew that the lad had been arrested," she said, "but she had not heard about Madame's valuables being found in the Colombes' cart-shed. I was just able to stop Adèle telling her. She is so fond of M'sieu' Amédé." Louise added with a sigh: "Oh! how I wish her father were here."

M'sieu' Duflos was watching Fleurette's trim little figure speeding across the square and then disappearing round the corner of the Rue Haute.

"She's run over to the *épicerie*," he commented drily. "The Colombes are fond of her. They'll be able to comfort one another. Come in and have a petit verre, Louise. The child will be back soon."

But Louise would not come in, she did not want to lose sight of Fleurette, so after thanking the kind butcher for his hospitality, she too turned to go in the direction of the Rue Haute. But at the last M'sieu' Duflos had one more word to say to her.

"There's one thing more, Ma'ame Louise," he said, with unwonted earnestness in his round, prominent eyes. "If I were you I would look after that wench of yours, Adèle, a bit sharper. No offence, you know, but people have been talking in the village. She was rather too familiar with all those draggled-tailed soldiers last night."

Old Louise, with all a peasant's philosophy, shrugged her fat shoulders.

"You may be right, M'sieu' Duflos," she said drily, "but the girl, you know, is no care of mine. My sister Amèlie looks after her."

After which she gave a friendly nod to the amiable butcher and made her way up to the Rue Haute as fast as she could, though this was not really so fast as Fleurette's nimble little feet had carried her.

Fifteen

There had been no need for words. As soon as Fleurette had entered the shop Ma'ame Colombe had stretched out her arms, and Fleurette ran to her at once to be enfolded in a great maternal embrace. With her fair hair resting on Ma'ame Colombe's ample bosom, the child began by having a good cry. She had had none since she heard the fatal news, for excitement had kept every other emotion in check. But now with those motherly arms round her, she felt free to let her sorrow and anxiety have free rein. But only for a moment or two. As soon as she felt Ma'ame Colombe's ample bosom heaving against hers, and the older woman's tears wetting the top of her fair head, Fleurette looked up, swiftly drying her eyes, and put on a reassuring smile.

It was difficult to speak at first with all those sobs choking one's voice; nevertheless, whilst mopping her eyes with her pocket-handkerchief, Fleurette contrived to say:

"You know, Ma'ame Colombe, that it is all right, don't you? About Amédé, I mean."

"All right, my dear? All right?" the poor woman reiterated, and shook her head with pathetic dubiousness. "How can it be all right, when my Amédé is accused of being a thief? And before the neighbours too!" she added, whilst a deeper tone of crimson than her kitchen-fire had lent to her kind old face, spread over her cheeks.

"That's just it, Ma'ame Colombe," Fleurette continued eagerly. "Presently – tonight I hope – everyone will know that it was not Amédé who took those things."

"Of course he didn't take them. But you know what village gossip is. If Amédé did not take Madame's valuables, they keep on saying, how came they to be in our cart-shed? Oh, mon Dieu! mon Dieu!" she moaned, "to think that my Hector and I should live to see such disgrace."

"But, Ma'ame Colombe," Fleurette put in, somewhat impatient with the older woman's lamentations, "I am going to Sisteron tonight to tell the gendarme how Madame's valuables came to be in your cart-shed, and who it was that stole them."

"You, child? How should you know?"

"Because it was I who took the valuables out of the secret place in Madame's room," Fleurette said glibly, "and I gave them to Amédé to take care of, and because it was I who gave them to him he hid them in a corner of the cart-shed."

"Holy Virgin!" was all that Ma'ame Colombe was able to say in response to this amazing story, "the child has taken leave of her senses."

"No, no, Ma'ame Colombe," Fleurette insisted earnestly; "it is just as I have told you. I took the valuables out of Madame's room while the soldiers were at the château, and I gave them to Amédé to take care of."

"But why?" the poor mother exclaimed, in an agony of bewilderment. "In Heaven's name why?"

"Because – "

And suddenly Fleurette hesitated. A hot flush rose to her cheeks and tears gathered in her eyes. She had felt Ma'ame Colombe's perplexed glance on her, and for the time a stinging doubt gripped her heart and made her physically almost sick. What views would other people – strangers or even friends – take of her amazing story? of the heavenly voice and the mysterious faggot-carrier with the wonderful twinkling eyes? Would they believe her? or would they deride the whole tale?

or again, like dear, kind Ma'ame Colombe, would they just feel anxious, perplexed, not wishing to condemn, and yet vaguely wondering what could have induced a girl like Fleurette to go rummaging about among Madame's things, and inducing young Amédé to help her to conceal them.

An overpowering impulse prompted her to keep her beloved secret to herself. The sight of Ma'ame Colombe's grief-stricken face almost shook her resolution, but in the end it was that first impulse which conquered. After all it was only a matter of a few days, hours perhaps, and everything would become crystal-clear. Fleurette's little handkerchief was now like a wet ball in her hot hands; she breathed on it and dabbed her eyes; she straightened her cap and smoothed down her kirtle.

"And so, dear Ma'ame Colombe," she said calmly, "I am just going to Sisteron. Probably I shall find Bibi there; but even if I don't, I shall go up to the Committee of Public Safety, and I shall tell them the whole truth, so that there'll be no question of Amédé going to fight the English with the stain of theft upon his name."

It was impossible to say anything more just then, because Louise had arrived at the *épicerie*, breathless, but happy to catch sight of Fleurette looking quite calm and reasonable.

"I hope you gave the child a good scolding, Ma'ame Colombe," she said. "The idea of her wanting to trapeze the high road today when all these ruffianly soldiers are still about."

But Fleurette only smiled. "Neither Ma'ame Colombe, nor anyone else," she said, "could dissuade me from going to see Bibi now."

"Why!" Louise exclaimed pettishly, "this morning it was M'sieu' Amédé you wanted to see."

"I do want to see Amédé," Fleurette rejoined simply, "but I must see Bibi first."

And Louise saw her exchange an understanding glance with Ma'ame Colombe. It was all very bewildering and very terrible. Of course she was terribly sorry for the Colombes, but, just for the moment, she wished them all at the bottom of the sea. A little feeling of jealousy had crept into her heart when she saw Fleurette clinging to Ma'ame Colombe and whispering words into her ears which she, Louise, could not hear, and this uncomfortable feeling added to her discomfort. What could Ma'ame Colombe be thinking about to encourage Fleurette in her obstinacy? Louise could only suppose that all common sense had been drowned in an ocean of grief for the beloved only son.

Ah! if only Monsieur Armand were here!

And with a last sigh and a none too cordial farewell to Ma'ame Colombe, Louise, dolefully shaking her head, followed Fleurette out of the shop.

Sixteen

It was long past sunset by the time the two women reached Sisteron. Louise was dog-tired, for the day had been hot and the roads heavy with dust, They had started from Lou Mas one hour before noon, and as they left the first outlying houses of the city behind them, the clock of the tower of Notre Dame was striking eight.

The road between Laragne and Sisteron goes uphill most of the way, but withal, it is a beautiful road, winding through the wide valley of the Buëche, past orchards of grey-green olives and almond trees laden with blossom. Once past the confluence of the Méouge with the Buëche, it rises in a gentle gradient and gradually reveals to the eye the magnificent panorama of the Basses Alpes with their rocky crests and wide flanks draped in the sombre cloaks of pinewoods: Mont de la Baume, St Géniez, Signal de Lure; as beautiful a picture as Nature has to offer for the delectation of travellers, but possessing no powers of fascination over the two women, who tramped along in weariness and with anxious hearts.

The road was lonely. Scarce anyone did they meet on the way; no one, at any rate, to inspire old Louise with alarm. Now and then, perhaps, a group of labourers toiling homewards would cast a bold glance on the pretty wench stepping it resolutely beside her old duenna. But after a ribald word or two, or at worst a coarse jest, they would pass on and the two women continued their way unmolested.

But the events of the day, subsequently those of the evening, were but one long string of disappointments. As soon as the first outlying houses of the city came in sight Fleurette began inquiring pluckily and determinedly.

"Citizen Armand," she would ask, "from Lou Mas, over beyond Laragne?"

"What about him?"

"He is an important personage in Sisteron, how could I find him?"

And because she was gentle and had pretty blue eyes, and because she looked weary and anxious, people would do their best to help her. Some suggested one place, some another; the posting-inn – he might be known there, if he sometimes posted to Paris – or else the commissariat. This latter place proved a danger spot. A ferocious-looking commissaire very nearly detained the two women on a charge of vagabondage. His ugly leers and unveiled threats nearly sent Louise off her head with terror; Fleurette, however, kept up her courage nobly. The thought of Amédé drove every other terror out of her heart. She had vaguely heard that her father had something to do with a certain Committee of Public Safety. When she told this to the commissaire his manner immediately underwent a complete change; he became almost obsequious, placed himself entirely at the disposal of the citizeness for any inquiries she might wish to make about her illustrious father. Unfortunately, he said, the hour was late; the offices of the Committee of Public Safety situated in the Town Hall were now closed for the night. Citizen Armand had probably found shelter under the roof of a friend. Until tomorrow morning nothing could be done.

One thing, however, appeared clear; the soldiers who had created so much stir in Laragne this morning had not come to Sisteron nor was anything known of them. There was, the now servile commissary explained, a detachment of the 87th regiment of the line in garrison in the city and two days ago a squad of the revolutionary army lately formed for the purpose of scouring the country for traitors and aristos had passed through Sisteron and gone on in the direction of Laragne. The commissary had heard something about a family named Frontenac against whom there was a black mark for treason against the Republic, but he did not know anything about the arrest of Monsieur or the escape of Madame and Mademoiselle – whom he persistently referred to as the ci-devants – nor did he know anything about the arrest of Amédé Colombe, citizen of Laragne.

It was all very disappointing. Fleurette, trying to be brave, nevertheless felt at times an overwhelming inclination to cry. For one thing she was very tired, and being young and healthy she was also hungry. She and Louise had consumed the contents of their provision basket when the day was still young. Now it was getting near bed-time and the goal of her efforts not even within sight. The sullenness and mistrust that seemed to hang over the whole city had the effect of further damping her spirits. The echo of the terrible doings in Orange, in Toulon and Lyons had penetrated as far as this hitherto peaceful little town. Tales of summary arrests, of death-sentences without trial, of wholesale massacres were on everybody's lips. Accusations of treason, it seems, were more frequent than daily bread. The women looked harassed, hugged their children to their sides, as they slunk down the ill-lit streets, whilst throwing furtive glances over their shoulders. The men stood about in groups of three or four in the dark angles of the streets or beneath the ill-lit doorways until roughly ordered to go their way by men dressed in nothing but rags, who wore a tricolour sash round their waist and a cockade on their worsted cap.

And so ultimately to Les Amandiers, a quiet little inn off the main streets of the town, that Louise knew of through the drovers from Laragne who frequented the place when they were in Sisteron on market-day. Baptiste Portal, the landlord, suspicious at first, not liking the look of the two unprotected women seeking for lodgings at this hour of the night, was mollified by seeing the colour of Louise's money and the blue of Fleurette's eyes. His temper, it seems, had not yet recovered from the assaults made upon it a couple of days ago by a set of ragamuffins who called themselves soldiers of the Republic, and by their loud-spoken and arrogant lieutenant; but he was willing enough to make the two women welcome, and to give them supper and a bed. Then only did they tell him who they were and what the purpose of their journey: to seek Citizen Armand of Lou Mas, whose daughter Fleurette had matters of the utmost importance to communicate to him.

"Qu'à ça ne tienne!" Baptiste Portal exclaimed. "Armand was here but a couple of hours after noon. He was on his way to Orange."

"To Orange!" A cry of terror from Louise; one of excitement from Fleurette. Orange, the tiger's den! How could two unprotected women hope to enter it without being devoured? Orange where the guillotine was at work night and day! where men and women and even children were massacred in droves, where innocent people hardly dared speak or smile or pray, lest they be seized and thrown into prison, only to be dragged out again to a horrible death.

Orange!

But Fleurette only smiled. What had they to fear seeing Bibi chéri would be there? Was not Bibi far, far more powerful than the whole of the revolutionary army? Fleurette had seen him at the château, with a great tricolour sash round his waist, giving orders, that the officer in command of the soldiers dared not disobey.

Orange! She was not afraid of Orange! Even if the great Robespierre was in Orange she would not be afraid to go.

After all, what did it mean? Two or three days' journey in the old *coche* which, it seems, left the Place d'Armes two days of the week, at nine o'clock in the morning, and lumbering along through Peipin, and Saint Etienne-les-Orgues, gave one the chance of getting a good bed for the night at Sault, and again at Carpentras, if one was too tired to continue one's journey then.

Orange indeed? Why should one fear Orange, when chance was all in one's favour. As luck would have it, it was the very next day that the *coche* would be starting from the Place d'Armes. All one needed was a few things, a clean pair of stockings, a handkerchief or two, a bit of soap and a towel, which dear, kind Ma'ame Portal was only too ready to lend; these were tied in a bundle and formed the only indispensable luggage which Fleurette and Louise would take with them. Fortunately Louise had plenty of money in her pocket, being always well supplied by Bibi, and then, of course, in Orange, Bibi would be there and he would provide further as necessity arose.

And thus it came to pass that among the passengers who took their places in the lumbering old vehicle that morning were two females, one of whom had corn-coloured hair and eyes bluer than forget-me-nots.

Seventeen

The Hôtel de Ville at Orange still stands, as it did then, in the newly named Place de la République; and if the tourist of today mounts its steps, enters the building through its central portal, crosses the wide vestibule and finally turns down a long corridor on his right, he will, almost at the end of this, come to a door which bears the legend: "Travaux Publics."

Should he be bold enough to push open the door, he will find himself in a perfectly banal room, with whitewashed walls covered with maps and plans that are of no interest to him, a large desk at one end, and a few wooden chairs. There is a thin carpet in the middle of the red-tiled floor and faded green rep curtains temper the glaring light of the afternoon sun. But on this day of May, 1794, there were no curtains to the window, and not even a strip of carpet on the floor. There was no desk either, only a long trestle-table covered with a tattered green cloth, behind which, on wooden chairs, sat three men, dressed alike in dark blue coats tightly buttoned across the chest, drab breeches and high-topped boots, and wearing tricolour sashes around their waist.

The one who sat in the centre and who appeared to be in supreme authority rested his elbow on the table, and his chin was supported in his hand. He was gazing intently on a man who stood before him, in the centre of the room, the other side of the table; a man who looked footsore and weary and who wore a military uniform all tattered and covered with slime and dust.

The two others also kept their eyes fixed on this man. They were listening with rapt interest to the story which he was relating. Early this morning he and a dozen others also attired in tattered uniforms had come into Orange in a state bordering on collapse. They had made their way to the barracks where the officer in command had mercifully given them food and drink. As soon as they had eaten and drunk, they tried to tell their story; but this was so amazing, not to say incredible, that the officer in command had thought it prudent to send for the superintendent of *gendarmerie*, who in turn had the men conveyed to the Hôtel de Ville, there to be brought before the Representative of the Convention on special mission who sat with the Committee of Public Safety. And now Lieutenant Godet stood alone to face the Committee; the others had been handed back to the *gendarmerie* to be dealt with later on. The representative on special mission who sat with the two other Members of the Committee at the table covered with the tattered green cloth, had questioned Godet, and he thereupon embarked upon the story of this amazing adventure. He began by relating the events which three days ago had set the quiet little commune of Laragne seething with excitement. He told of the arrival of the squad of soldiers in magnificent uniforms, under the command of an officer more superb than anything that had ever been seen in the countryside before. He told of the perquisition in the house of Citizen Colombe the grocer, by those magnificent soldiers, of the finding there by them of certain valuables belonging to the ci-devant Frontenacs, valuables which he himself had vainly searched for in the château, the evening before. He told of the arrest of young Colombe: of the high-handed manner in which the superb officer had relieved him, Godet, of his command, and ordered him and his men, together with the ci-devant Frontenac, to join his squad, and to march with him out of Laragne. He had told it all with a wealth of detail, and the members of the Committee had listened in silence and with rapt interest.

But now the man at the table who was the representative on special mission, and who appeared chief in authority, broke in with an exclamation that was almost one of rage.

"And do you mean to tell me, citizen lieutenant," he said in a harsh, rasping voice, "that you could mistake a lot of English spies – for that is what they were, you may take it from me – that you could mistake them, I say, for soldiers of our army. Where were your eyes?"

Lieutenant Godet gave a shrug which he hoped would pass for unconcern. In reality he felt physically sick; a prey to overwhelming terror. At first, when he and his men had come in sight of the city, they had felt nothing but relief to see the end of what had been almost martyrdom. It was only afterwards, when he found himself in this narrow room, with its white-washed walls and its silence, and face to face with those three men, that fear had entered his heart. He felt like an animal in a cage – a mouse looking into the pale, piercing eyes of a cat. He passed his tongue once or twice over his parched lips before he gave reply.

"I was not the only one, citizen," he said sullenly, "who was deceived. The whole commune of Laragne was at the heels of those soldiers. My own men were mustered before the pseudo-captain and heard him give words of command."

"But Englishmen, citizen lieutenant," the man at the table argued; "Englishmen! Their appearance! Their speech!"

"They spoke as you and I would, Citizen Chauvelin," Godet retorted, still sullenly. "As for appearance, one man is like another. I could not be expected to know every officer of our army by sight."

"But you said they were splendidly dressed!"

"They were. I knew the uniform well enough. Had there been a doubtful button or a galloon wanting I should have spotted it."

"But so clean!" one of the others at the table remarked with a sigh, that might have been of envy, "so magnificent!"

"I knew that there were some compagnies d'élite," the lieutenant rejoined, "attached to certain regiments. How could I guess?"

"It might have been better for you if you had," the man in the centre remarked drily.

Godet's wan face took on a more ashen hue; again he passed his tongue over his parched lips.

"Haven't we had enough of this?" one of the others at the table now put in impatiently. "We are satisfied that those English spies, or whatever they were, acted with amazing effrontery, which makes me think that perhaps they are a part of that gang that we all know of, and of which Citizen Chauvelin spoke just now. We are also satisfied that Citizen Lieutenant Godet did not show that acumen which an officer in his responsible position should have done. What we want to know now is, what happened after the pseudo-captain of the so-called 33rd division had arrested that young Colombe and marched out of Laragne?"

"And in your interest, citizen lieutenant," the man in the centre rejoined sternly, "I advise you to make a statement that is truthful in every detail."

"Had I wished to tell lies," the soldier retorted sullenly, "I shouldn't be here now. I should have – "

"No matter," the other broke in curtly, "what you would have done. The State desires to know what you did."

"Well!" Lieutenant Godet began after a moment or two during which he appeared to collect his thoughts. "We marched out of Laragne in the direction of Serres. The captain – I still, of course, looked upon him as a captain – had so disposed us that I and my own men were between two squads of his. We were footsore, all of us, because we had had three days' tramping in the dust, one day battling against hard wind, another with long hours spent in scouring the château of those traitors Frontenacs;

we were also very hungry. Remember that we had been dragged out of our beds in the early morning, and not given a chance of getting a bite or drink before starting on the march. But they, the others, were fresh as if they had just come out of barracks with their bellies full... They marched along at a swinging pace, and it was as much as we could do to keep step with them."

The man's voice became somewhat more steady as he talked. The note of terror which had been so conspicuous in it at first had given place to one of dull resentment. Encouraged by the obvious interest which his story had evoked in his hearers, he resumed more glibly:

"About half a league north of Laragne, a bridle-path branches off the high road; into this the captain ordered his company to turn, and we continued to plod along through the dust and in the midday heat, till we came to a tumbledown cottage by the roadside; a cottage flanked by a dilapidated shed, and a bit of garden all overgrown with weeds. Here a halt was called, and the prisoners were ordered out of the wagon. A moment or two later a woman appeared at the cottage door, some words were exchanged between her and the captain, and subsequently, when order to march was given, the prisoners marched along with us; the wagon and horses having been left behind at the cottage."

"Didn't you think this very strange, citizen lieutenant?" one of the men at the table asked; "a wagon and horses which you would naturally presume belonged to the State, being thus left at a tumbledown roadside cottage?"

"Whatever I may have thought," the lieutenant replied, "it was not my place to make observations to my superior officer."

"Superior officer!" the man in the centre remarked, with a gesture of contemptuous wrath.

"I think, Citizen Chauvelin," the accused now put in a little more firmly, "that you are unnecessarily hard on me. There was really nothing to indicate – "

But the other broke in with a vicious snarl:

"Nothing to indicate – ? Nothing? The eyes of a patriot should be sharp enough to detect a spy or a traitor through any disguise – "

He paused abruptly, and cast a quick, inquisitorial glance at his two colleagues first, then at the soldier before him. Had he detected a trace, a sign, a flicker of the eyelid that betrayed knowledge of his own past? of the times – numberless now – that he too had been hoodwinked by those bold adventurers who called themselves the League of the Scarlet Pimpernel, and by their chief whose prowess in the art of disguise had marked some of the most humiliating hours in Chauvelin's career? Calais, Boulogne, Nantes, Paris; each of those great cities had a record of the Terrorist's discomfiture when brought face to face with that mysterious and elusive Scarlet Pimpernel. Even now, crushed in the hot palm of his hand, he held a scrap of paper which had revealed the author of the plot to which that fool Lieutenant Godet had fallen a victim – just as he, himself, Chauvelin, had done – just like that – and so many times – The penalty for him had always been more humiliation, a further fall from the original high place which he had once occupied in Paris: and with it the knowledge that one day the masters of France would tire of his failures. Ah! he knew that well enough, he knew that they would tire, and then they would crush him as they had crushed others, whose only crime, like his, had been failure.

His only claim to immunity, so far, had been the fact that he alone, of all the members of the National Assembly, of all the members of Committees, or of the Executive, knew who the Scarlet Pimpernel really was; he had seen him without disguise; he knew him by name, not only him but some of his more important followers; and when some of the ferocious tyrants, who for the time being were the masters of France, did at times loudly demand the suppression of Citizen Chauvelin, for incompetence that amounted to treason, there were always others who pleaded for him because of that knowledge. Many felt that with the death of Chauvelin, the last hope of capturing that band of English spies would have to be abandoned; and so they pleaded for his retention and their fellow-tyrants allowed him another few months' grace so that he might accomplish that which they knew was the great purpose of his life. And whenever in the opinion of those bloodthirsty tigers, who held France under their domination, some outlying provincial districts had need of what they called "purging from the pestilence of traitors," whenever wholesale arrests, perquisitions, wholesale death-sentences or brutal massacres were the order of the day, Citizen Chauvelin was sent down with special powers, always in the vain hope that the Scarlet Pimpernel, emboldened by success, would fall into the trap perpetually set for him. The English spy's predilection for aristos, his sympathies so quickly aroused when traitors happened to be women or young children, was sure to draw his activities to any region where prisons were full and the guillotine kept busy.

Thus it was that Citizen Chauvelin had been sent to Orange. The Southern provinces of France had been left far too long to welter in a morass of treason; there were veritable nests of traitors in the châteaux and farms of Provence and Dauphiné. The country had to be purged: the traitors extirpated; the magnificent Law of the Suspect be set in motion to do this cleansing process. Any man who ventured to criticize the government, who complained of taxation or restrictions was a traitor; any man or woman who owned more than they needed for bare subsistence, who refused to pour off their surplus into the lap of patriots, was a traitor, and the country must be purged of them, until the dictatorship of the proletariat was firmly established, until every man, woman and child in the whole of France had been dragged down to the same level of mental and physical wreckage.

There had been a dramatic pause after Chauvelin's outburst of contemptuous wrath; for a minute or two, while the old clock up on the wall ticked away with slow monotony, a strange silence remained hanging over the scene. Whatever the other three men may have known or remembered of the noted Terrorist's past history, they thought it wiser to say nothing. In these days of universal brotherhood and Liberty, every man in France was frightened of his neighbour. The time had come when the lustful tigers, satiated with the blood of those whom they deemed their enemies, had turned, thirsting, for that of their whilom friends. The makers of the Terror had started digging their fangs into each other's throats. The victory now was to the most ferocious. After the Girondins, Danton, he, who had ordered the September massacres, two and a half years ago, had had to yield to a more vengeful, more merciless power than his own.

Chauvelin knew that. The victory today was to the most ferocious. He who would sacrifice friends, brother, sister, child, was the true patriot; the man who stayed his hand in face of a revolting crime that would put a wild beast to the blush, was unworthy the name of citizen of France. Therefore death to him. Death to the weakling. To the Moderate. This was the era of the Universal Brotherhood of Death.

What chance then had this unfortunate Lieutenant Godet now? brought to justice – save the mark! – before a man who knew that to show weakness was to court death. No wonder that all the swagger and the arrogance which made him but a day or two ago the terror of a lot of peasants of Sisteron or Laragne, was knocked out of him, by a mere glance from those pale, piercing eyes. And he – a mere notary's clerk born and bred in the depth of Dauphiné and thrust into the army, as a mule is thrust into harness – knew nothing of Paris save from hearsay, and nothing of the men whose word had even sent a king and queen to the scaffold. He knew nothing of Citizen Chauvelin, save that he was a man of power, before whose piercing glance and tricolour sash every man instinctively cringed and trembled. He knew nothing of Chauvelin's tussles with those same English spies who had so effectually led him,

Godet, by the nose; nothing of Citizen Chauvelin's past life, very little of the present. He was just a mouse in the power of a cat; allowed a little freedom just now, while he told his tale of failure.

"Continue, citizen lieutenant," Chauvelin now said more calmly. "We are listening."

"Let me see," Godet rejoined vaguely, "where was I?"

"On the bridle-path off the main road," Chauvelin responded with a sneer; "half a league north of Laragne. The wagon and horses presumably belonging to the State left in a tumbledown cottage by the roadside. A thrilling situation forsooth. An ordinary situation you would have us believe. Pray continue. What happened after that?"

"We marched and we marched and we marched," the lieutenant resumed sullenly. "We marched until we were ready to drop. We had had three days of marching, and had started in the morning without a bite, hungry! Nom d'un nom! how hungry we were! and weak and faint! The hours sped on; we could see the sun mounting the heavens and then start on its descent. The heat was intense, the dust terrible. It filled our eyes, our nostrils, our mouths. The soles of our feet were bleeding, sweat poured down our faces and obscured our vision. We marched and we marched, through two villages, the names of which I do not know; then over mountain passes, across rocky gorges, stepping over streams, climbing the sides of hills, the banks of rivers. I am a stranger in these parts. And I was tired. Tired! I knew not where we were, whither we were going. March! March! March! Ceaselessly. Even had I dared, I would no longer have had the strength to ask questions or to beg for mercy."

And at the recollection of those hours of agony, Lieutenant Godet wiped the perspiration from his streaming brow.

"Well?" Chauvelin queried drily, "and the others, the Englishmen?"

"They marched along at a swinging pace," Godet replied, smothering a savage oath. "Without turning a hair. They kicked up no dust. They did not sweat. They just marched. No doubt their bellies were well filled."

"And the prisoners?"

"They set to with a will. And I make no doubt but they had fed and drunk while they sat in the wagon. At any rate they showed no fatigue."

"How long did you continue on the march?"

"Till one by one we – my comrades and I – fell out by the roadside."

"And those who fell out were left, while the others went on?"

"Yes! We had gone through the second village, and were marching along the edge of a stream, when the first lot of us dropped out. Three of my men. They just rolled down the bank of the stream; and there lay on their stomachs trying to drink. The captain – or whatever he was, curse him! – called "Halt!" and one of his men ran down the bank and had a look at those three poor fellows who lay there striving to slake their hunger as well as their thirst in the cool mountain stream. But, nom de nom! They – the miscreants! – had no bowels of compassion. I believe – for in truth I was too tired to see anything clearly – that one of them did leave a hunk of bread by the side of the stream: perhaps he was afraid that those poor fellows would die of inanition and then their death would be upon his conscience."

"Well! And did all the men fall out that way?"

"Yes! We were marching three abreast: and three by three we all fell out. Always beside the stream, for we suffered from thirst as much as from hunger. The stream seemed to draw us, and three of us, as if by common understanding, would just roll down the bank and lie on our stomachs and try to drink. The captain no longer called a halt when that happened. One of his own men would just throw pieces of bread down to the edge of the stream, just as they would to a dog."

"And you were the last to fall out?"

"The very last. I verily believe, when I rolled down the bank and felt the cool stream against my face, that I had died and reached the Elysian fields. A piece of bread was thrown to me, and I fell on it like a starved beast."

"And then what happened?"

"Nothing."

"What do you mean? Nothing?"

"Nothing as far as we were concerned. The bank of the stream, for a length of two kilometres or more, was strewn with our dead – that is not dead, you understand, but fatigued, and only half-conscious with hunger: while those miscreants, those limbs of Satan, marched off without as much as a last look at us! Gaily they marched away singing. Yes, singing, some awful gibberish, in a tongue I did not understand. That is," poor Godet went on ruefully, "when first I had an inkling of the awful truth. That strange tongue gave it away. You understand?"

The others nodded.

"And then, by chance, I put my hand in the back pocket of my tunic, and felt that piece of paper."

With finger that quivered slightly, he pointed to Chauvelin's hand; between the clenched claw-like fingers there protruded the corner of a scrap of paper. Chauvelin failed to suppress the exclamation of rage which rose to his lips.

"Nom de nom!" he muttered savagely through his teeth, and with his handkerchief he wiped the beads of moisture that had risen to the roots of his hair.

"And so they marched away," one of the others remarked drily. "In which direction?"

"Straight on," the soldier replied laconically.

"On the way to Nyons, I suppose, and Walreas?"

"I suppose so. I don't know the neighbourhood."

"You do not seem to have known much, Lieutenant Godet," Chauvelin put in with a sneer.

"I come from the other side of the Drac," Godet retorted. "I could not – "

But Chauvelin broke in with an oath:

"Wherever you come from, citizen," he said sternly, "it was your duty to become acquainted with the country through which you were ordered to march your men."

"I had no orders to take them through mountain passes," Godet remarked sullenly. "We came through here a month ago and have kept to the high road. At Sisteron I had my orders to arrest the ci-devant Frontenacs. You, Citizen Chauvelin, must know how conscientiously I did my duty. All the orders you gave me I fulfilled. After Sisteron you ordered me to go to Laragne, and thence to Serres. It was you ordered me to halt at Laragne for the night."

"All this is beside the point," one of the others broke in roughly. "All we can gather from this confused tale is that all traces of the English spies have completely vanished."

"For the moment," Chauvelin assented drily. "It is for Lieutenant Godet to find those traces again."

He spoke now with extreme bitterness, and the glances which he levelled at Godet were both hostile and threatening. It would be curious to try and follow the mental processes which had given rise to this hostility. Godet, after all said and done, had only failed in the same manner as he himself, Chauvelin, had so often done. He had been hoodwinked by a particularly astute and daring adventurer who was an avowed enemy of France: and if being thus hoodwinked was a crime against the State, then the powerful member of the Committee of Public Safety and the humble lieutenant of infantry were fellow-criminals. This, of course, Godet did not know. Not yet: or he would not have been in such dread of this man with the pale eyes and the talon-like hands. The others he did not fear nearly so much. No doubt they too were cruel and vengeful these days. Strike or the blow will fall on you, was the rule of every man's conduct. Pochart and Danou took their cue from Chauvelin; his was the master-mind, his the more ruthless nature, all they did was to try and show their zeal by saying Amen to every suggestion, every sarcasm, every accusation put forth by their colleague.

In fact the proceedings by now had developed into a kind of duel between the accused and the principal judge; it was a duel made up of acrimonious accusations on the one hand, and of defence that weakened perceptibly as the accused became more and more confused through ever-increasing terror. The other two only put in a word here and there. They wished to know how the adventure had finally come to an end.

"In a long, weary tramp to Orange," Godet replied; "weary beyond what words can describe, footsore, hungry and thirsty we tramped."

They had to cover three leagues. How they lived through it, they none of them knew. At one or two villages which they encountered, they obtained a little food, and some drink. For the space of a league and a half, he, Godet, and two others got a lift in a farmer's wagon. On the way they asked news of the English spies. They had been seen marching merrily; but soon all traces of them had vanished.

"Had I been the traitor you say I am, Citizen Chauvelin," Godet said in the end, "would I have come into Orange with my tale? I would have tried to run away and to hide. Made my way to Toulons, what? and joined the army there. You would not have found me then; months would have gone by before you heard of my adventure."

"You underestimate the power which is in my hands, citizen lieutenant," was Chauvelin's curt comment. "Only one thing could save you from the consequences of your treachery, and that was to speak the truth and to redeem your crime."

He paused a moment, and then addressing his two colleagues, he said with slow deliberation:

"We all agree, I think, that Citizen Lieutenant Godet has been guilty of gross negligence, which today, when France is threatened by traitors within as well as by her enemies on her frontier, amounts to treason against the State. Silence!" he went on, throwing a stern glance on Godet who had uttered a violent word of protest. "Listen to what hope of indulgence it is in my power to give you. The State against whom you have sinned will grant you the chance of retrieving your crime. We will grant you full powers under the new Law of the Suspect. You shall go into the highways and the byways with full power to seize any man, woman or child, whom you as much as vaguely suspect of complicity in this affair. Do you understand?"

"I think I do," Godet replied dully.

"The State," Pochart put in sagely, "would rather have the English spies than your head, citizen lieutenant."

"The State will have Citizen Godet's head," Chauveun rejoined drily, "or the English spies. The choice rests with Citizen Godet himself."

There was a moment's pause. The eyes of the soldier were fixed upon the pale, determined face of his ruthless judge. He knew that his life hung upon the decision uttered by those thin, bloodless lips. He was in the grip of a white terror; his teeth were clenched and his tongue clove, hard and dry, against the roof of his mouth. He was terrified, and in his wildly beating heart there was an immense hatred for the man who thus terrorized him. He longed to get at him, to grip him by the throat, to scream out insults into that pale, stern, colourless face. He longed to see that same fear of death which was paralysing him, dim the light of those pale eyes. His own impotence made that hatred more intense. It shone out of his eyes, and Chauvelin meeting them caught the glance like that of an enraged cur, ready to spring. Indifferent, he shrugged his shoulders and the ghost of a sneer curled round his thin lips. He was accustomed to hatred and desire for revenge.

"Citizen lieutenant," he said at last, "you have heard the decision of the committee. It has been found expedient to withhold punishment from you, because it is in your power to serve the State in a way that no other man could do at this moment. You have seen the English spies face to face; you know something of their appearance, something of their mode of speech. Go then into the highways and byways, the men who with you were guilty of negligence shall go with you. It is for you to use the full powers which the Law of the Suspect has placed in your hands. Go scour the country. Yours is the power to seize any man, woman or child whom you suspect of treason to the State, make use of that power in order to track down to their lair the English foxes who have outwitted you. Only let me add a word of warning in your ear. Do not be led by the nose a second time. If you are, no power on earth will save you. The State may forgive incompetence once: the second time it will bear the ugly name of treason."

He had risen to his feet, and just for a moment the muscles of his hand relaxed, and the scrap of paper which he had crushed into a ball rolled upon the table.

His colleague Pochart picked it up and idly opened and smoothed it out: he studied for a moment or two the close writing upon it, then looked inquiringly up at Chauvelin.

"Can you tell us what is written on this paper, citizen?" he asked.

And while he spoke he tossed the paper across to his colleague Danou.

"Is it English?" Danou asked, puzzled.

"Yes," Chauvelin replied curtly.

"It looks like poetry," Pochart remarked.

"Doggerel verses," commented Chauvelin.

"And you can't read it?"

"No!"

"I thought you knew English."

"Not I."

"Strange why a bit of doggerel verse should have been slipped into the pocket of Citizen Godet's tunic," Pochart remarked drily. "And there's your name, Citizen Chauvelin," he added, pointing to the words "À mon ami Chauvelin," which preceded the four lines of poetry written in English, a language which, apparently, no one here understood.

But Chauvelin was at the end of his patience. He seized the scrap of paper and tore it savagely into innumerable little pieces.

"Enough of this futility," he said, and brought his clenched fist down with a crash on the table. "The English spies have been facetious, that is all. We do them too much honour by attaching importance to this senseless, childish verse. Lieutenant Godet," he went on, once more addressing the accused, "you are dismissed, under the conditions I told you of just now. When next we meet face to face, you will either be the lucky man who has helped to lay these impudent English adventurers by the heel, or you will stand before me arraigned for treason and preparing for death. Now you can go."

Without another word Godet turned on his heel and went out of the room. Past the guard at the door, he went with head erect, and with a firm step he walked the whole length of the corridor. But there was one moment when in the vestibule he found himself alone. Unwatched. At any rate he thought so. So he paused and looked over his shoulder in the direction of the room where he had just spent an uncomfortable two hours. He paused and raising his fist, he shook it at the unseen presence of the man who had so terrorized him, and whom he hated because of the terror which he inspired.

"With a bit of luck," he muttered through his teeth, "we shall be even yet, you and I, mon ami Chauvelin."

Then once more with a firm step he walked out of the Town Hall.

Eighteen

It was on the following day that the *coche* from Sisteron was due
to arrive at Orange, and Lieutenant Godet, his mind set on the
one purpose, to find a clue to his mysterious adventure with
the English spies, hied him to the posting-inn which is situated
in the Rue de la République.

At noon the *coche*, covered with dust, unloaded its wearied
passengers; a farmer and his son come to negotiate a sale of
stock; the wife of Citizen Henriot, the lawyer, home from her
annual visit to her mother; two or three skilled artisans from the
country, come to seek their fortune in town, and so on; and
finally there descended from the *coche* two women, one of
whom carried a small bundle, while the other – well! at sight
of the other Citizen Lieutenant Godet uttered such a cry of
surprise and of excitement that the crowd around him thought
that here was a poor soldier who had taken leave of his senses.

The woman who had caused Lieutenant Godet thus to lose
his self-control, was a perfectly self-possessed young woman
wrapped in a cloak and hood from beneath which peeped
strands of golden curls that vied in colour with the ripe corn of
the Dauphiné, and eyes bluer than the sky that spread over
Orange on this exquisite midday in May. The older woman who
accompanied her appeared travel-stained, weary and cross; not
so this beautiful girl, who tripped lightly from the *coche* towards
the parlour of the posting-inn and with a little air of triumph
and encouragement called gaily to her companion:

"The end of our journey, my Louise! And now to find Bibi!"

Even in these days of advanced democracy which in Orange had of late reached its apogee, the shattering of ancient manners and customs had not got to the stage where a beautiful woman would not command the attention and services of im-pressionable males, to the exclusion of others less favoured. And thus it came to pass that while the other weary and travel-stained passengers were left to look after themselves and their bits of luggage, and to wait their turn until such time as the servants of the inn were pleased to get them refreshments, the landlord himself, a florid man in shirt sleeves and baize apron, bustled obsequiously around Fleurette and Louise, offering wine, bread and advice, polishing the chairs on which they were invited to sit, and generally placing himself and his house at the disposal of this attractive customer.

Fleurette took all these attentions as a matter of course. She was accustomed to being the centre of attraction at Lou Mas or in the house of M'sieu' and Ma'ame Colombe, and although her trust in the goodwill of men had received one or two somewhat rude shocks of late, she still retained that self-possession and gentle air of mingled modesty and graciousness which is the attribute of every pretty, unspoilt woman. She asked for a room where she and her companion might tidy their kerchiefs and caps, and use their precious piece of scented soap, and she felt so triumphant and so elated that when she found herself in the privacy of that room she took poor old Louise by the waist and twirled her round and round in a mad dance.

"We are in Orange, Louise darling!" she cried. "We are here! here! here! and in less than an hour we shall have found Bibi, and Bibi will have commanded Amédé to be set free! Just think of it, Louise," she went on more seriously, "four whole days since he was arrested! Poor, poor Amédé, under a horrible accusation of a sin which he never committed! What he must have suffered! What he must have thought of me who knew the truth and did not at once set to work to obtain his freedom..."

Gradually her tone became more and more dull, all the excitement died out of it. She saw Amédé in prison, with irons round his wrists and ankles, or else standing before stern judges who condemned him to a terrible punishment, because he held his tongue, and would not accuse the real delinquent, who was none other than she, Fleurette. She sighed, and her eyes now were full of tears, while old Louise, stolidly, and with much grumbling, got some water and proceeded to wash her face and hands and to tidy her dress.

"Come, child," she said drily after a while, "we'll go down now and get something to eat."

She had never ceased to protest against the madness of this adventure, prophesying every kind of calamity for them both: but Fleurette with the quiet obstinacy of the habitually meek had persisted. She had begun by wheedling the money out of Louise, then obtained the passes for places in the *coche*. Once on the way, it would of course have been ridiculous to turn tail and go back, and Louise, led unconsciously by a force of will stronger than her own, had found herself meekly acquiescing in all the arrangements which Fleurette made on the way. As a matter of fact she had not ceased to marvel at the child. Here was this young thing, who had never travelled in a *coche* before, who had never in her life been further than Serres and Sisteron, calmly undertaking a three days' journey, sleeping and eating in strange inns, and arriving at her destination unscathed. There certainly was a miracle in all this good luck, for old Louise had heard many a tale of what terrible adventures usually befell unprotected females upon the high roads. What she did not realize was that the miracle merely consisted in the fact that in these outlying corners of beautiful France, in Dauphiné and in Provence, there was still plenty of the good old kindly stock left, some of the chivalry, the warmth of heart, the bonhomie, which all the tyranny and the cruelty perpetrated in the great cities had not contrived to kill; and that there was something in Fleurette's beauty, her simplicity as well as her determination, which brought forth that chivalry and bonhomie and helped her to win through.

When the two women returned to the parlour, where hot milk and country bread awaited them, they were met by a young soldier, who very politely and deferentially claimed acquaintance with them.

"You would not remember me, citizeness," he said, more particularly addressing Fleurette, "but I and some very weary soldiers under my command are deeply indebted to you for your kindness to us, when, like a good Samaritan, you gave us food and drink, on the bridge near your home. Do you remember?"

He looked very bedraggled and out-at-elbows, but frank and kind. Fleurette raised shy, blue eyes up to his, and gave a little gasp of recognition. She well remembered the soldier. She remembered how sorry she had been for them all, in their shabby clothes and stockingless feet, weary and thirsty, and how she had sent Adèle out to them with food and drink. She also remembered, though she would not remind him of that, that he had been very curt and uncivil with her, had made a sneering remark when she told him that she was Citizen Armand's daughter, and also that the men under his command had been positively cruel to a poor inoffensive old man whom she afterwards befriended.

However, for the moment, she was perhaps conscious of a slight feeling of relief at sight of a familiar face; she had seen nothing but strangers ever since she left Laragne four days ago. So when the soldier, still speaking quite deferentially, reiterated his: "Do you remember?" she replied simply: "Of course I do, citizen lieutenant." Which goes to prove that Fleurette had learned a great deal in the past three days, and the word "citizen" now came quite glibly to her tongue.

Lieutenant Godet had told her his name, told her that he was a native of Orange and was home on leave for a few days.

"A real piece of luck," he went on lightly, "seeing that perhaps I might be of service to you."

The two women sat down at the table and he helped to wait on them, brought them bread and cheese and a jug of hot milk, and bustled the maid of the inn if the latter appeared negligent. He made himself very agreeable to Louise, talked of his own journey, and inquired after her adventures. Louise, despite her innate suspicion of soldiers, gradually unbent to him. The warm food further put her into a good temper, and presently the three of them were conversing in the most amicable manner.

When the meal had been duly paid for, the soldier once more offered his services. Could he pilot the citizenesses through the town?

"Well yes, you can," Louise said resolutely, "we want to find M'sieu' Armand."

"Citizen Armand," Fleurette broke in, "my father. I think you know him, citizen lieutenant."

"Know him?" he exclaimed, "of course I know Armand. Who does not know Citizen Armand in Orange?"

"Then he is here now?" Fleurette cried eagerly.

"Of a surety he is."

"You know where he lodges?"

"Everyone in Orange knows where Citizen Armand lodges."

"Then you can take me to him?"

"At your service, citizeness."

"Now?"

"When you wish."

With a little cry of delight Fleurette gathered up her cloak.

"Let us go," she said simply.

Louise sighing, but stolid, followed meekly. The thought that she would soon relinquish her wayward charge into the keeping of M'sieu' Armand was a comforting one; Fleurette was tripping it gaily beside the soldier, but the latter's dirty clothes and bedraggled appearance still filled old Louise with mistrust.

They crossed the river by the old bridge and then trudged along the dusty streets to a great open place, now called Place de la République. The soldier led the way across the square to a tall stone building, flanked by a square tower, to which a flight of steps gave access. He seemed to know his way about. At the top of the steps a couple of soldiers in somewhat tidier uniforms than his own, were on guard. They stood in what Louise, who had old-fashioned notions as to the behaviour of soldiers on duty, put down as a slouchy and disrespectful attitude. When Lieutenant Godet walked past them they did not salute. This want of respect of the soldier for his officer was another manifestation, it seems, of Equality and Fraternity. Louise, with her nose in the air, sailed past in the wake of Godet and Fleurette.

After crossing a wide vestibule and turning on the right into a long paved corridor, Lieutenant Godet came to a halt before a door which bore the legend: "Committee of Public Safety, Section III." Beside the door another soldier, also in very shabby uniform, stood leaning upon his bayonet. Fleurette, overawed by the vastness and silence of the place, gazed with vague terror at this man who without uttering a word had put his bayonet athwart the door and held it there, barring the way, motionless as a statue. Lieutenant Godet then spoke to him:

"The citizeness," he said, "is the daughter of Citizen Chauvelin. She desires to speak with him!"

The daughter of Citizen Chauvelin? What did the man mean? Fleurette, puzzled and frowning, pulled him by the sleeve. She was the daughter of Citizen Armand: she'd never heard the name of Chauvelin before. Nevertheless the soldier on guard lowered his bayonet. Godet pushed open the door and the next moment Fleurette found herself facing a large desk which was covered with papers, and behind which Bibi was sitting, writing. A voice said loudly:

"Citizen Chauvelin, here's your daughter come to see you."

Whereupon Bibi raised his head and looked at her, staring as if he had seen a ghost.

Forgetting everything save the joy of seeing chéri Bibi at last, Fleurette gave a glad little cry, ran round the table, and came to a halt on her knees beside Bibi's chair, with her arms round his neck.

She felt so glad, so glad that she was ready to cry.

"Bibi," she said softly, whispering in his ear, "chéri Bibi, are you not glad to see me?"

Nineteen

At sight of Fleurette, Chauvelin had stared as if he had seen a ghost. He did not trust his eyes: they were obviously playing him a trick. It was only a a second or two later that he realized it was indeed the child, come, Heaven only knew why and how, but here in this awful city where treachery, hatred and cruelty were holding sway under his own command.

Half-dazed, he yielded to the caresses of this one being in the whole wide world whom his tigerish heart had ever loved. His arms closed round her beloved form, whose sweet breath as of thyme and violets filled his soul with joy. Then, looking up, he saw Louise standing there: silent, stolid, mutely accusing, and he asked roughly:

"How the hell did you both get here?"

Louise shrugged her shoulders.

"By the *coche*," she said, "from Sisteron."

"I know," he rejoined. "But why did you come?"

"Ask her," Louise replied curtly. "She would come. I could not let her travel alone."

Bibi's two hands were clasped round Fleurette's head, his fingers were buried in her hair: he pressed that dearly beloved head closer and closer to his breast; joy at sight of her had already given place to terror. What was the child doing here? How and why had she come? He had kept her so completely aloof from real life, that it seemed to him that some awful cataclysm must have occurred over in that peaceful home in Dauphiné, else she were not here.

His pale, restless eyes searched Louise's impassive face:

"Who brought you here?" he reiterated roughly.

"An officer in a draggle-tailed uniform," Louise replied, still speaking curtly, whilst with a glance that was distinctly hostile her eyes swept round the room. "I thought," she added, "that he followed us into the room."

"What was he like?"

She described him as closely as she could, and then added: "I don't remember his name."

She too had heard the name "Chauvelin" spoken by the soldier and for a moment had pondered. Marvelled. In her downright peasant mind vague doubts, doubts that were eighteen years old now, turned to more definite suspicions. She knew well enough that some kind of mystery hung around the personality of Fleurette's father; she knew for instance that he was really a wealthy and high-born gentleman; but eighteen years ago, in the days of the old régime, the fact that a high-born gentleman chose to hide a love-romance from the eyes of his equally high-born friends was not an infrequent occurrence. If at any time during the past eighteen years she had learned that M'sieu' Armand was really a great Duke or Prince or Ambassador, she would have been neither surprised nor suspicious. But Chauvelin!!! For the past three years whenever rumours of cruelty or ruthless persecution of innocent men and women had penetrated to these distant corners of Dauphiné or Provence, the name of Armand Chauvelin had stood out as the protagonist of these terrible tragedies; people spoke of Danton the lion of the revolution, and also of Marat its tiger, of Robespierre and of Chauvelin.

Chauvelin!!!

And he, meeting her glance, understood what went on in her mind. As to this he was indifferent. What Louise thought of him was less than nothing. It was the child that mattered now: the child who clung to him quivering with excitement. The terror in his heart grew in intensity: it gripped him till he felt physically sick. The mad dogs of hatred and cruelty, which he himself had helped to unchain, seemed to be snarling at him and threatening his Fleurette. With a hand that trembled visibly, he stroked the pretty golden hair.

"Now, little one," he said, steadying his voice as much as he could, "are you going to tell me why you've come?"

Fleurette struggled to her feet. Self-possessed she stood before her father and said firmly:

"Chéri Bibi, I came in order to right a great wrong. I believe that you are strong and powerful and that you will help me to see justice done. That is why I came to you."

He frowned, more puzzled than before, angered with himself for being so dull-witted, for not making a guess at what had brought the child along. His mind just before she came had been so completely absorbed in the latest adventure of his arch-enemy the Scarlet Pimpernel, that the presence of Fleurette, here and now, had been for him like a sudden stunning blow on the head. He felt dazed and stupid: unable to turn his thoughts into this fresh channel.

"Fleurette, my darling," he pleaded, "try and tell me more clearly. I don't understand. What do you mean by righting a wrong? What wrong?"

"Why," she replied simply, "the arrest of M'sieu' Amédé for a crime which he did not commit.

"You knew M'sieu' Amédé had been arrested?" she insisted.

Yes, he knew that. The mock arrest of young Colombe was one of the tricks played on that fool Godet by those impudent English spies. But what had Fleurette's presence here to do with that?

She was trying to explain.

"Then you know, chéri Bibi," she was saying in that sweet, eager way of hers, "that some valuables belonging to Madame over at the château were found in the shed behind M'sieu' Colombe's shop?"

Yes, he knew that too. But what had she…?

"And that the soldiers accused M'sieu' Amédé of having stolen them?"

A sigh of relief escaped him. He was beginning to understand. Nothing to worry about apparently. Indeed he might have guessed. The child had come to plead for that young fool Amédé, and –

"And what I had come to tell you, chéri Bibi," she went on glibly, "is that it is not Amédé who stole the things belonging to Madame."

She paused for a second or two. What she was about to say required courage: and how Bibi would take it she did not know. But Fleurette had come all the way from Lou Mas, had journeyed three days, so that Bibi might right a great wrong, as only he could do, and, once more sinking on her knees beside her father's chair, she added in a clear voice, rendered somewhat shrill with excitement:

"I stole the valuables out of Madame's room, chéri Bibi."

With a hoarse cry he clapped his hand against her mouth. My God, if someone had heard! The guard outside, or one of these innumerable spies whom he himself had set in motion, and whose ears were trained to penetrate through the most solid walls.

His pale eyes in which now lurked a kind of vague terror, wandered furtively round the room, whilst Louise, equally horrified and frightened, exclaimed almost involuntarily:

"The child is mad, M'sieu', do not listen to her."

Fleurette alone remained self-possessed: she was still on her knees, but at Bibi's rough gesture she had fallen back, steadying herself with one hand against the floor. Slowly, noiselessly, Chauvelin had risen and tiptoed across the room, Louise, wide-eyed and scared, following his every movement. They were furtive like those of a cat on the prowl, and his face was the colour of ashes. He went to the door and abruptly pulled it open. Outside the soldier on guard was quietly chatting with Lieutenant Godet; at sight of Citizen Chauvelin they stood at attention and saluted.

"Go and tell Captain Moisson over at the barracks," Chauvelin said curtly, addressing Godet, "that I shall want to see him here at two o'clock."

"Very good, citizen."

Godet saluted again and turned on his heel. Chauvelin looked at him closely, but his face was expressionless. He watched him for a moment or two, as he, Godet, strode along the corridor. Then he closed the door and went back to his seat behind the table.

He had made an almost superhuman effort to regain his composure. He wanted to hear more, and did not want to scare the child. The sight of Godet standing outside the door talking to the man on guard, had made him physically sick, raised that same terror in his heart which his presence and his glance were wont to raise in others. The expression of his face must at one moment have been absolutely terrifying, for Fleurette could hardly bear to look at him; but when he sat down again his face was just like a mask, waxen and grey. He turned to her, and rested his elbow on the table, shading his eyes with his long, thin hand. And Fleurette felt how dreadful it must be for him to think that his daughter was a thief.

So before he had time to ask her any questions she embarked on glib explanations.

"You must not think, chéri Bibi," she said, "that I stole those things for a bad motive. I did it because – "

She checked herself, and went on after a second or two:

"You remember, chéri Bibi, that evening at the château when we met, you and I, by the stable door?"

Yes, he remembered. "But speak softly, child! these walls have ears!"

"I had taken the things out of Madame's room then," Fleurette continued, speaking in an agitated whisper, "and hidden them under my shawl." She gave a nervous little laugh: "Oh! I was terrified, I can tell you," she said, "that you would notice."

He had his nerves under control by now. His mind, keen, active, was concentrated on her story, his indomitable will was slowly mastering his terror. What had he to fear? Godet was out of the way, and the child's whispers could not be heard outside these four walls. If only that fool Louise did not look so scared: the sight of her face, open-mouthed and with big, round eyes, got on his nerves. He tried not to look her way. While his glance was fixed on Fleurette he felt that he could think of her, scheme for her and above all protect her – he, so important in the councils of State. So powerful. He could shield her even against the consequences of her own folly.

Of course, he must make light of the whole affair. Oh! above all make light of it. The child was silly, wilful and ignorant, but he would know how to protect her, and how to make her hold her tongue. Louise was a fool, but she was safe and these walls were solid, there was really no cause for this insane terror which had turned him giddy and faint, and at first paralysed his brain.

So he forced his quaking voice into tones of gentle banter, forced himself to smile, to tweak her cheek and to look gaily, almost incredulously into her eyes.

"Allons, allons," he said lightly, "what story is this? My little Fleurette taking things that belong to others? I won't believe it."

"Only pour le bon motif, chéri Bibi," she insisted; "because you see the soldiers were at the château, and they were ruining and stealing everything they could lay their hands on... And also because – "

Once more she checked herself, loath to give away that one cherished little secret: The mysterious voice at which perhaps

Bibi would scoff. But she did tell Bibi how with the precious burden under her shawl she had hurried homewards until, fearing that she would be overtaken by the soldiers on the road, she had sought refuge in the widow Tronchet's cottage. She told him how she had watched him riding past, heading towards Lou Mas, and how she had become scared lest, if he spent the night at home, he would find out what it was that she was keeping so carefully hidden underneath her shawl.

And then she told him how she had thought of M'sieu' Amédé and had asked Adèle to tell him to meet her outside the widow's cottage, and how she had entrusted him with the precious treasure and he had undertaken to hide it in the shed outside his father's shop. But how it came to pass that those other soldiers, who were as magnificently dressed as anything Fleurette had seen in all her life, how they had come to suspect M'sieu' Amédé of the theft, she could not conjecture. All she knew was that M'sieu' Amédé was innocent and that he must be proclaimed innocent at once. At once.

"I stole the things, Bibi," she concluded, "not for a bad motive, I swear, but I did steal them and gave them to M'sieu' Amédé to keep. If anyone is to be punished, then it must be I, not he."

She was sitting on her heels, and looking up boldly, and with a little wilful air at her father. Her dear little hands were resting on her knees. She looked adorable. Chauvelin mutely put out his arms and she snuggled into them, pressing her cheek against his breast with a nervous little gesture, twiddling one of the buttons of his coat.

Old Louise, sitting at the far end of the room, had listened, open-mouthed, wide-eyed, to the tale. Her furrowed face was a mirror of all the different expressions with which Chauvelin regarded her from time to time. Terror and slow reassurance. "If that is all, then I can deal with it!" he seemed to be telling her now, when it was all over, and he knew the worst. He held the child very close to him, and there was a certain nervous terror still lurking in his eyes as he buried his face in the soft waves of her hair.

"Bibi chéri," Fleurette insisted, "I must find those who are going to sit in judgment on M'sieu' Amédé. And you will help me find them, won't you? I must tell them the truth. Mustn't I?"

"You shall, child, you shall," he babbled incoherently. He was trying to steady his voice, so as not to let her know how scared he had been.

"When Adèle told us the next morning about the soldiers having found Madame's valuables and arrested M'sieu' Amédé, I knew at once that you would help me to put everything right. So Louise and I just started then and there, as I thought we would find you in Sisteron."

"The child told me nothing," Louise protested in answer to a mute challenge from Chauvelin. "I only thought she wanted to see you in order to plead for young Colombe."

"There is no need," he said steadily, "for me or anyone else to plead for him. Amédé Colombe is a free man at this hour."

Fleurette's little cry of rapture gave him a short, sharp pang of jealousy.

"Do you love him so much as all that, little one?" he asked almost involuntarily.

She blushed, and without replying hung her head.

For a second or two he debated within himself whether he would tell her the whole truth, then came to the conclusion that on the whole it would be best that she should know. Doubtless she would hear the story, anyhow, from others and so he told it her just as he had had it the day before from Lieutenant Godet. The magnificent soldiers who had come that morning into Laragne were not real soldiers of the revolutionary army, they were a band of English spies whose chief was known throughout France as the Scarlet Pimpernel: a cynical, impudent adventurer whose business it was to incite French men and women to desert their country in the hour of her greatest need, and who doubtless would incite Amédé Colombe to treachery and desertion. It was that chief, no doubt, who had spied on Fleurette and seen her that night hand over Madame's valuables to Amédé Colombe. He had taken this means of obtaining possession of the valuables, as well as of the persons of the ci-devant Frontenac and Amédé. Both men and money he would use against France, for the English were great enemies of this glorious revolution, the friends of all the aristos and tyrants whom the people were determined to wipe off the face of the earth.

Wide-eyed and dumb, Fleurette listened to him. After the first moment of intense joy, when she heard that Amédé was safe, there had come a sense of exultation that the mysterious voice which had urged her to find Madame's valuables had spoken with a purpose and that that purpose was now accomplished. Monsieur, Madame and Mademoiselle had all been saved by what she believed was a supernatural agency – whatever Bibi might say. No man who was a mere spy and an enemy of France could have accomplished all that this mysterious being had done, from the moment when disguised as a faggot-carrier he had commanded her to look after Madame's valuables, until the hour when clad in a magnificent uniform, daring and fearless, he had found such glorious means of saving Amédé and M'sieu' de Frontenac too, from prison and perhaps death.

And after the joy and the exultation there had crept into Fleurette's heart a feeling of awe and dread for the father who apparently she had never really known until this hour. She had only known him as kind, indulgent, loving – loving in a kind of fierce way at times, snarling like a wild cat if she thwarted him – but always indulgent and always secretive. Now he seemed to lay his soul bare before her. His love of France, of that revolution which apparently he had helped to make. His hatred of those whom he called traitors and enemies of France, the aristocrats, the men who owned land and property, who had ancestors and family pride, and then the English who were the real enemies, who worked against the people, against democracy, and against liberty, who had harboured every traitor that plotted against France. Bibi hated them all and Fleurette felt awed and chilled thus to hear him speak. He, who was so gentle with her always, now spoke as if he approved of all the cruelty perpetrated against those who did not think as he did, and whom he hated with such passionate intensity.

Instinctively, and she hoped imperceptibly, she recoiled from him when he once more tried to clasp her in his arms. This man with the pale eyes and the cruel sneer was not the Bibi she loved. He was just a man whom she feared. All she wanted now was to get away, to get back to Lou Mas. Since Amédé was safe, why should she stay any more in this awful place where even Bibi seemed like a stranger?

Louise now was standing near her, and Bibi was giving Louise some peremptory orders:

"You will go back now to the 'Chat Noir'," he said, "the inn where you were this morning. There you will wait quietly until I come to fetch you. We will get on the way as early as we can, so as to get to Vaison before dark."

"Vaison?" Louise asked, perplexed. "But the *coche*..."

"We are not travelling by the public *coche*," Bibi broke in impatiently. "My private *calèche* will take us as far as Lou Mas, and I'll not leave you till I've seen you safely home."

"A *calèche!*" Louise exclaimed. "Holy Virgin!"

"Silence, woman," Bibi cried with an oath. "There is no Holy Virgin now."

Well! of course, Bibi had said that sort of thing before now, but never in such a rough, almost savage tone. Slowly Fleurette struggled to her feet. All of a sudden she was feeling very, very tired. For four whole days excitement and anxiety had kept her up; but now excitement had died down and dull reaction had set in. A sense of unreality came over her: the voice of Bibi giving all sorts of instructions to Louise came to her muffled as if through a thick veil. All that she knew – and this was comforting – was that soon they would all be starting for home: not in a crowded, jostling old *coche*, but in a *calèche*. What a wonderful man Bibi was: so grand and powerful and rich, that he had a *calèche* of his own and could come and go as he pleased. She remembered how deferential the soldiers had been to him that night at the château, and even now her eyes fastened on the beautiful tricolour sash which he wore, the visible sign of his influence and power.

When Bibi finally took her in his arms and kissed her as affectionately, as tenderly as was his wont, she swayed a little when he released her and the things in the room started to go round and round before her eyes. Louise put her strong arm round her and Fleurette heard her say: "Leave her to me, she'll be all right!" She felt herself being led out of the room, past the sentry at the door, and then along a corridor.

When she felt the soft, spring air strike her in the face she felt revived, and walked steadily beside Louise as far as the inn.

Twenty

Bibi's orders to Louise had been to go back to the inn and there to wait until he came in his *calèche* to take them home to Lou Mas. And the two women, ready for the journey home, so tired that only excitement kept them from breaking down, waited for him patiently in the parlour downstairs.

The travellers who had arrived in the early morning by the old *coche*, had all disappeared by now; some had found accommodation at the "Chat Noir", others had gone to their homes or to friends in the city: the hour for dinner was not yet, and the personnel of the inn was busy in the kitchen.

The place was deserted and silent; the room itself hot and stuffy. The air was heavy with the mingled odour of dust, stale grease and boiled food. Up on the wall a large white-faced clock ticked with noisy monotony, and against the small window-pane a lazy fly kept up an intermittent buzz. Now and again from a remote part of the house came the sound of a human voice or the barking of a dog, or the rattling of pots and pans.

Louise, sitting in a large, old-fashioned armchair by the side of the great hearth, had closed her eyes. The monotonous ticking of the clock, the buzzing of the fly, the heat and the silence lulled her to sleep. Fleurette, on a straight-backed chair, sat wide awake, unable to keep her eyes closed even for a few minutes, although they ached terribly and she was very, very tired. But there was so much to keep her brain busy. In the past four days more exciting events had been crowded into her life

152

than in all the eighteen years that lay behind her. And round and round they went – these events – beginning with the first sight of the squad of soldiers marching down the high road and coming to a halt on the bridge, until the happy moment when Bibi had assured her that M'sieu' Amédé was safe and free, under the protection of that mysterious personage whom Bibi called an impudent spy and enemy of France, but whom she, Fleurette, believed to be an agent of the *bon Dieu* Himself.

It seemed a part of her confused thoughts, presently, when she saw the door of the parlour slowly open and the kind soldier who had conducted her to Bibi standing in the doorway. He cast a quick glance all over the room, and as Fleurette was obviously on the point of uttering a cry of surprise, he put up a warning finger to his lips and then beckoned to her to come. She rose, eager as well as mystified, and once more he made a gesture of warning, pointing to Louise and then raising a finger to his lips. A warning it was to make no noise, and not to waken Louise. Fleurette tiptoed across the room to him.

"Your father sent me round," he said in a whisper. He beckoned to her to come outside. She cast a last look at Louise who was obviously peacefully asleep, and then slipped out past him into the street.

"There is something your father forgot to say to you," the soldier said as soon as he had closed the door behind Fleurette. "But he told me not to bring the old woman along, and so as she was asleep – "

"But if she wakes and finds me gone – ?" Fleurette rejoined, and turned to go back to the inn. "I must just tell her – "

Immediately he seized hold of her hand.

"Your father," he said, "told me to bring you along as quickly as I could. You know how impatient he is. It is but a step to the Hôtel de Ville. We'll be there and back before the old woman wakes."

No one knew better than Fleurette how impatient Bibi could

be. If he said anything it had to be done at once. At once. So, without further protest, she followed the kind soldier down the narrow street. A few minutes later she was back in the Hôtel de Ville, outside the door which bore the legend: "Committee of Public Safety, Section III." The same soldier in the shabby uniform was lounging, bayonet in hand, outside the door, but at sight of Lieutenant Godet he stood up at attention and made no attempt this time to bar the way. Godet pushed the door open and at a sign from him Fleurette stepped into the room. Of course she had expected to see Bibi sitting as before behind the table, alone, busy writing.

Bibi certainly was there, she saw that at a glance, also that at sight of her he jumped to his feet with an expression on his face, far, far more terrible than when she had told him that it was she who had stolen Madame's valuables. But Bibi was not alone. To right and left of him two men were sitting, dressed very much like he was himself and wearing the same kind of tricolour sash round their waist. There was a moment of tense silence while Fleurette, a little scared, but not really frightened, stepped further into the room. She could not take her eyes off Bibi, whose dear face had become the colour of lead. He raised his hand and passed it across his forehead. He seemed as if he wanted to speak, yet could not articulate a sound. After a second or two he looked down first at the man on his right, and then at the one on his left, then back again at her, and over her head at Lieutenant Godet.

It was Fleurette who first broke the silence.

"What is it, father?" she said. "You sent for me?"

She did not call him Bibi just then; he seemed so very, very unlike Bibi.

But all he said was:

"What – is the meaning of – of this?" and the words seemed to come through his lips with a terrible effort.

"It means, Citizen Chauvelin, that I am trying to do my duty, and redeeming my faults of negligence and incompetence, for which you passed such severe strictures on me yesterday."

The voice was that of Lieutenant Godet. Fleurette could not see him because he stood immediately behind her, but she recognized the voice, even though it was no longer amiable and almost servile as it had been earlier in the day. It had, in fact, the same tone in it which Fleurette had so deeply resented that day upon the bridge when first she had told him that she was Citizen Armand's daughter.

"You ordered me," Godet went on deliberately, "to go into the highways and the byways, and you gave me full power to arrest any man, woman or child whom I suspected of connivance with the enemies of France. This I have done. I have cause to suspect this woman of such connivance, and in accordance with your instructions I have brought her before you on a charge of treason."

Whereupon the man sitting on the right of Bibi nodded approvingly and said:

"If indeed you have cause to suspect this woman, citizen lieutenant, you did well to arrest her."

And the man on Bibi's left asked: "Who is this woman, citizen lieutenant?"

Then only did Bibi appear to find his voice, and it came through his lips just as if someone held him by the throat and were trying to choke him before he had time to speak.

"My daughter," was all he said.

As a matter of fact Fleurette did not understand. That something terrible had occurred, she could see well enough, but for the moment the fact that she was in any way involved had not reached her inner consciousness. She did not realize that when Lieutenant Godet spoke of having arrested a woman he was referring to her. Thinking that she was probably in the way amongst these serious and busy men, she asked timidly:

"Shall I go, father?" whereat the man on the left gave a short, dry laugh.

"Not just yet, citizeness," he said; "we shall have to ask you one or two questions before we let you go."

"Citizen Pochart," Bibi now rejoined somewhat more steadily, "there is obviously some grave error here on the part of the citizen lieutenant and – "

"Grave error," Pochart broke in with a sneer. "We have heard nothing in the way of witnesses or details of the accusation so far, so why should you think there is an error, Citizen Chauvelin?"

Fleurette could see the struggle on Bibi's face; she could see the great drops of moisture on his forehead, the swollen veins upon his temples; she saw his hands clenched one against the other, and how he passed his tongue once or twice over his lips.

"The citizen lieutenant," he said with a marvellous assumption of calm, "has shown too much zeal. My daughter is as good a patriot as I am myself – "

"How do you know that, Citizen Chauvelin?" the other man asked, the one on the left of Bibi.

"Because she has led a modest and a sheltered life, Citizen Danou," Bibi replied firmly. "Knowing nothing of town life, nothing of intrigues or plots against the State."

"It is impossible," Pochart put in sententiously, "for any man to know what goes on in a woman's head. The soundest patriot may have a traitor for a wife – or else a daughter."

Bibi was obviously making a superhuman effort to control himself. No one knew better than Fleurette how violent could be his temper when he was thwarted, and here were those two men, not to mention Lieutenant Godet, taunting and contradicting him, and she could see the veins swelling upon his temples and his hands clenched until the knuckles shone like polished ivory under the skin.

"My daughter is not a traitor, Citizen Pochart," he said loudly and firmly.

"Lieutenant Godet says she is," Pochart retorted drily.

"I challenge him to prove it."

"You forget, Citizen Chauvelin," Danou put in suavely, "that it is not for the citizen lieutenant to prove this woman guilty; rather it is for her to prove her innocence."

"The Law of the Suspect," Pochart added, "has been framed expressly to meet such cases as these."

The Law of the Suspect! Ye gods! He himself, Chauvelin, had in the National Assembly voted for its adoption.

"Are we not ordered instantly to arrest all persons who by their actions, their speaking, their writing or their connections have become suspect?" This from Danou who spoke slowly, unctuously, without a trace of spite or anger in his voice. And Pochart, more rough of tone, but equally conciliatory added:

"The Law tells us that if suspect of nothing else, a man, or a woman, or even a child, may be 'suspect of being suspect'. Is that not so, Citizen Chauvelin? Methinks you yourself had something to do with the framing of that law."

"It was aimed at traitors – "

"No! No! at the suspect – "

"My daughter – "

"Ah ça, Citizen Chauvelin," here interposed Pochart with an expressive oath, "are you by any chance on the side of traitors? What has the State to do with the fact that this woman is your daughter? A patriot has no relatives these days. He is a son of the State, a child of France, what? Her enemies are his enemies, his hatred of traitors should over-ride every other sentiment."

"A patriot has no sentiment," Danou echoed suavely.

Chauvelin now looked like an animal at bay. Caught in a net turning round and round, wildly, impotently; seeking an egress and only succeeding in getting more and more firmly enmeshed. But he kept himself under control nevertheless. He felt the eyes of those three men probing his soul. Exulting over his misery. Hatred all around him. Cruelty. Godet openly hostile, vengeful, with a grievance for his own humiliation; ready to hit back, to demand humiliation for humiliation, and terror for terror. Revenge! My God! who but a fiend could dream of such revenge? And the other two: that fool Danou and that brute Pochart! No actual hostility about them. Only envy: a mad desire to save their own skins, to purchase notoriety, advancement at any price – even at the price of innocent blood.

And as a wild beast twirling and turning in the trap will pause from time to time and glare out into the open, which means all that its life has stood for until now, so did Chauvelin, with soul enmeshed in vengeance and envy, pause a moment in his mad struggle for freedom. He paused and with wildly dilated eyes gazed upon a swift, accusing vision of all the innocent blood he himself had helped to shed. Those clenched hands of his, on which his gaze for one instant rested, fascinated, how many times had they signed the decree which had deprived a father of his son, a wife of her husband, a lover of his mistress. And through the meshes that tightened round him now, Chauvelin gazing into space saw before his eyes the awful word "*Retribution*" written in letters of fire and blood.

And seeing the writing on the wall, he felt an immense rage against these men who dared to taunt him, who dared to hit at him, through the one vulnerable spot in his armour of callousness and of cruelty.

How dared they stand up to him, these miserable creatures whose existence was of less account than that of a buzzing fly? And throwing back his head he gazed upon them all one after the other, meeting their sneering glance with a bold challenge. How dared they defy him? Him, Chauvelin? The trusted friend of Robespierre, one of the makers of this glorious revolution; one of its most firm props? Now a representative of the National Convention on special mission? There stood the child, his daughter, his little Fleurette, silent, wide-eyed, obviously not fully aware of the terrible position in which she stood: and they dared to hit at her, to accuse her, without rhyme or reason, just in order to hit at him through her. It was Godet, of course, that vile, incompetent brute: savage and cruel like the fool he was:

vengeful for the bad half-hour he had been made to spend in this very room. He must have heard something of what the child had said. At one moment her sweet voice had risen to shrill tones. Oh! what a senseless, mad confession! and he had seized upon it so that he might hit back: have his revenge. But he could prove nothing. It would be one man's word against another, and he, Chauvelin, representative on special mission, with the ear of all the great men up in Paris, would see to it that his word carried all the weight. He would deny everything, swear that Godet lied. His was the power, he was more influential, more unscrupulous than most.

If only the child held her tongue! She would if she was assured that her Amédé was in no danger. How thankful he, Chauvelin, was that he had told her the truth this morning. He couldn't bear to look at her just at this moment, she looking so innocent, so unconscious of danger, but nevertheless he tried to convey to her with eyes and lips the warning to hold her tongue.

Chauvelin had been silent for quite a little while; the others thought that they had cowed him. In their hearts Pochart and Danou were not a little afraid of him. A representative on special mission had unlimited power and this Chauvelin was always a crouching beast, ready to snarl and to spring, and they knew well enough how influential he was. But here was a double chance to show their zeal, and to get even with the man whom they had always feared. As for Godet, he had obviously staked everything on this throw. His life was anyhow forfeit; Chauvelin's threats yesterday had left him no loophole for hope. But here was revenge to his hand, and at worst a powerful lever wherewith to force his enemy's hand.

Chauvelin's mind had been so busily at work that for a while he lost consciousness of these men. After his rage against them he forgot their very presence. Nothing mattered – no one – except the child, and his own power to save her. Through that semiconsciousness he only heard vague words. Snatches of phrases that passed rapidly between those two men and Godet. "Proofs –" "Witnesses –" And then Danou's voice soft and unctuous as usual:

"Of course the more solid your proofs –"

And Pochart's rough and determined:

"Why should we not hear that witness now?"

Godet replied lightly: "I have her here. Perhaps it would be best."

It seemed as if they were determined to ignore him, Chauvelin; to shut him out of their counsels. He was so silent, so self-absorbed; they thought that he was cowed, and dared not raise his voice in defence of his daughter. They were all alike these men – these masters of France as they liked to be called – overbearing, arrogant, always menacing, until you hit back, when all the starch would go out of them, and they would cringe, or else become surly and defiant like any aristo.

"Go and fetch your witness, citizen lieutenant," Pochart said in the end.

Then Chauvelin woke, like a tiger out of his sleep.

"What?" he queried abruptly, "what is this?"

"A witness, citizen representative," came in unctuous tones from Danou. "It will be more satisfactory in this case – the Law does not demand witnesses – suspicion is enough – but –"

"Out of deference to your position, citizen," Pochart broke in with a short laugh. "Go and fetch your witness, Citizen Godet," he added drily.

Chauvelin brought his clenched fist down with a crash on the table.

"I'll not allow you –" he began in thundering accents, and met Danou's sneering, inquiring gaze.

"Allow what, citizen representative?" Pochart asked roughly.

"Refuse to hear witnesses? On what grounds?" Danou put in in smooth, velvety accents.

Godet said nothing. It was not for him to speak; but he met Chauvelin's glance just then, and almost drained his cup of revenge to its dreg.

"No one," now put in Pochart significantly, "has more respect for family ties than I have. But I am first of all a patriot, and then only a family man. I happen to be a single man, but if I were married and discovered my wife to be a traitor to the State, and an enemy of the people, I would with my own hand adjust the guillotine which would end such a worthless and miserable life."

"Now you, Citizen Chauvelin," Danou said, taking up his colleague's point, "are doing your daughter no good by trying to shield her from punishment if she be guilty."

"You would not dare – "

"Dare what, Citizen Chauvelin? Act up to the principles which you yourself have helped to promulgate in France? Indeed we dare! We dare strike at the enemies of the State whoever they may be. That woman," he added, indicating Fleurette, "is suspect; the Law of the Suspect gives our Committee power to arrest her. If she be proved innocent she shall go free. If she be guilty, you, by defending her, cannot save her and do but condemn yourself."

And that was true! No one knew it better than Chauvelin, who but a few weeks ago in Paris had helped Merlin and Douai to frame that abominable Law. The heavy hand of Retribution was indeed upon him. The voice of the innocent had cried out for Vengeance before the Lord, and Nemesis, hour-glass in hand, had stalked him now at last. All that was left him at this moment, out of all that arrogance which had imposed his personality upon the masters of France, made them forget his failures and fear him even in the hour of humiliation, was just a shred of pride, which enabled him to hide his misery and his despair behind a mask of impassiveness. He even succeeded in hiding his hatred and contempt of these three curs who were yapping at his heels. And when Pochart for the third time reiterated his order to Godet to go and fetch his witness, Chauvelin made no further protest. He rose from the table and went round to where Fleurette was standing, silent and bewildered, with great tears, like those of a frightened child, running down her cheeks.

He held his hands tightly clenched behind his back, to prevent himself from seizing her in his arms and raining kisses upon her golden hair, letting those sneering men see how terribly he had been hit and how he suffered. Godet had gone out of the room to fetch the witness – what witness? and the other two were sitting at the table, whispering together. Chauvelin, through compressed lips, murmured in Fleurette's ears:

"Try not to be frightened, little one! Don't let them see you are frightened. They dare not do anything to you."

"I am not frightened, chéri Bibi," she replied, smiling at him through her tears.

"And you will hold your tongue, Fleurette," he urged under his breath, "about what you told me this morning? Swear to me that you will."

"If M'sieu' Amédé is safe –"

"I swear to you on my soul, that we do not even know where he is."

"In that case, Bibi chéri –"

Quick footsteps outside the door. A challenge from the man on guard. The opening of the door. Then Godet's voice saying loudly:

"The witness, citizens."

Chauvelin looked up and saw beside Godet a woman with a shawl wrapped round her head; she came forward boldly, then threw back her shawl. Chauvelin uttered a savage oath, whilst Fleurette gasped in amazement.

"Adèle!" she cried.

Twenty-one

It seemed almost the worst moment of this awful day to see Adèle – Adèle! – standing there, like some sly and furtive rodent, snapping at the hand that had fed and tended it. The lessons taught by all these makers of a revolution which was going to be a millennium for the people, and inaugurate an era of brotherly love, had been well learnt by all those who had nothing to lose and everything to gain by venality, by treachery and the blackest of ingratitude. And Chauvelin himself had been head master in that school, where this wretched little bastard had learned how to hate; she was the personification of that proletariat which he had striven to exalt, of the low, mean mind that never tries to rise, and only strives to drag down others to the level of its own crass ignorance. Adèle was only a product of that levelling process which was going to make of mankind one great family, full of love for one another, of pity for the weak and contempt of the strong, and which had only succeeded in arousing a universal hatred in every breast and envy of everything that was lofty and pure. The levelling process according to its early protagonists – idealists for the most part – was destined to eliminate all tyranny and to protect those who were too weak to protect themselves; but all it had succeeded in doing was to substitute one tyranny for another; it had not levelled the classes, made one man as good as another; what it had done was to hurl down from his self-imposed altitude of nobility or of virtue every man who was unwilling to step down

163

of his own accord. It had set every beggar on horseback who was a beggar by nature, and kept him there by virtue of ruthlessness and of cruelty. None but a fellow-beggar, more ruthless perhaps, and more cruel, could unseat him. Death was the only real leveller, and this glorious revolution had become a fraternity of death. The Republic of France must march to Liberty over corpses, one of its makers had said, and another added sententiously that no traitor failed to return, except the dead. Terror reigned now everywhere, marching hand in hand with its hand-maiden the guillotine.

The time was no longer far distant when this titanic battle between all these beggars on horseback would reach its fiercest struggle ere it ended in a gigantic cataclysm, and when the gorge of all these tigers would rise at last in face of the daily hecatombs which had made a graveyard of the fair lands of France. But that time was not yet. Men like Chauvelin had seen visions of Retribution like fiery Fata Morgana pointing to the inevitable hour, but the Godets, the Danous, the Pocharts and the Adèles knew not the signs of the times. They had learnt their lesson and were applying it for their own advancement and above all for their own safety, destroying all that was destructible, taking Earth and Heaven to witness that they whose lives had been nought but misery and hunger would henceforth sweep off the face of the earth all those who had only known ease and comfort, who had practised virtue, and never known despair.

And Adèle, whose hatred of Fleurette had thriven all these years as in a forcing-house, had learnt her lesson well. Fleurette to her meant tyranny, the tyranny of riches over her poverty, of good food over her empty stomach, of neat kirtle over her rags. Poverty and Hunger had enchained her to Fleurette's wheel, had forced her to wash dishes, to scrub floors, to sleep on a straw pallet. But now her turn had come. Her very misery had put it in her power to drag Fleurette down to her own level. She had imbibed the principles of this glorious revolution until she felt herself to be one of its prophets. She had spied on

Fleurette and denounced her because she had seen at last a way to satisfy her hatred and to lull her envy to rest.

She had plenty to say when questioned by Pochart and Danou; proud of the fact that for over two years now she had supplied the Sisteron section of the Committee of Public Safety with information about the district. She had known the ci-devant Frontenacs and it was – she was proud to state – chiefly owing to her that they came to be suspected of treason. They used to turn one of their rooms into a chapel on Sundays and a ci-devant priest, who was not Constitutional, performed there rites and ceremonies with wafer and cup which had long since been decreed treasonable against the State. Adèle had been forced by the ci-devant Frontenac women to be present at these treasonable practices; she had even been made to scrub the floor of that temple of superstition and to remove the dust from the so-called altar. Her patriotic soul had risen in revolt and she had journeyed to Sisteron one day when she was free and placed the matter before the Committee of Public Safety who had commended her for her zeal.

"Adèle!" Fleurette exclaimed involuntarily. "How could you? Indeed *le bon Dieu* will punish you for this."

At which remark everybody laughed – except Chauvelin, who smothered a groan. Oh! the child! the senseless, foolish, adorable child! She seemed wilfully to run her darling head into the noose. Adèle turned a sneering glance on Fleurette.

"I'll chance a punishment from your *bon Dieu*," she said flippantly, "for the joy of seeing you punished by the Revolutionary Tribunal."

And strange to say Chauvelin did not strike her, though she stood quite near him, with only the width of the table between her and his avenging hand. But he did not strike her, even though his muscles ached with the desire to strike her on the mouth. It was pride that held him back. How those men would have laughed to see him lose his self-control with this wench

165

who was only emitting principles that he indirectly had taught her. Retribution! Nemesis at every turn.

And now Adèle embarked upon her main story. Her spying on Fleurette. Long, long had she suspected her with her airs of virtue and bunches of forget-me-nots in front of a statue representing a ci-devant saint. "Saint Antoine de Padoue, priez pour nous!" every time she placed a fresh bunch of flowers before that statue. Bah! such superstition made a patriot's gorge rise with disgust. But Adèle had said nothing. Not for a long time. She knew that Citizen Chauvelin – he was known as Armand over at Laragne – was a great patriot and an intimate friend of Citizen Robespierre over in Paris. So Adèle decided to bide her time, and she did. Until that evening when at last the Frontenacs were arrested and the château ransacked. That night Adèle had had her suspicions aroused by Fleurette's strange airs of mystery, her desire to meet Citizen Colombe alone on a dark night. Fleurette had always been such a *Sainte Nitouche* that Adèle guessed that something serious was in the wind.

Like a zealous patriot she had watched, and she had seen Fleurette hand over a casket and a wallet to young Colombe. She had heard the two talk over the question of hiding these things in a shed behind Citizen Colombe's shop, and finally seen them locked in each other's arms, which confirmed her in the idea that Fleurette, with all her appearances of virtue, was a woman guilty of moral turpitude.

And still Chauvelin did not strike her on the mouth. He fell to wondering what crime he had committed that was heinous enough to deserve this punishment of impotence.

The others listened for the most part in silence. Only occasionally did one or the other break into a chuckle. *Nom de nom*, what an event! Representative Chauvelin! the man of almost arrogant integrity, sent to Orange to spy and report on the workings of the Committee of Public Safety, one of the makers of the Terror, a man whose every glance was a menace, and every word a threat of death! When Adèle had finished speaking Pochart winked across at Danou. Here was a find that would exalt them both, bring their names to the notice of the great men over in Paris. All sorts of possibilities of reward and advancement loomed largely before them. And Pochart rubbed his large, coarse hands contentedly together, and Danou poured himself out a glass of water and drank it down. All these possibilities had made him thirsty.

Fleurette too was silent. For the first time in her life she had come in contact with human passions of which hitherto she had not even dreamed. Adèle, the little maid of all work, with the coarse hands, the red elbows and narrow rat-like face, who wore Fleurette's cast-off clothes and worn-out shoes, had suddenly become an ununderstandable and terrifying enigma. Fleurette felt as if she could not utter a sound, that any word of protest which she might raise would choke her. The girl's words, her bitter accusations, spoken in an even monotone, gave her a feeling as of an icy-cold grip upon her heart. Surrounded from her cradle onwards with love and care, this first glimpse of spite and hatred paralysed her. Only when Adèle spoke of M'sieu' Amédé and of that kiss which had tokened him to Fleurette, that delicious kiss under the almond trees, only then did a hot blush rise to her cheeks, and tears of shame gather in her eyes.

Beyond that she felt like an automaton, while these four creatures who hated her and who hated Bibi were discussing her fate. Bibi was strangely silent and motionless, although from time to time the others referred a question or two to him in which case he replied in curt monosyllables. There was much talk of "detention" and of "revolutionary tribunal". Of course Fleurette did not understand what these meant. Since Bibi appeared so indifferent she supposed that nothing very serious was going to happen to her.

Presently Adèle and Godet were dismissed. Adèle swept past her with her shawl once more over her head, hiding the expression of her face. Her eyes did not meet Fleurette's as she glided past like a little rat seeking its burrow. Perhaps she was ashamed. Godet was ordered to send two men along – they would be wanted to take the citoyenne to the house of detention. Godet gave the salute and followed Adèle out of the room.

Fleurette's feet were aching. She had been standing quite still for over half an hour, and was longing to sit down. Bibi's eyes were upon her now, and his long thin hands were fidgeting nervously with a paper-knife. At one time he clutched it so tightly, and half raised it, as if he meant to strike one or the other of his colleagues. Fleurette, tired and a little dizzy, only caught snatches of their conversation. At one time Bibi said very quietly:

"You are very bold, Citizen Danou, to measure your influence against mine."

And the man on Bibi's left retorted very suavely:

"If I have transgressed, citizen representative, I'll answer for it."

"You will," Bibi rejoined, and his words came through his thin, compressed lips harsh and dry, like blows from a wooden mallet against a metal plate. "And with your head, probably."

"Is that a threat, Citizen Chauvelin?" the other asked with a sneer.

"You may take it so if you wish."

The man on Chauvelin's right, Citizen Pochart, had in the meanwhile been writing assiduously on a large piece of paper. Now he pushed the paper in front of Chauvelin and said curtly:

"Will you sign this, citizen representative?"

"What is it?" Chauvelin asked.

"Order for the provisional arrest of one Fleur Chauvelin, suspect of treasonable connections with the enemies of France, pending her appearance before the Revolutionary Tribunal."

Chauvelin raised the paper and read it through carefully. His hand that held the paper was perfectly steady.

"Your signature," Pochart went on, and held out the quill pen invitingly toward Chauvelin, "as Representative of the National Convention on special mission, is necessary on this order."

"You may take that as a threat too, Citizen Chauvelin," Danou added with a sly wink directed at his colleague Pochart, "for if you do not sign there's others that will, and sign one too that will be even more unpleasant for you."

Chauvelin took the pen, and the two men, Pochart and Danou, sprawling over the table, had the satisfaction of seeing him sign the order for the arrest of his own child – her death probably. Not the first time either that something of the sort had occurred, that a man put his seal on the death-warrant of his kith or kin. Had not Philippe d'Orléans voted for the death of his cousin the King? Chauvelin signed with a steady hand, his lips tightly pressed one against the other. They should not see, these fiends, what torture he was enduring; they should not see that at this moment he felt just like a brute beast writhing in agony. Not that he had abandoned hope with regard to Fleurette. He felt confident that he could turn the order into a mere scrap of paper presently, and see those two snarling dogs fawning at his feet once more, kicked with the toe of his boot and howling in vain for mercy.

It was only from humiliation that, conscious of his power, he had decided that silence and outward acquiescence were his best policy. He had certain cards up his sleeve which the others wot not of, but he could only play them if he succeeded in lulling them into a sense of security by his obvious indifference. Fortunately his reputation stood him in good stead. He was known by his enemies to be so ruthtess and so unscrupulous – such an ardent patriot, declared his friends – that his indifference now where his own daughter was concerned, did not even astonish Pochart and Danou. It was just like Citizen Chauvellin to send his own daughter to the guillotine. And this estimate of his character helped him to play the role that would mean life to Fleurette.

So there he sat for a few minutes, perfectly impassive, his face a mask, his hand perfectly steady, perusing the paper, and then deliberately drawing his pen through one of the words and substituting another.

"We'll say the house of Caristie," he said drily, "the other is already full."

Pochart shrugged his shoulders. Why not concede this point? It was so fine to have the citizen representative under one's thumb. What matter if his daughter was thrust into one prison rather than another?

"Is the guard there?" Danou asked. "We have plenty of business to see to. This one has lasted quite long enough."

"There is still that report from Avignon to look through," Pochart added. "It will need your attention, citizen representative."

"I'll be with you in one moment," Chauvelin replied calmly.

He rose and went to the door. Opened it. Yes! there was the guard sent hither by Godet, two men to escort his Fleurette to the house of Caristie the architect, now transformed into a house of detention. Chauvelin did not even wince at sight of them. He closed the door quietly and then approached Fleurette. He took hold of her hand and drew her to the furthest corner of the room, out of earshot.

"You are not frightened, little one?" he whispered to her.

"No, Bibi chéri," she replied simply. "If you tell me not to be."

"There is nothing to be frightened at, Fleurette. These brutes wish you ill; but – "

"Why should they?"

"But I can protect you."

"I know you can, chéri Bibi."

"And you won't see that wretch Adèle again."

"I wonder why she hates me! I thought we were friends."

170

"There are no friends these days, little one," he said almost involuntarily. "Only enemies or the indifferent – They are the least dangerous."

"There are those whom we love."

"You are thinking of Amédé?"

"And of you, chéri Bibi."

"You believed me, didn't you, little one, when I told you that young Colombe is safely out of harm's way?"

"Yes," she said, "I believed you."

"Then you will hold your tongue about – about what you know?"

"I promise you, chéri Bibi. But I won't allow Amédé to suffer for what I did," she added with that determined little air of hers, which Chauvelin had learned to dread.

"He won't. He can't," he declared, whilst an exclamation of impatience at her obstinacy almost escaped him. "Have I not told you –"

"We are waiting, Citizen Chauvelin," Danou's unctuous voice broke in at this point. "As you are near the door perhaps you will call the guard."

He did. And stood silently by, while Fleurette was ordered to follow the men. She obeyed, after a last, smiling glance at Bibi. No! she was not frightened; she felt sure that he could protect her, and so long as M'sieu' Amédé was safe –

The last words she said before she finally passed through the door were:

"Poor old Louise! You'll tell her, won't you, Bibi, not to fret for me? and tell her to send me my crochet work if she can. I shall have plenty of time on my hands to get on with it."

Twenty-two

At four o'clock that afternoon the President of the Revolutionary Tribunal sitting at Orange received a summons to accompany Citizen Chauvelin, Representative of the National Convention on special mission, to Paris, there to present his last reports of the cases tried by him since the beginning of the year.

Public Prosecutor Isnard received the same summons; he hastened all in a flurry to the Hôtel de Ville to find Citizen Chauvelin.

"What does it all mean, citizen?" he asked.

Chauvelin shrugged his shoulders.

"I know not," he replied. "The summons came by courier an hour ago. I have my *calèche* here. We could start at daybreak tomorrow and be in Valence before dark. The next day should see us in Lyons, and the middle of next week in Paris."

"Can you not conjecture – ?"

Once more Chauvelin shrugged.

"One never knows," he said. "There must have come some denunciation. You and the President have your enemies, no doubt, as everyone else."

Public Prosecutor Isnard's flabby cheeks were the colour of lead.

"I have always done my duty," he stammered.

"No doubt, no doubt," Chauvelin responded lightly. "You'll be able to justify yourself, I feel sure, citizen. But you know what these summons are. Impossible to argue – or to disobey."

172

"Yes, I know that. But the business here – "

"What of it?"

"Our prisons are full. A batch of twenty at least should be tried every day. I have forty or fifty indictments ready now and we can keep the guillotine busy for at least a week. All that business will be at a standstill."

"You will have to work twice as hard on your return, citizen," Chauvelin retorted drily.

The arrival of the President of the Tribunal put a temporary stop to the colloquy. He too was flurried and not a little scared. He knew about these summonses that would come from time to time from Paris without any warning. They meant re-primands of a certainty. Perhaps worse. One never knows with leaders of the Government over there. One moment they would shout: "Strike! Strike!" at the top of their voices, "let not the guillotine be idle!" They would frame laws to expedite the extermination of all traitors and suspected traitors. The next, they would draw back, accuse you of over-zeal, over-cruelty, what not? See how Carrier had suffered! He had been sent to Nantes to purge the city of aristos and bourgeois and calotins; he had done his best; invented a new way of disposing of ninety priests all at once by the mere unmooring of a flat-bottomed craft, laden with those traitors, and on a given signal opening all the hatches and sinking the whole craft with her cargo.

Well! Carrier had done that. He had effectually purged Nantes of traitors. Nevertheless he was summoned to Paris, and his head rolled into the basket on the Place de la République, just as if he had been an aristo. Look at Danton, and at – but why recall it all? Anyhow, what a week of desperate anxiety this would be until Paris was reached. President Legrange had thoughts of flight, of taking refuge in the mountains as others had done. But Public Prosecutor Isnard dissuaded him. What was the good of running away? One always got caught, and then it would of a certainty be the guillotine. Chauvelin too was for immediate obedience.

"I too am summoned," he said. "We are all in the same boat. As for the business here, it will have to wait until our return."

Public Prosecutor Isnard could not suppress a taunt.

"There's your daughter, Citizen Chauvelin," he said. "We were going to make quick work of her. I had her indictment all ready. In fact the chief witness – a wench who looks like an anaemic rat – was in my study when your summons came."

"I know, I know," Chauvelin said with perfect indifference. "Well! all that can wait till our return."

After which he added lightly: "At daybreak, citizens, my *calèche* will be ready outside the 'Chat Noir'. I await you then and advise you to eat a good breakfast. Our first stop will be Montélimar, where we can get relays. In the meanwhile I bid you adieu. I still have much work to see to before the close of day."

For the first time this day Chauvelin heaved a genuine sigh of satisfaction when the two men had departed. His first manoeuvre had succeeded admirably. With the President of the Tribunal and the Public Prosecutor out of the way the business of the State would be at a standstill in Orange, and he would have at least three weeks of freedom before him in which to act. He had planned this summons, and intended to accompany the two men as far as Lyons. There he would find some pretext for sending them on their way without him, whilst he returned in secret to Orange. That was his plan, a risky one at best; but in less than three weeks he would either have found a way of getting Fleurette out of the clutches of these fiends, or he and she would both be dead. Strangely enough at this moment he fell to wondering what his arch-enemy, the Scarlet Pimpernel, would do under the circumstances and he longed for the possession of that same imaginative brain, that marvellous resource and unbounded pluck which had foiled him, Chauvelin, at every turn.

The Scarlet Pimpernel! If that bold adventurer were to know that his bitterest foe was now probing the lowest depths of sorrow, that this cruel Nemesis had overtaken him at last, how he would exult, how jeer at his enemy. And of the many pin-pricks which Chauvelin had had to endure today, he felt that none could hurt him so deeply as the thought that the Scarlet Pimpernel might hear of his trouble and hold jubilee over his soul agony.

Twenty-three

That first night the party slept at Valence in the Maison des Têtes, the quaint old house with its unique façade which stands to this day in the Grand' Rue, and which in that year of grace 1794 had been requisitioned by the Drôme section of the Committee of Public Safety for its offices. A concierge with wife and family were in charge of the house, and there were two or three additional rooms in it which were often placed at the disposal of any official personage who happened to be passing through Valence. Chauvelin had often stayed there on his way through to Paris and was a familiar figure to the concierge and his family; there was no difficulty whatever in finding accommodation for himself and his two friends in the Maison des Têtes for the night. *Calèche* and horses, together with driver and postilion, were put up in the stables at the back of the house.

Night had overtaken the party when some five kilometres outside Valence, and this last part of the way had to be done at walking pace. Thus it was nearly ten o'clock before the *calèche* drew up in the Grand' Rue outside the Maison des Têtes, and the concierge, hurrying to greet the unexpected and important guest, had regretfully to inform him that neither the President nor any of the officials were here to welcome him as they had already gone to their respective homes. But the rooms were there, quite ready, at the disposal of Citizen Chauvelin and his friends, and supper would be got immediately for them. The three travellers stepping out of the *calèche* were more than thankful to find shelter and food at this hour. Already at sunset the sky had been threatening; great banks of cloud came rolling up from the south-west, driven by tearing gusts of wind; by night-time a few heavy drops were falling, presaging the coming storm. No sooner were the travellers installed in the dining-hall in front of an excellent supper, than the storm broke in all its fury. It was accompanied by torrential rain and a tearing wind. Such wild weather during the month of May was almost unparalleled in the valley of the Rhône, so the concierge hastened to explain to the two strangers who accompanied Chauvelin. The night was very dark too, the very weather, in fact, for foot-pads and malefactors who, alas! infested the countryside more than ever now.

"What would you?" the man added with a shrug, "so many are starving these days; they get their existence as best they can. Honesty is no longer the best policy."

And then he caught Citizen Chauvelin's eye and, nervously clearing his throat, began to talk of something else. It was not prudent to grumble at anything, or to make any remark that might be constructed into criticism of the present tyrants of France.

Supper drew to an end mostly in silence. Chauvelin was never of a loquacious turn of mind, and neither of the other two were in a mood to talk. After a curt good night the latter retired to the room which had been assigned to them. Chauvelin before doing the same gave orders to his driver and postilion to have the *calèche* at the door by seven o'clock on the following morning. Then he too went to bed, there to toss ceaselessly through the endless hours of wakefulness, his mind tortured with thoughts of his darling Fleurette, wondering how she would bear this first night in prison, the propinquity, the want of privacy, the lewd talk perhaps, or coarse jests of some of her room-mates. It was only in the early dawn that, wearied at last in body and mind, he was able to close his eyes and snatch an hour or two's sleep.

When the concierge brought him a steaming mug of wine in the early morning his first inquiry was after the *calèche*. Was it being got ready?

Yes! the concierge had seen the driver and postilion at work this hour past. Everything would doubtless be ready for a start by seven o'clock. It was now half-past six. Chauvelin drank the hot wine eagerly; his sleepless night and all his anxiety had produced a racking headache and a state of mental inertia difficult to combat. Slightly refreshed by the drink, he proceeded to dress. While he did so he heard a great clatter of horses' hoofs striking the cobble-stones, a good deal of shouting and rattling of wheels. His windows gave on the Grand' Rue, and looking out he expected presently to see the *calèche* being driven round from the stable-yard at the back. But nothing came. He felt nervy and impatient, hoping that nothing would go wrong. Angered too with himself for feeling so flat on this very morning when he would need all his brain-power to carry his scheme successfully to the end.

He intended journeying with the two men as far as Lyons, and there to invent a pretext for separating from them, sending them on to Paris by the stagecoach, and then returning quietly and secretly to Orange alone. Already he was fully dressed and ready to go downstairs. He heard the clock in the tower of St Apollinaire striking seven. A minute or two later the concierge, wide-eyed and babbling incoherently, came bursting into the room.

"Citizen! Citizen! Nom de nom, quel malheur!" These ejaculations were followed by a string of lamentations, and a confused narrative of some untoward event out of which the only intelligible words that struck clearly on Chauvelin's ears were: "*Calèche*," and "cursed malefactors!" His questions remained unanswered; the man continuing to lament and to curse alternately.

Finally, bereft of all patience, Chauvelin seized him by the shoulder and shook him vigorously.

"If you don't speak clearly, man," he said roughly, "I'll lay my stick across your shoulders."

The man fell on his knees and swore it was not his fault.

"I could not be in two places at once, citizen," he lamented. "I was looking after your two friends and my wife –"

Chauvelin raised his stick. "What is it that was not your fault?" he shouted at the top of his voice.

"That your *calèche* has been stolen, citizen!"

"What?"

"It is those cursed brigands! They have infested the town these past –"

The words died in his throat in a loud cry of pain. Chauvelin had brought his stick crashing upon his back.

"It was not my fault, citizen," he reiterated, protesting. "I could not be in two places at once –"

But Chauvelin no longer stayed to listen. Picking up his hat and coat he hastened downstairs, to be met in the corridor by the concierge's wife and two sons all incoherent and lamenting. The whole house by now was astir. Public Prosecutor Isnard came clattering down the stairs followed by President Legrange, both in more or less hastily completed toilette. And thus the whole party with Chauvelin *en tête* proceeded at full speed to the stable-yard, where the yawning coach-house and empty stalls told their mute tale. Of *calèche*, horses, driver or postilion not a sign. The stableman, an old fellow, and his aid, a very young lad, were busy at the moment telling the amazing story to a small crowd of gaffers and market-women who had pushed their way into the yard from the back and were listening, open-mouthed, to a tale of turpitude and effrontery, unparalleled in the annals of Valence.

At sight of Chauvelin and his tricolour sash the crowd of gaffers and women respectfully made way for him, and he, seizing the old stableman by the shoulder, commanded him to tell him clearly and briefly just what had happened. Thus it was that at last he was put in possession of the facts that touched him so nearly. It seems that his own driver and postilion, up betimes, had got the *calèche* and horses quite ready and standing in the middle of the yard. They had in fact just put the horses to, and the postilion and driver were standing by the *calèche* door drinking a last mug of wine, when from the narrow lane which connects the yard with the rue Latour at the back, a band composed of four ruffians came rushing in. Before he, the stableman, could as much as wink an eyelid, three of these ruffians had seized the driver and postilion round their middle and thrust them into the *calèche*, followed them in, banged the coach door to, whilst the fourth climbed up to the box with the rapidity of a monkey, gathered up the reins and drove away.

In the meanwhile the lad who had been at work in the stables and heard the clatter came running out. Stableman and lad then ran to the lane and out into the rue Latour, only to see the *calèche* rattling away at break-neck speed. They shouted and strained their lungs to attract the notice of passers-by, and they did attract their attention, but before they could explain what had happened the *calèche* was well out of sight. The lad ran as fast as he could to the nearest *poste de gendarmerie*, but before the gendarmes could get to horse, no doubt those ruffians would have got well away with their booty.

That was in substance the story to which Chauvelin had to listen, and through which he was forced to keep his temper in check. As soon as the stableman had finished speaking the lad had put in his own comments, whilst the gaffers and gossips started arguing, talking, conjecturing, giving advice, suggesting, lamenting. Oh! above all lamenting! That the high roads were not safe, everyone knew that to his cost. Masked highway robbers held up coaches, attacked pedestrians, robbed and pillaged the countryside. That the streets of Valence were not safe was, alas! only too true. The *gendarmerie* was either incompetent or venal, and lucky the man who possessed nothing that could be taken from him. But this outrage today in broad daylight surpassed anything that had been seen or heard before. A *calèche* and pair, *pardieu!* was not like a purse that could be hidden in one's waistcoat pocket. And so on, and so on, while Chauvelin, still silent and curbing his impatience, went back into the house, followed by his crestfallen friends and by the staff of the Maison des Têtes still lamenting and protesting their innocence, and withal beginning to feel doubtful as to what the consequences might be to themselves of this untoward adventure.

The stable-lad was then sent back to the *poste de gendarmerie*, with orders from Citizen Representative Chauvelin that the chief officer in charge present himself immediately at the Maison des Têtes. Whilst waiting for this officer, Chauvelin, sitting in the small parlour, had a few moments' peace in which to co-ordinate his thoughts. The inertia which had weighed upon his spirits the first thing in the morning had been suddenly dissipated. Already his keen, imaginative brain had seized upon this catastrophe, and planned how to turn it to the furtherance of his scheme. And while his friends, no whit less voluble or more coherent than the concierge or his kind, were loudly lamenting: "What a misfortune, citizens! what bad luck!" and throwing up their arms in utter helplessness, Chauvelin broke in impatiently upon their wailings:

"We must make the best of it, citizens," he said, "I shall certainly be held up here a day or two, on this stupid business, but it certainly need not detain you. The stagecoach leaves for Lyons at half-past eight if I mistake not. As soon as my *calèche* is recovered, which I doubt not it will be in a couple of days, I'll follow you on. You in the meanwhile can proceed to Paris all the way by the stagecoach. It will be perhaps not quite as comfortable as my *calèche*, but it will serve."

They demurred a little. The stagecoach would certainly not be as comfortable as Citizen Chauvelin's luxurious *calèche*, and perhaps a day or two's delay would not be very serious.

"It would be fatal," Chauvelin said emphatically. Orders from Paris such as they had received must be obeyed in the least possible delay, a couple of days idling in Valence, when a stage-coach was available, would certainly be put down to pusillanimity and want of zeal.

He could be eloquent when he liked, could Citizen Chauvelin, and on this occasion he was determined to gain his point – to send these two packing, post-haste, off to Paris, and leave himself free to return to Orange immediately. As to what would happen presently, when those two arrived in Paris and found that they had been hoaxed, that they had not been sent for, and would have to return biting the dust and chewing the cud of their wrath, as to that in truth, Chauvelin had not given a thought. To save his Fleurette, to get her away out of the country, at the cost of his own life if need be, was all he thought about, and while the business of trying and condemning prisoners was at a standstill through the absence of these two men, there was a hundred to one chance that he could accomplish his purpose.

Therefore he put forth all his powers of persuasion – and they were great. He drew lurid pictures of what happened to those who were thought to be guilty of dilatoriness or want of zeal. So much so that he reduced President Legrange and Public Prosecutor Isnard – at no time very valiant heroes – to a state of abject fear, and half an hour later had the satisfaction of bidding them *au revoir*, in the yard of the posting-inn, they having found seats in the stagecoach to Lyons.

As soon as he had seen the last of them, he made haste to requisition a chaise and the only horses to be had in Valence, to take him forthwith to Orange.

As for his own *calèche*, he wished the foot-pads joy in its possession and cared less than nothing what became of his driver or his postilion.

Twenty-four

Could Citizen Chauvelin have seen his *calèche* and horses a couple of hours later on the road, he would perhaps not have been quite so complacent as to its fate. After rattling over the cobble-stones of Valence and tearing down the high road at maddening speed, it slackened a little for the hill, and worked its way slowly up through the small township of Livron. A quarter of a league or so further, it turned off at the cross-roads in the direction of Cest and after another half-hour came to a halt at that small cottage which still nestles to this day, with its tumbledown roof and vine-covered harbour, beside the celebrated Roman ruins at the foot of the hill, not far from the banks of the Drôme.

Three ruffians, grimy from the roots of their hair to their down-at-heel shoes, jumped out of the *calèche*, dragging after them in the open the driver and postilion lately in the employ of Citizen Chauvelin, Representative of the National Convention on special mission. Whilst thus journeying between Valence and Livron these two poor wretches had been securely pinioned with ropes, but they were not gagged, and they used the freedom left to their tongues by uttering oaths and protests which appeared vastly to amuse their captors.

The fourth ruffian – for ruffian he was – despite the fact that he had donned a bourgeois' dress, the better to carry out his coup and pass unnoticed on the road, had in the meanwhile scrambled down from the box.

"Quite successful so far," he remarked lightly, speaking in English, and rubbing his hands, which were slender and long and firm, contentedly together.

"What shall we do with these?" one of his companions asked, laughing, and pointing to the two woebegone prisoners, who had ceased to curse and to protest, chiefly owing to want of breath, but also through astonishment at finding themselves the victims of some kind of foreign brigands whose language they did not understand.

"Poor beggars!" the other said lightly. "We'll place them in front of an excellent breakfast and I'll warrant we need not as much as tie their legs to their chairs. Get them inside, Ffoulkes, will you, and I'll talk to them as soon as Tony and I have seen to the horses."

"You don't think the gendarmerie from Valence will be after us, Blakeney, do you?"

"Not they," Sir Percy replied. "They are very short of horses in these parts, and the best will, I doubt not, be requisitioned by my friend M. Chambertin for his own use. I wonder now," he added musing, "what he is after, taking those two ruffians with him to Paris; and whether his errand is sufficiently urgent to cause him to travel in the stagecoach, now that we have borrowed his *calèche*…"

He paused, slightly frowning, evidently a little puzzled.

"I wonder," he added, "if our friend in there can throw some light upon the matter."

After which Sir Percy Blakeney and Lord Antony Dewhurst took the streaming horses out of the shafts, relieved them of their harness and gave them a good rub down, a drink and a feed, while Sir Andrew Ffoulkes and Lord Hastings went into the cottage and busied themselves with their prisoners.

My Lord Stowmaries was for the moment in charge of this untenanted cottage, which was a stronghold as well as a rallying place of the League of the Scarlet Pimpernel, as it lay perdu, off both the main and the secondary roads. He it was who had prepared food for his chief and his comrades with the assistance of one Amédé Colombe. The cottage consisted of four rooms; unsecurely sheltered against the weather by a cracked roof, and against damp by broken floors. There were a few very rare pieces of furniture in the place, abandoned there by the late owner and his family, worthy farmers whom the League of the Scarlet Pimpernel had conveyed safely out of France when their loyal adherence to their exiled seigneurs had brought them under the ban of the Revolutionary Government.

In one of the rooms the two prisoners were busy for the moment pinching one another to see if they were really awake. After thinking that they were within sight of death at the hands of a band of malefactors, they found themselves sitting at a table in front of an excellent plate of soup, some bread and cheese and a very large mug of excellent wine, while the cords round their bodies had been removed. Anyway, a very pleasant dream. Leaving conjecture to take care of itself, they fell to on this welcome repast with a healthy appetite. The door which gave on the larger room had been left open, and through it the two men could see the band of malefactors falling to, just like themselves, in front of an excellent meal, laughing and talking in that same gibberish language which they did not understand.

"They don't look to me much like brigands," the driver remarked presently, speaking with his mouth full, "in spite of their dirty clothes."

"And that tall one," the postilion added thoughtfully, "he seems to be their captain. If you ask me I think he is an aristo."

"Or an English spy."

The other shook his head.

"Not he. English spies would have murdered us."

"Then what in the name of hell –"

He got no further, the postilion had gripped him by the arm.

"Nom de nom!" the postilion exclaimed; and expressed further amazement by a prolonged whistle. "If that is not Amédé Colombe."

"Qui çà Amédé Colombe?" the other asked.

"The son of the grocer over at Laragne. I know, I come from those parts. But what the hell is he doing here?"

Amédé Colombe, sitting at the table with his wonderful new friends, caught the sound of his name, and gave an anxious start.

"Do not worry about them, my young friend," Sir Percy Blakeney said reassuringly. "Before they could do you any harm we shall be many leagues out of the way."

At which postilion and driver gazed at one another, more puzzled than ever before. Were they really dreaming, or had they actually heard that foreigner speaking their own language? – and perfectly. The driver was inclined to think that the wine which they had been drinking was potent enough to be the cause of an hallucination. Not that this deterred him from pouring himself out another mugful, and drinking it down with much smacking of the lips and sighs of contentment. It was such very excellent wine. Didn't his friend the postilion agree with him? Why of course, and the filling and refilling of the two mugs continued apace and at a great rate.

"They'll be blind in a few moments," Lord Antony Dewhurst remarked, glancing over his shoulder at the two men.

And he was right in this surmise. In less than a quarter of an hour driver and postilion were blind to the world with arms stretched out across the table, their heads buried in the bend of their elbows, breathing stertorously.

"You are not eating, my friend," my Lord Stowmanes remarked to Amédé Colombe, who in truth had been sitting silent, self-absorbed, neither eating nor drinking.

"Friend Amédé does not appreciate your cooking, old man," Blakeney put in lightly. "It is fairly bad, I confess. Is it not, Monsieur Amédé?"

"It is excellent, milor'," the young man sighed, "but I ask you, how can I eat or drink when I am in such terrible anxiety?"

"We were just going to discuss the best way – and the quickest – of alleviating your anxiety, mon ami," Sir Percy rejoined, "all we were waiting for was for those two amiable gentlemen over there to become deaf temporarily as well as blind."

"It is not for myself that I am anxious, milor'," the young man said timidly. He was over-shy of these wonderful men, who had led him from adventure to adventure, in a manner that had almost addled his poor brain. His unsophisticated mind was still vibrating with the excitement of the unforgettable hour, when throwing disguise aside these strangers had revealed themselves not as revolutionary soldiers at all, but as mysterious beings, whose actions had appeared to him to savour of the supernatural. It took him a long time to understand the situation. It seems that his being in possession of Madame de Frontenac's valuables was known to the girl Adèle who was nothing but a spy in the pay of the Committee of Public Safety. She had that night spied upon him and the girl he loved, seen the girl hand over the valuables to him, and revealed the fact to the Committee. Had these mysterious strangers not played the part of revolutionary soldiers and got him, Amédé, safely out of the way, before the real soldiers appeared upon the scene, he would at this moment be languishing in a prison at Sisteron or Orange preparatory to being sent either to the guillotine or for cannon-fodder on the frontier.

All this Amédé understood well enough; he cursed Adèle a thousand times in his heart for being such a snake in the grass. What he could not understand was why these strangers should take an interest in him and in his fate. When to his timid query on that subject their leader laughingly replied: "Sport! mon ami, the fun, the excitement! nothing more philanthropic, I assure you, than just sport!" he understood still less.

No wonder that to him, Amédé Colombe, the whole adventure had come as a manifestation of something supernatural. As for M. de Frontenac, his fellow-sufferer, on the other hand, he had apparently been prepared for that manifestation. It appeared that Madame and Mademoiselle had already been rescued from peril and taken to a place of safety, where presently M. de Frontenac would be able to join them, always through the instrumentality of these wonder-working strangers. The last thing M. de Frontenac had said to him, Amédé, when he took leave of him a couple of days ago, somewhere in the lonely mountain paths where the party had called a halt, was: "Trust these Englishmen, Amédé, trust them with everything you hold dear. Look at me, had I not trusted them with my wife' and daughter I should have seen my dear ones first, and myself afterwards, facing the guillotine at this very hour!"

It was with these words ringing in his ears that Amédé, sitting now amongst these men to whom he owed his life, had mustered up sufficient courage to reiterate more firmly: "It is not for myself I am anxious, milor'."

"I know that, mon ami," Sir Percy replied, "you are thinking of that brave little girl – Fleurette. Isn't that her name?"

"Yes, milor'," Amédé whispered timidly.

"Some of my friends and I are going straightway back to look after her now."

"And you will hurry, milor', you will hurry, will you not? Every day may be fatal for her."

"I think not," Blakeney said in that decisive way of his, which carried so much conviction. "You told me she was the daughter of a man high up in the councils of the revolutionary government."

"One Armand, milor'," Amédé continued. "Little is known of him in the neighbourhood, save that he is a widower and apparently has influence with the government."

"Fleurette is an only child?"

"Yes. She has lived at Lou Mas all her life."

"If her father has influence he can protect her for a time."

"For a time – yes! But – oh, milor'!" the poor young man suddenly burst out with passionate vehemence, "if anything were to happen to Fleurette I would curse you for having saved my life."

Blakeney smiled at the young man's eagerness.

"Listen, friend Amédé," he said lightly, "are you going to trust me and my friends?"

And Amédé, who remembered those last solemn words spoken by M. de Frontenac, looked into those lazy grey eyes, meeting that half-earnest, half-humorous glance beneath the heavy lids, replied simply: "Yes, milor'!"

"And you will accord me what my friends accord so ungrudgingly, bless them, implicit obedience?"

Again Amédé replied simply: "Yes, milor'!" And then he added: "What am I to do?"

"For the moment nothing," Sir Percy replied, "but remain here quietly and alone until you hear from me again. Can you do it?"

"If you command."

"You won't mind the loneliness?"

"I shall be thinking of Fleurette and trusting you."

"Come, that's brave!" Sir Percy concluded lightly. "You will find some provisions in the armoire in this room: but apart from that you will find your way every day down to the river, and, turning to your right, you will walk along its bank till you come to a derelict shed hidden from view by two old walnut trees. In a corner of the shed, beneath a pile of leaves, you will find something to comfort you, either a loaf of bread, or a piece of cheese, sometimes a jug of milk or a bottle of wine. Scanty fare probably, but it will suffice to keep the wolf from the door. Those who supply it are poor and risk much to do it. They owe my friends and me a debt which they pay in this fashion. Now are you prepared to live this life of a lonely anchorite while my friends and I return to Laragne and gather news of your Fleurette?"

"If I could only come with you, milor'!" Amédé sighed.

"Tush, man, what were the good of that?" Sin Percy retorted with a slight note of impatience in his pleasant voice. "You would only lead us all – and your Fleurette into trouble."

"But you will bring me news of her soon?" Amédé entreated with tears in his kind, innocent-looking eyes.

"Either news of her – or Fleurette herself."

Amédé shook his head. "She would not leave her father," he said dolefully.

"Then she will be safe with him, until better times come along, which will be very soon, friend Amédé, you may take that from me. Another few months – very few – and the dragon's own teeth will be turned against itself. This anarchy cannot endure for ever, because all evil, friend Amédé, is by the grace of God finite."

He spoke these last words with unwonted earnestness, and simple Amédé Colombe looked up to him with awe as to a prophet standing there, magnificent in energy and strength, head thrown back, the lazy eyes beneath their heavy lids flashing with unquenchable inner fire. And suddenly he checked himself, laughter chased away earnestness, the eyes twinkled with merriment like those of a carefree schoolboy, rather than a seer.

"La!" he said lightly, "I verily believe we were waxing serious. No cause for that, eh, friend Amédé? My friends and I are off on a gay adventure. To take a message of love from you to a brave little girl who loves you, a shade better, methinks, than she loves that mysterious father of hers. Write your love-letter, my friend, but be sure and make it brief, and I'll deliver it myself in her own little hands. I saw her, that sweet wench of yours, no woman ever showed more pluck than she did when she went to seek Madame de Frontenac's valuables."

"You saw her, milor'?" Amédé exclaimed, wide-eyed. "Mon Dieu! is there anything that you do not see?"

"There is, mon ami," Sir Percy replied gaily. "I have never seen your pretty Fleurette's mysterious father. He must be a fine man to keep the love of so sweet a daughter. So write your letter, my friend," he went on, and pointing to an oaken desk at the further end of the room on which were quill-pen, inkpot and sand, "and I promise you that I will deliver it, if only for the pleasure of having a squint at the mysterious owner of Lou Mas. Heigh-ho!" he added with a contented sigh, "but this promises to be fine sport. What say you, Ffoulkes, or you, Tony? We are going to put our heads into the wolf's jaws again, eh? Stowmaries, you too, and Hastings. But we'll do it, and I promise you that the sight of pretty Fleurette will be a fitting compensation for some very unpleasant half-hours we may have to go through. Now then, friend Amédé! your love missive, and two of you put the horses to, we'll have to make Montélimar by nightfall! there we'll either abandon the *calèche*, steal a couple of horses and cut across the hills to Sisteron, or keep to the *calèche* and the road as far as the neighbourhood of Orange, where much information can always be gleaned about the district. We'll make no plans now and trust to luck and chance. What?"

Lord Tony then pointed, smiling, to the driver and postilion still fast asleep in the adjoining room.

"What is to happen to those mudlarks?" he asked.

"We'll take them along, of course," Blakeney replied. "So thrust them into the bottom of the *calèche*, under the seat for choice, and those who sit inside can use them as footstools. Where we leave the *calèche*, there we leave them too, to find their way back to the bosom of their families in due course."

He looked so gay and so full of life and strength, so sure of himself, such pure joy in this new adventure radiated from his entire person, that some of that divine spark in him set Amédé Colombe's blood tingling through his veins. Anxiety, melancholy, doubt fell away from him at a glance from those lazy eyes now twinkling with joy, at sight of that firm mouth, even softened by a smile; of those long, slender hands, delicate as a woman's, firm as those of a leader of men. Poor Amédé was almost happy at this moment, feeling that he was one with this band of heroes, that just by obedience and self-effacement, he could feel that he was one of them.

In cramped schoolboy hand, he wrote a brief, very brief little line to Fleurette, and told her how he adored her and longed for her nearness. He also told her that whatever else happened he implored her to trust the bearer of this note, who would be the means of bringing her back one day to the shelter of her Amédé's arms.

Less than an hour later he was all alone in the tumbledown cottage that nestled against the ruins of a former, long-since-dead civilization. The late afternoon was soothing and balmy, the sky of a pale turquoise, clear and translucent, and as Amédé, standing somewhat forlorn at the cottage door, watching the narrow road over which the *calèche* had lumbered awhile ago, bearing away his mysterious new friends, the pale crescent of the moon appeared above the snow-capped crest of La Lance, and Amédé, remembering the old superstition, bowed solemnly nine times to the moon.

Twenty-five

What irked Fleurette most in her prison life was the monotony of it: the want of something to do. After she had cleaned out the room which she shared with ten others, and put herself and everything tidy, the day appeared interminably long. She did her crochet work while her supply of thread lasted; old Louise had been allowed to make up a bundle of some clothes for her, and in it she had also put the crochet work and a few hanks of thread, but a few days saw the end of this supply, after which there was nothing with which Fleunette could occupy her fingers. Some of her fellow-prisoners had needles, cotton and thimbles, and presently Fleurette, always willing and always smiling, was asked to darn and mend their clothes. She was glad enough to do it, as a means of killing time.

They were a heterogeneous crowd these fellow-prisoners of hers, culled from every social grade from the great lady to the troll out of the street. Misfortune and the precariousness of existence had brought these usually warring elements closely together: friendships sprang up where in the past even a nod of recognition would have been grudged. The Comtesse de Mornas, who belonged to the highest aristocracy of Provence, would take her morning exercise with her arm round the waist of Eugénie Blanc, daughter of a second-hand clothes dealer of Orange. Hélène de Mornas' husband had been guillotined three months ago on some trumped-up charge or other, and Eugénie Blanc's father, accused of traffic with the enemy – whoever that enemy might be no one knew – had perished in that awful wholesale massacre perpetrated in Orange last month. Sorrow brought these two women together, as it did many others, and when Claire de Châtelard, obviously a woman of evil reputation, sought Fleurette's compassion with a tale of hunger, misery and arrest, that compassion was freely given, and the girl who had led such a sheltered life at Lou Mas, knowing nothing of temptation or of evil, had for daily companion after that, one Claire de Châtelard, the most notorious jade of Orange.

Thus the first few days went by. In the prison – it is Architect Caristie's house with all the furniture turned out of it and the rooms left bare of everything save a few benches, a few paillasses, a table, a wash-hand basin or two – in the prison great puzzlement prevails. Hitherto every day, just before sunset, a captain of the guard with half a dozen men would enter the courtyard and, standing there, would in a loud voice read out a list of names. That list was the Roll-call, the decrees of the Revolutionary Tribunal condemning so many to the guillotine on the morrow. And at all the windows of the houses around the courtyard, heads would appear: men and women – yes! and children too – clutching their prison bars, and listening. Listening if their name be upon that list, And then a sigh of relief if that name was not called: another day's respite! another day in which to drag this miserable, precarious existence. As for the others, the ones whose names were read out in a loud voice by the captain of the guard, there was nothing for it but to clasp their loved ones, or mayhap only the newly found friend, in their arms – for the last time. That same night they were transferred to the prison of the Hôtel de Ville, and in the morning the guillotine. Sometimes not that. Just driven like a herd to the slaughter: on the bridge or the Place de la République. And there the guns. And death pell-mell. Like cattle, with ne'er a grave nor a prayer.

That was how it had been before Fleurette's arrival. That cinder-wench Claire de Châtelard told her how it used to be.

But Fleurette never saw anything of that. The very day after her arrival was marked by the non-appearance of the captain of the guard with his list. They all wondered, put their heads together, and for an hour or two after the usual time there was whispering, conjecturing going on. Respite for everybody: that was of course what it meant. But why? Had that awful Revolution really come to an end, as everybody had prophesied it would? Had all those tigers up in Paris really devoured one another, and was there no one left to carry on the infamy? Well! that was perhaps how it was. But no one knew anything. Not the warders. Not the prisoners. Not anybody. Inside these walls wherein news was wont to penetrate with extraordinary pre-cision and rapidity, nothing was known. Nothing. Except that there was no list and that on the morrow the guillotine was idle.

This new departure from regular routine was accepted with the same stoicism as everything else. It was the stoicism of supreme helplessness, or rather of despair, and it had engendered in all these people, men and women, herded here together on the eve of death, a kind of levity which it is difficult for modern thought to understand. Death was so familiar to them, such a daily companion, that they had ceased to think of him with awe. Familiarity had bred contempt. And deriding Death, they turned him into ridicule. Made game of him, defied him to break their spirit. It was a species of madness born of intense horror and absolute despair. Fleurette at first felt sick and wretched at sight of these people – proud countesses and high-bonn seigneurs, as well as muckworms and jades – acting the guillotine, as they called it, in the great hall of Architect Caristie's house which was assigned to them for recreation. She, poor little soul, had never learned to envisage death as anything but awesome for which the Holy Church was at pains to prepare doomed mankind with sacraments and prayers.

The first time she saw them all in their gruesome mummery, she fled affrighted back to the dank, noisome room where she slept, and throwing herself on her miserable paillasse, she sobbed her little heart out with horror and grief, stuffed her fingers into her ears so as not to hear the voices and the laughter that came from the great hall. Here Claire de Châtelard found her an hour later, and I think this was the beginning of their friendship, for the wench found just the right words wherewith to console this ignorant little country mouse.

"Their one recreation," she urged. "They mean no irreverence. Just think of them face to face with death. Always. Deprived of every consolation: mocked, jeered at. This play-acting is only a blind to hide their own misery, the despair which they are too proud to display."

After a while Fleurette dried her tears. But she slept ill that night. Nightmares pursued her. Visions of that mock tribunal, with the mock prosecutor, and the mock culprit. And then the setting up of two chairs, and draping them with bits of crimson rags to represent the guillotine. Once or twice she sat up on her hard paillasse, hardly able to smother a scream which would have roused her room-mates from their sleep. She had seen in retrospect one of the warders, who had helped in the acting of the gruesome play, dressed as Satan with horns and tail and entering the hall with a bound and a whoop. His rôle was to snatch the President of the Tribunal and the Prosecutor from their seats and to drag them away with him into everlasting fire, while a weird voice boomed the query: "What hour is it?" and another replied: "Eternity."

Poor little Fleurette! It was her first experience of life. And what an experience! Yet, it had only been one step from Lou Mas with its almond trees and rippling mill-streams, with Bibi and old Louise, one step from there to this barrack of a house converted into a prison, with all its humiliating propinquities, and all its horrors. Her companions in misfortune were very kind to her. All of them. The men as well as the women. Claire de Châtelard and the Comtesse de Mornas. They all seemed to understand her position, her helplessness, her ignorance. They were so kind! so kind! They admired her crochet-work, and talked to her of Laragne, or the snows of Pelvoux, or the almond trees of the Dauphiné. They thanked her and kissed her when she offered to ply her needle for them: to mend their clothes or darn their stockings. Within a few days she became one of themselves. A younger sister in this family of the despairing. Within a week, on mayhap ten days, she had lost her sense of horror at their mummeries, could laugh at the antics of the mock Satan come to carry the mock judges off to hell. The only thing to which she could not get accustomed was the representation of the guillotine, the inverted chairs and the bits of red rags, the cords, the victim, the basket and the executioner. Oh! that executioner! He was terrible! Especially of late. The role, like that of Satan, had always been undertaken by one of the warders; rough fellows these, culled from the lowest scum of the city; men who delighted in all the physical and moral torture inflicted on the aristos under their charge, who would gloat over the sight of a father torn away from his children and led to the guillotine, who would regale the unfortunate prisoners with tales culled from the *Moniteur* of wholesale executions or brutal massacres. The idea of acting the part of executioner to the mock representations of the guillotine delighted a certain grim sense of humour which most Southerners possess. There was one man in particular, lately come to replace another who was sick, who threw himself into the gruesome rôle with zest. He would strip almost naked for the part, and then cover his face and his large body with a mixture of soot and charcoal and oil so that he looked like a huge negro, with gleaming teeth and long, lank hair, of a pale blond colour, speckled with dirt.

Poor Fleurette could not bear to look at him, nor at the mock execution when one or other of her fellow-prisoners would allow himself to be tied to the mock guillotine, amidst the well-acted laughter and jeers of men and women who impersonated the awful rabble that was always to be found around the real guillotine. It was horrible, and Fleurette would run out into the corridor, or back to her miserable paillasse, anywhere where she could shut her ears to that gruesome mockery.

Unfortunately there came a day when the warder declared that an order had come through, that prisoners must remain together in the hall during the hour of recreation. He said it was so, and there was no one to contradict him. Of all the tyrants that had been set over their fellow-men, these days, none were more dreaded because more autocratic, than prison-wardens. As far as prisoners knew, these tyrants' power over them was absolute. In any case they could, if contradicted or thwarted, make it ten thousand times worse than before for those who did not cringe. This order then had to be obeyed and Fleurette, cowering alone in a corner of the hall, kept her eyes tightly shut while the impish scene was being enacted.

Madame de Mornas, aristocratic, dignified, with her arm round Eugénie Blanc's waist, spoke to her very kindly.

"My dear," she said in her gentle, well-bred voice, "if we did not make a mockery of all these horrors we should brood over them, and some of us would go mad."

And Eugénie Blanc, the "old clo" dealer's daughter, added with a shrug: "You dear innocent! You have seen nothing of life as it is. You don't know what it is when memory sets to work and you see things – you see –" She gave a shudder and then a harsh laugh. "This at any rate takes one's mind off memory for a time."

Claire de Châtelard's sympathy too was sincere, though rather more grim: "We've all got to go through the real thing presently; the mockery of it now will make the reality tomorrow more endurable."

"We must practise today," M. de St Luce, the great scientist, said lightly, "our attitude of tomorrow."

That was the general tenor of everyone's feelings upon the subject. Fleurette, touched by so much sympathy, tried to smile through her tears, and promised to school herself to the same philosophy. But as soon as all these kindly creatures had left her, in order to join, laughing, in the grim spectacle, she once more closed her eyes and sat in the dank corner, quite still, hoping that no one would notice her. But the laughter at one time was so loud, everyone's mood so hilarious, that involuntarily she opened her eyes and looked. The mock executioner had just completed his task. It seems he was complaining that Madame la Guillotine was still unsatisfied: she was putting out her arms, ready to embrace another lover. M. de Bollène – a minor poet well known in Provence – was declaiming some verses of his own composition, in praise of that promised embrace. The executioner's coal-black face shone like polished ebony in the flickering light of the tallow candles that guttered in their sconces. Madame de Mornas, almost unrecognizable in ragged kirtle and with a crimson scarf tied round her head, was flourishing her knitting and humming the tune of the *Carmagnole* as an accompaniment to M. de Bollène's verses, whilst Claire de Châtelard sprawled at the foot of the mock guillotine with a red streak across her throat.

And suddenly, to her horror, Fleurette saw the executioner stride towards her corner.

"What?" he cried aloud, "tears? Tears are for aristos. To the guillotine with her!" or words to that effect. Fleurette did not rightly understand what he did say, all she knew was that this hideous, horrible man came striding towards her with hands outstretched, and that everyone was laughing or singing or clapping their hands. The next moment she felt that horrible hand upon her shoulder, on her kerchief, her breast. She gave a loud scream and cowered further into the corner thinking that she would faint with terror, until she heard a peremptory voice calling our loudly: "Leave the child alone, man, can't you see she is frightened?"

"Frightened? Of course she is frightened," the loathsome creature retorted with a laugh. "Did I not say that she was an aristo? Let me just call the warder and – "

A woman's voice was raised in protest:

"No, no, don't call the warder. She's done nothing wrong – and he might – "

And Madame de Mornas it was who added:

"You coveted this ring this morning, man, it is yours if you leave the child alone and say nothing to the warder."

How kind people were! How kind! As nothing further seemed to happen, Fleurette ventured to open her eyes: Claire de Châtelard was sitting beside her, trying to comfort her. The gruesome play had apparently come to an end; the prisoners in groups of three or more stood about talking and laughing, preparatory to be driven back to the sleeping-rooms for the night. The black executioner was no longer there.

"He is not a bad man really," Claire de Châtelard said to Fleurette, fondling her hand and smoothing the golden curls that clung to her moist forehead! "only very rough and coarse. Bah! these men!" she went on with a shudder. "The warder is a veritable fiend: a genius in inventing means to punish you if you do not bribe him or give in to him. All my little treasures, which I was able to bring here with me, have gone into his rapacious hands. This man is not so bad, he is new to his work, he came a day or two ago to replace one who was ill. But he is only a scavenger. When the warder is dead drunk he takes his place, the rest of the time he does all the dirtiest work in the house. A loathsome creature, what? If he were not so big, we should not be so frightened of him. But he is better than the warder."

Fleurette only listened with half an ear. She still felt bruised and ill after the fright she had had. That horrible black hand touching her breast. It was worse than any nightmare.

She was glad when the bell clanged and the warder accompanied by his new aide – only partially relieved of the soot and the grime of his rôle – drove the prisoners like a herd of cattle back into their pens. So many women in one room, so many men in another. He had his list, and with a stout stick in his hand which he flourished as he read out the names, he drove them all in, into their respective night quarters and locked the doors upon them.

Fleurette shared her wretched paillasse with Claire de Châtelard. There was no dressing or undressing in this overcrowded room. No privacy. One just lay down in one's clothes and snatched what rest one could. Oh! the horror of it all to these women, most of them accustomed to dainty homes. Fleurette never knew which moment she dreaded most, that of opening her eyes to another awful day, or trying to close them in intermittent sleep.

Claire de Châtelard, less impressionable, was already asleep. Fleurette slipped out of her kirtle which she laid tidily across the foot of the paillasse; then she took off her muslin kerchief. As she did so something fluttered to the ground. A piece of paper neatly folded. Smothering an involuntary cry of surprise, she stooped to pick it up. Yet she hardly dared to touch the thing at first. How had it got between the folds of her kerchief? Who could possibly have put it there unbeknown to her? This was the second time within a very little while that Fleurette had come in contact with something that savoured of the supernatural. Still timorous, and with a trembling hand, she picked the paper up. Claire was asleep and most of the others had already stretched out their limbs upon their hard paillasses. No one paid any heed to Fleurette.

There was no direct light in the room itself, but an oil lamp which hung from the ceiling in the corridor threw a feeble ray of light through the fan-light over the door. Fleurette unfolded the paper and smoothed out its creases against her knee. She made her way to the centre of the room where she could just contrive, by that dim light from above, to decipher the handwriting upon the paper. But the first word that caught her eye, nearly caused her to utter a cry of joy; it was the signature: *Amédé*.

Amédé! At once her eyes grew dim with tears. Amédé! Those five letters in the clumsy, schoolboyish handwriting meant happiness and home. Amédé! Before trying to read further she pressed the paper against her cheek, fondled it, laid it against her lips.

Amédé! He had written to her. Where from? How? She did not care to think. What did it matter after all? He was thinking of her. Had written to her. And some divine messenger had conveyed his missive to Fleurette. Though he was safe and well – Bibi had assured her that he was – he had thought of her and sent her this letter through one of God's own angels.

And then Fleurette dried her eyes, for she remembered that presently the bell would clang again, when all the lights would be put out and she might have to wait until tomorrow to read Amédé's letter.

It was short, very, very short. Amédé had never been a scholar, but in it he told her how he adored his Fleurette and longed for her nearness. He also told her that whatever else happened, he implored her to trust the bearer of this note who would be the means of bringing her back one day to the shelter of his arms.

The bearer of this note? Who was he? Surely, surely, one of God's angels! and so of course she trusted him. And it was only *le bon Dieu* who would so guide Bibi that all this trouble would come to an end and she, Fleurette, would of a certainty find a shelter once more in her Amédé's arms.

She read and re-read the few brief lines over and over again, and presently when the bell clanged, and she was forced to make her way hurriedly to her paillasse before the room was plunged into utter darkness, she laid down on the hard straw with a little sigh of contentment and of peace. Her evening prayer was one entirely of gratitude to *le bon Dieu* for His gift of Amédé's love and Bibi's protection. And that night Fleurette slept quite soundly, with her cheek resting against the letter from Amédé.

Twenty-six

For two whole days Citizens Pochart and Danou of the 137th Section of the Committee of Public Safety had been sorely puzzled. They had received a curt note from Representative Chauvelin telling them that he would be absent from Orange for a brief while, and bidding them suspend all business until his return. Suspend all business? In very truth all business was perforce at a standstill, not because of the absence of the representative on special mission, but because of that of two high officers of State: the President of the Tribunal and the Public Prosecutor.

Representative Chauvelin in his note had also alluded to this absence, stating that by direct orders from the Central Committee of Public Safety, President Legrange and Prosecutor Isnard had been obliged to proceed to Paris.

It was all very puzzling, not to say suspicious. Pochart and Danou put their heads together and came to the conclusion that here undoubtedly were some machinations at work on the part of Representative Chauvelin with a view to getting his daughter out of harm's way. The question was how to make use of these machinations. Of their knowledge that they were machinations. How in fact to turn them against the man who hitherto had carried himself with such consummate arrogance, lording it over every officer of State in Orange, with thinly-veiled threats that had roused ire, malice and hatred in these men, whose rule of life was "strike ere you yourself be struck".

One thing, however, was crystal-clear. Representative Chauvelin was hard hit. He put on an air of lofty indifference; he continued to bluster and to threaten, but he was hard hit by the arrest of his daughter, as indeed any family man would be. Pochart and Danou did not care one worthless assignat what became of the daughter, but they did feel that the pleasure of threatening and terrorizing the representative on special mission, perhaps even of dragging him down from his exalted position and sending him in his turn to the guillotine, was not one to be missed. Up to the hour when Lieutenant Godet had arrested the wench Fleurette on suspicion, Representative Chauvelin had been a living threat to every patriot in Orange. He seemed, as it were, to be always walking hand in hand with the guillotine, or else in its shadow; sheltered himself, yet a menace to others. But now the tables were reversed, and Pochart and Danou had in one hour learned to substitute threats for soft words, arrogance for servility. And they vastly enjoyed the substitution.

But the trouble was that they were void of imagination. Representative Chauvelin could be brought down, they knew that. But how? Judging other men by themselves, they quite envisaged the possibility of a father sacrificing his own daughter in order to save himself. And there was also the possibility that a representative on special mission was powerful enough to save both his daughter and himself. Strong forces would have to be marshalled against him. Pochart and Danou with heads together passed these forces in review.

There was Lieutenant Godet who hated Representative Chauvelin with a hatred born of fear – the deadliest hatred of all. There was that rat-faced little spy, Adèle, a mixture of petty spite and malice. She would be useful. Others might be found, for Representative Chauvelin had many enemies who had not until this hour dared to come out into the open, but who would readily show themselves once the powerful representative was attacked.

And in the meanwhile the business of purging the countryside of aristos, suspects and traitors was at a standstill. With no Public Prosecutor to frame indictments and no President to try the accused, the order: "Que la Terreur soit à l'ordre du jour": "Let Terror be the order of the day", had become a dead letter. This could not go on, of course. Pochart and Danou, quite apart from their schemes against Representative Chauvelin, felt that a solution must be found – and that quickly – for this impossible situation. If allowed to continue they stood in very great risk of a reprimand from Paris for allowing the business of the State to be at a standstill. They might be accused of want of zeal. Those great patriots up in Paris were so unreasonable, one never knew what they might do. Having sent for President Legrange and Public Prosecutor Isnard, they probably expected "the order of the day" to go on just the same. But how, *nom de nom*? How?

They were still seeking a solution, these two, Pochart and Danou, on the third morning, when to their surprise Representative Chauvelin walked in, as calm and indifferent as you please.

He had completed his business, he explained to them, sooner than he had anticipated. President Legrange and Public Prosecutor Isnard on the other hand had continued their journey to Paris.

Danou, suave as ever, expressed satisfaction at the return of the citizen representative. It was indeed a matter of congratulation, he added, for them all, seeing that the business of the State was so completely at a standstill.

Pochart was somewhat more emphatic.

"There are at least one hundred and sixty traitors," he said, "who should have been dealt with days ago. Your absence, citizen, and that of two other public servants should not have occurred at this critical hour – "

"It was inevitable, Citizen Pochart," Chauvelin broke in drily. "Orders from Paris, you know – "

"I was just proposing to Citizen Pochart," Danou put in mildly, "that we send a message to Paris by this new aerial telegraph to ask for further orders. There is one installed at Avignon, and a courier – "

"The aerial telegraph is required for more important business than yours, Citizen Danou," Chauvelin once more broke in, and this time with some impatience.

"What can be more important than the suppression of traitors?" Pochart argued with an obvious sneer. "I marvel at you, citizen representative, that you should think otherwise."

"The very latest decree of the National Convention," Danou added, "was that Terror be the order of the day. I too marvel at you, Citizen Chauvelin."

"There is no cause for marvel," Chauvelin rejoined with well-assumed indifference. "I have not been in Orange more than a few hours. I have not had time to devise for this new situation."

"Well then, tomorrow, citizen," Danou suggested, "will you be ready to consult with us on the best means of meeting this impossible situation? Otherwise, I am still of the opinion that the aerial telegraph, or perhaps a courier to Paris – "

He went on mumbling for a few seconds. His tone had been quite suave, not to say deferential; but Chauvelin's keen ear had not failed to detect the threat that lurked behind those smooth, velvety tones.

"Tomorrow, as you say," he concluded drily.

All through the wearisome journey back from Valence he had been busy scheming and planning; alternately adopting and rejecting one plan after another. He knew well enough that Pochart and Danou were stalking him like wild beasts, ready to pounce on him, to come to grips with him in a life and death struggle in which his darling Fleurette would also be involved.

Now after his interview with the two men, he knew that already they scented victory, that they too were scheming and planning, planning his overthrow, and using Fleurette as the deadliest weapon against him. These last three years of titanic struggle of man against man, of the strong against the weak, of the weak against the strong, had taught him that he could expect nothing, neither mercy nor consideration, from enemies whom he himself would never have hesitated to sacrifice to his own whim or his own tyranny. His only hope lay in his avowedly superior brain-power. He no longer could dominate these snarling wild beasts, now that they were showing their fangs, but he could outwit them, before they sprang and devoured him. Brain-power as against blind lust. And Chauvelin thought that he could win.

Twenty-seven

Representative Chauvelin was quite calm, businesslike, armed with sheaves of papers and documents, when he met his colleagues the following morning in the bureau of the Committee.

"I have found," he announced as soon as they were seated, "a solution to our difficulty."

"Ah!" Danou ejaculated simply. And Pochart also said "Ah," but in a different tone.

"I have here," Chauvelin continued, and selected an official document from the pile which he had deposited upon the table. "I have here a decree which exactly meets our case. It was promulgated by the National Convention on the motion of Citizen Cabot on the 6th of Brumaire last."

Leaning back in his chair, he began to read from the official document in his hand. The others, elbows on table, chin cupped in hand, listened with what we might call mixed feelings.

"Should it occur that through any cause whatsoever, one of the chief officers of State be absent from duty for a period exceeding seven days, the Representative on special mission shall then assume his functions and continue to discharge them for as long as seems expedient. And in the event of more than one important officer of State being so absent, the Representative on special mission shall himself appoint a substitute who will also discharge such duties as the Representative on special mission shall have assigned to him for the time being."

Having finished reading, Chauvelin put the document down, and with a gesture of finality let his thin, claw-like hand rest upon it.

"The decree is clear enough, methinks," he said coldly.

There was a pause. A silence lasting perhaps thirty seconds; then Danou said mildly:

"I have never heard of this decree."

"Nor I," Pochart echoed.

"The Central Committee in Paris," Chauvelin put in drily, "has often remarked on the strange ignorance displayed by avowed patriots of the decrees promulgated for the welfare of the State. The Committee deems that such ignorance almost amounts to treason."

"May I look at the document?" Danou rejoined simply, choosing to ignore the reprimand – and the thinly veiled threat.

"Certainly," Chauvelin replied, and handed the document over to his colleague.

"Is it a copy?" Pochart asked, looking over his friend's shoulder.

"An attested copy, as you can see," Chauvelin replied. "It is countersigned by Citizens Robespierre, Billaud, Couthon and Saint Just. You are not thinking of disputing the order, Citizen Danou?"

Once more and still that arrogance, those veiled threats. The situation being entirely different from what it was yesterday, Danou and Pochart dared not persist in their mood of defiance. Not before they had consulted one another, marshalled those forces – Godet, Adèle, the proofs against the wench Fleurette – and decided on the mode of attack. Representative Chauvelin must have something up his sleeve, some hidden power, or he would not be so arrogant, so threatening.

Danou wiped the sweat from his bald cranium and handed the document back to Chauvelin. Pochart shaking himself like a wet dog, returned to his seat.

"I'll take over the office of President Legrange," Chauvelin said calmly, "and preside over the Tribunal until his return."

"Then I," Danou put in boldly, "had best take over the work of the Public Prosecutor."

"Impossible, citizen," Chauvelin rejoined firmly; "I must have a lawyer for that office."

"But –"

"You do not seem to have listened very carefully, Citizen Danou," Chauvelin broke in quietly, "to my reading of the decree, or you would remember that it is for the representative on special mission to appoint a substitute, in case of absence on the part of a second important officer of State."

"And whom do you propose to appoint, citizen representative?" Pochart inquired with a sneer.

"I will let you know my decision as to that tomorrow."

"The sooner the better, citizen representative," Danou concluded unctuously. "Remember that it is my colleague and I of the 137th Section of the Committee of Public Safety who will have to collect the evidence against the accused and place it before the Public Prosecutor whom you will appoint. That is a duty from which only the Central Committee can relieve us. There are one hundred and sixty prisoners," he went on slowly, "arrested under the Law of the Suspect. Some of them gravely accused, and by witnesses too."

"I am well aware of that, Citizen Danou," Chauveun replied calmly. Not by the quiver of an eyelid did be betray the fact that the shaft had gone home. With a perfectly steady hand he collected his papers and placed a weight upon them. After which he dismissed the others with a curt nod.

"Your pardon, citizens," he said, "I have still work to do. You too doubtless. I shall require your attendance here tomorrow at this same hour."

When the door had finally closed behind the two men, the mask fell from Chauvelin's face. Leaning his elbow on the table, he buried his burning head in his hands; a heartrending groan broke from his parched lips, his eyes felt as if seared with glowing charcoal! Ah! if he had not only forgotten these years past how to pray, what fervent orisons would he not have sent heavenwards at this hour. Help! where could he find help out of this web which his enemies had woven round him? How he hated them! longed to smite them before they had time to accomplish their fell purpose. They had determined on striking at Fleurette. Out of revenge or hatred, or was it fear? they had determined on striking at him, Chauvelin, through this being whom he loved beyond everything in the world. And he who had been one of the first protagonists of hatred and revenge and mutual distrust, he who had the will and the power, seemed so inextricably enmeshed that he could do nothing to save her. Fight? he would fight, inch by inch, step by step. Fight to save his Fleurette. Fight while he had breath in his body; fight until he fell vanquished by her side. For if he failed he would not let her die alone. He could not think of her being dragged through the streets in that awful tumbril which he himself had so often helped to fill; could not – heavens above no – could not think of her mounting the steps of the guillotine, which so many innocent feet had mounted at his bidding. Retribution! It had come nearer, more inexorable now! Death by his Fleurette's side seemed the only possible issue.

And even as he sat there alone, in that room wherein the hatred of his fellow-men seemed still to linger like noisome ghosts, a pale ray of sunlight found its way through the closed window and played upon the myriads and myriads of dust atoms that hovered in the air. Chauvelin's hands dropped down upon the table. His weary eyes rested vacantly upon that shaft of dust-laden light. And inside its very heart he saw a face, smiling and debonair, with lazy eyes and smiling lips mocking him in his grief. It was a vision, gone as soon as seen, but vivid enough during that one brief second to bring a savage curse upon the lonely man's lips. His claw-like hand clenched so tightly that the knuckles shone like polished ivory.

"My evil genius!" he muttered through his teeth. "Had I succeeded in bringing you down, had I seen that mocking head fall under the guillotine, this devastating misery would never have come upon me. If only I could be even with you, I would die happier – even now."

Twenty-eight

Ever afterwards to Chauvelin, it seemed as if the Scarlet Pimpernel had heard his challenge, and come in response to his thoughts: for hardly had a couple of days gone before the first rumour reached him of the nearness of his arch-enemy. Twenty-four hours later the hue and cry was all over Orange after a gang of English spies who, it was averred, made it their business to cheat Madame la Guillotine out of her dues.

Citizen Pochart brought Representative Chauvelin the news which already was all over the town, namely that Architect Caristie and his family, consisting of his wife and the small son now aged ten, who was destined one day to become one of Orange's most distinguished citizens, had unaccountably disappeared from their tumbledown lodgings in the Rue de la République, where they had taken refuge after their house had been requisitioned by the State and turned into a prison-house.

For some time the Sectional Members of the Committee of Public Safety, Citizens Pochart and Danou, ardent patriots, had had their eyes on the Caristie family. Aristos, what? Architect Caristie had designed and built houses in the past for tyrants and ci-devants. The arrest of the entire family had been decided on. It was to have taken place that very evening. Orders to that effect were out, their place of incarceration fixed in the very house where they had once sat in luxury, whilst patriots had' starved outside their gates.

And suddenly the news had spread like wildfire through the town that Architect Caristie, his wife and son had disappeared. Disappeared? Where? asked every patriot. But no one knew. One evening they had still been seen, as usual, taking walking exercise on the river-bank, and the next day when the soldiers of the revolutionary army presented themselves at the door of their lodgings in the Rue de la République and demanded admittance, lo! they received no answer: the lodgings were deserted, the birds had flown from their nests. Nor could the guard at any of the gates of the city throw light upon this mysterious occurrence. No one had passed the gates without duly authenticated passes. Pochart was at his wits' end and asked counsel of Representative Chauvelin. What was to be done in face of this mystery? Exercise strict supervision at the gates, Chauvelin advised. All passes in future to be signed by himself as well as by the Sectional Members of the Committee of Public Safety.

The news of the presence of the Scarlet Pimpernel in Orange had acted upon his nerves like a whiplash. Fate, it seemed, was hitting at him from every side: and he felt like a fighter who has been downed once, twice, and then suddenly feels the strength of giants in his blood; the agility of a cat spurring him to a new and stupendous effort. In a vague, fatalistic kind of way the safety of Fleurette and the destruction of the Scarlet Pimpernel appeared to him as inextricably involved. If he allowed his arch-enemy to baffle him now and here, in this city, then Fleurette was doomed and he himself must perish.

This was the immediate state of mind into which the news of the nearness of the Scarlet Pimpernel had thrown him. A wild desire to link the destruction of his enemy with the safety of his child, to deserve so well of the State, in fact, that the life of Fleurette would be ceded to him as a reward. A drowning man will catch at a straw, and so did Chauvelin catch at this hope, cling to it, turn the thought over and over in his mind. With feverish activity then he spurred those about him into additional vigilance, combated that superstitious terror with which every official these days regarded the gang of English spies and their mysterious chief. He brought to every man's notice the handsome reward offered by the Revolutionary Government for the capture of the Scarlet Pimpernel, described the Englishman's appearance, his methods, his motives, worked up every man in Orange, aye, and every woman too, into a state of enthusiasm for the possible capture of this inveterate and daring enemy of France.

But this particular frame of mind was not destined to endure. Soon memory got to work, recalled unpleasant moments in Calais, Boulogne, in Paris, in Nantes. What if here too, in Orange, the Scarlet Pimpernel should triumph and he, Chauvelin, once more be forced to eat the bread of humiliation? What if baffled once more, he should lose, at one terrible swoop, both his revenge and his last hope of saving Fleurette? And then it was that first the insidious, the stupendous thought penetrated his brain. Was it Satan himself who had whispered it into his ear? or some army of mocking imps intent upon torturing him to madness? But heavens above, what a thought! The Scarlet Pimpernel and Fleurette! Was that going to be the solution of this terrible impasse? The thought feverishly driven back at first, returned more insistent. Why not? And then again, why not? A young girl, sweet, pretty, innocent, was she not one to arouse those instincts of chivalry which Chauvelin had hitherto affected to despise?

What a possibility! Heavens above, what a possibility! His very senses reeled now at the thought. But he allowed his mind to dwell upon it, to weigh its possibilities: to familiarize itself more and more with it. At first it had seemed like madness, but no longer now! His Fleurette! Already Amédé Colombe was far away, under the protection of the Scarlet Pimpernel, what more likely than that – No! no! it could not be! His daughter! His, Chauvelin's! And in a swift vision he saw himself luring Marguerite Blakeney, the beloved and beautiful wife of the

Scarlet Pimpernel to her death, holding her as hostage, threatening her, torturing her. His enemy's wife! What agonies she had endured at his hands! And now Fleurette! Would not the Scarlet Pimpernel, triumphant and revengeful, gloat over her death, rather than raise a finger to save her life? Would he not gaze with joy on the misery endured by his bitterest foe?

And then once more torturing thoughts would assail him: torturing fears and torturing hopes, hopes? Yes, hopes! "Why should you not hope, man?" whispered an insidious demon in his ear: "the Scarlet Pimpernel does not know, cannot know that Fleurette is your daughter; the daughter of his enemy Armand Chauvelin. To him she is just the sweet, pretty, innocent victim of a system of government which he hates and which he combats. Then why not hope?" And the floating, racking visions of Juliette Marny, and Yvonne de Kernogan, of the Abbé Foucquet and Madèleine Lanoy, would once more haunt the daydreams of this man already steeped in misery, and hope insidious, ever-living hope, would whisper in its turn: "To that long list of innocents snatched from prison and from death by the insolent adventurer whom you hate, why should not the name of Fleurette be added? Fleurette of unknown parentage, just a sweet girl dwelling at Lou Mas, with old Louise and a father known as Armand? Why not?"

And day after day, whilst presiding, self-appointed, over a tribunal of infamy, Chauvelin's mind became more and more familiarized with the vision of his Fleurette snatched out of the jaws of death by the man with the lazy eyes and the mocking lips, the demmed, elusive Pimpernel of his daydreams and his sleepless nights.

Twenty-nine

Meanwhile in Architect Caristie's house, transformed for the necessities of the State into a prison, the old routine is now restored. Daily, once more, an hour before sunset, the captain of the guard with his half-dozen men, enters the courtyard, and in a loud voice reads the names that appear upon his Roll-call. They are the names of those who on the morrow are summoned before the Revolutionary Tribunal, there to answer the charges that are trumped up against them by the venal spies, who make their living out of the blood of innocent men and women and children.

Impossible to refute those charges, since the law has decreed that it is a crime to be merely suspected of treason against the State. Foucquier-Tinville, the great Public Prosecutor in Paris, no longer troubles, it seems, to prepare fresh indictments against every accused in turn. He has a printed formula of accusation, with just the name left in blank, presently to be filled in as convenience arises. Therefore in other greater and lesser cities of France, patriots desirous of showing their zeal, can do no better than emulate the example set by so great a man. Local sections of the Committee of Public Safety prepare the indictments – set formulae with the names left in blank. These they pass on to the Public Prosecutor who mumbles as he reads them before the Tribunal with the President sitting up on the dais, and the accused – names left in blank – brought up to the bar, not allowed to say a word in their own justification, nor to question the witnesses brought up to testify against them.

Abandon all hope then, ye whose names are upon that Roll-call! tomorrow the Tribunal, the next day the guillotine! And once again now, day after day, the captain of the guard comes to the house, late of Architect Caristie, and reads; and at all the windows that overlook the courtyard heads appear, men, women and little children – clutching the bars and listening. Listening for their own name or that of one who is dear. Sighing with relief if neither has been called, or with resignation if tomorrow is destined to bring this miserable existence to an end.

And day after day Chauvelin presides over this tribunal of infamy. Self-appointed, he sits upon the dais and sees before him pass a daily file of doomed, and dying. Sometimes ten, sometimes as many as twenty in a day, and still the prisons are full – fresh arrests made up for those whom the guillotine has claimed. Acquittals are rare, for moderation now has become a crime. Danton – aye! even Danton, the lion, has perished, he who ordered the September massacres, he who thundered forth from the tribune, "Liberty! Fraternity! Equality! or Death!" he has perished because he became guilty of this crime of moderation. The glorious revolution has no use for two such of its products as Danton and Robespierre – for the reality of the one and the canting hypocrisy of the other: so Danton it was who perished. "It is right," he had dared to say once, "to repress the Royalists: but we should not confound the innocent with the guilty!"

"And who told thee," Robespierre retorted, sea-green with hatred, "that one single innocent has perished by our hand?"

And because Danton had dared to raise his voice in the cause of the innocent, Danton had perished.

What chance then has Chauvelin to defend his Fleurette? His power is great. He can make or unmake your Pocharts and your Danous, your President Legrange or Public Prosecutor

Isnard, but he cannot accord special privileges in prison for his own daughter. He cannot see her in private, comfort her, warn her if need be, tell her not to be afraid, for Bibi chéri is there, on the watch, ready to protect her with his body, to stand by her in the last hour. He cannot. Pochart and Danou are on the watch. "We must not confound the innocent with the guilty:" Danton had dared to say. And for this he had perished: and though he perished, could not save one single innocent.

And all evening, after the sittings of the Tribunal are over, and ten – or mayhap fifteen or twenty – condemned to the guillotine, Chauvelin like a pale, thin ghost haunts the purlieus of Architect Caristie's house. On pretext of his office he enters the courtyard with the captain of the guard and looks up at the windows to see if *she* is there. Once he saw her: just her little face peeping behind the opulent shoulders of one Claire de Châtelard, the best noted strumpet in Orange. The woman had one arm round Fleurette's waist and when the captain of the guard read out the name of Claire known as Châtelard upon his list, Fleurette threw her arms round her, and laid her head upon the trollop's breast.

Chauvelin turned away from the spectacle with a groan, and all night he lay awake thinking of his sweet flower laying her head upon the breast of a Claire de Châtelard.

Yet Claire de Châtelard bore herself bravely before him the next day, and when, on the day after that, he watched her from the window of the Hôtel de Ville mounting the steps of the guillotine, saw her standing there, superb and defiant with a coarse jest upon her sensual lips, he gloated over the thought that his Fleurette would no longer pillow her innocent head upon that breast. He tried to picture her, grieving for this friend, the propinquity, the squalor of that house of detention, from which there was but one egress, that egress the gate of Death. Claire de Châtelard today – Fleurette when? Every day the indictments are sent up to him for examination, the printed forms of accusation with the names left in blank, to be filled in as convenience demands: and every day a list of ten, perhaps fifteen names are sent along with these printed forms, and it is his business to direct the Public Prosecutor, a man of his own choosing, which of these names are to be inserted in the blank spaces, on the forms of accusation. Up to now he has been able to keep Fleurette's name out, but it has been sent up to him on two consecutive days. The fight then was getting at close quarters. Pochart and Danou were pressing him, showing their teeth like snarling dogs ready to spring. And time was hurrying on. Time would presently bring back President Legrange and Prosecutor Isnard from Paris, time would inevitably bring to light his machinations for keeping those two men out of the way. Aye! time was hurrying on, and Fleurette's name had twice appeared upon the list.

And for the past three days not a word in the town about the English spies. After Architect Caristie and his family, it had been the widow Colmars and her daughter, and then General Paulieu and his family. Disappeared as if the earth had swallowed them up. Always traitors and aristos whose arrest was imminent, whose subsequent condemnation certain. But after that, three days' respite: the Scarlet Pimpernel and his gang seemed to have disappeared in their turn. The hopes which insidious demons had whispered in Chauvelin's ears were once more merged in a sea of despair. He derided himself for these hopes, lashed himself into a state of fury against himself for having allowed his mind to dwell upon them.

One scheme after another now did he devise and then reject. He would defy his enemies, the jury, the populace: loudly denounce the witnesses against Fleurette as liars and perjurers, pronounce her acquittal in the face of all opposition. Had he not made a point day after day of pronouncing acquittal on one or the other of the accused? just to test his power – to see how his enemies would behave? And he saw them lying low. Sneering. Whispering. Ogling him and laughing. They knew! They saw behind his schemes and his hopes. They reserved their counter-attack. They could afford to wait, whilst he could not.

If only Fleurette bore herself well: did not allow herself to be carried away with admissions or inconsidered words, out of sentiment for that fool Amédé Colombe. Chauvelin longed to see her, if only to impress this one thing upon her; to say nothing. To admit nothing. To hold her tongue and to trust chéri Bibi. If only she did that, he felt that he might save her yet. And obsessed by this idea, devoured with the desire to convey this message to her, without compromising her or giving yet another advantage to his enemies, Chauvelin at evening would wander like a restless ghost through the city.

That afternoon after he watched Claire de Châtelard mount the steps of the guillotine, a joke upon her lips, this restlessness became exquisite torture, and racked with tumultuous thoughts, wrapped in a black mantle, he sallied forth into the streets. It was now early in June: nearly three weeks since that last carefree day, Fleurette's eighteenth birthday, spent with her over at Lou Mas, when the scent of almond-blossom had been in the air and the nightingale had sung in the old walnut tree. The day had been sunless and chilly, after sunset the rain began to fall. But rain and weather held no terrors for Chauvelin in his present mood. Holding his mantle tightly round his shoulders and pulling his hat down over his eyes, he wandered aimlessly through the streets, over the river and back again, down unpaved streets and lonely lanes, now and then sitting down to rest in some obscure little outlying café, where no one knew or heeded him, and then starting off again on his restless course. But always drifting back instinctively to the purlieus of Architect Caristie's house.

Almost opposite to it there was a small café: no one sitting outside because of the rain, but the interior lighted up, and sounds of merriment proceeding from within. Chauvelin thought of going inside, feeling that if he sat down there, close to the window, he could watch the walls behind which lived and suffered his little Fleurette. He did not dare go in for fear of being recognized. He was just debating within himself whether he would go or stay, when he saw a man come out of the house of Architect Caristie, cross over to the café, then disappear behind its creaking door. A scavenger, no doubt, ragged and dirty – not a warder, he was too ill-clad for that – just a scavenger – but perhaps he had seen Fleurette. The thought fascinated Chauvelin. His mind clung to it: turned it over and over. The thought that here was a man who perhaps had seen Fleurette within the last few minutes, had swept corridor or staircase when she was passing by. And with that thought there was still the burning desire to send her a message, to tell her to be brave and trust in Bibi, but above all, oh! above all, not to be led into making any admission about those valuables belonging to Madame de Frontenac, or about her association with Amédé Colombe.

Chauvelin, leaning against the wall which faced the little café, dwelt on his thoughts and his desire. He allowed the rain to drip upon his hat and upon his shoulders from the roof above him. He no longer felt restless. He just wanted to stand there and watch for the return of the man, who perhaps would be seeing Fleurette again within the next few minutes. He wondered if he dare approach him, always with the idea of possibly conveying a message to Fleurette. But the fear that the man might know who he was, deterred him from entering the café himself. He had been a fairly conspicuous figure in the courtyard of Caristie's house, standing by the side of the captain of the guard: if that scavenger was at work in the corridor, he might have looked out of the window and seen him, learned who he was. All through he had been at pains to show an indifferent attitude before his enemies: if this man happened to be a spy, would the knowledge that he, Chauvelin, was trying to establish communication with Fleurette compromise him hopelessly and do no good to her?

As he stood there, pondering and debating what he had better do, he saw the scavenger come out of the café. For a minute or two the man stood at the door, his hands buried in the pockets of his ragged breeches, contemplating the rain. The next moment another equally dirty and bedraggled ruffian came down the street, paused at the entrance of the café and passed the time of day with the scavenger. The two mudlarks remained talking for a few moments, after which they parted, each going his own way. The scavenger recrossed the road and entered the Caristie House. The other passed on in the opposite direction and Chauvelin, after an instant's hesitation, followed him. He came up with the man at the angle of the Rue Longue: and putting out his arm, touched him on the shoulder. With a cry of terror the man fell on his knees.

"Mercy! I've done nothing!" he babbled almost incoherently.

"I dare say not," Chauvelin said drily, "but it will be to thine advantage if thou'lt come along quietly with me."

He seized the man by the arm and dragged him up from his knees. The poor wretch tried to wriggle himself free, but Chauvelin held him tightly, and without another word drew him within the shelter of the nearest doorway. Fortunately, though the man kept up a ceaseless litany of lamentations and cries for mercy, he did so under his breath, thus creating no disturbance nor exciting the attention of the few passers-by who were hurrying homewards through the rain-swept streets.

"Are you willing, citizen," Chauvelin began abruptly, as soon as he had assured himself that the doorway was deserted and no eavesdropper nigh, "are you willing to earn fifty livres tournoi?"

The man gave no immediate reply, it seemed as if he was shaking himself free from his first terror and pondering over this extraordinary proposal, so different to what he had anticipated. Then he cleared his throat, expectorated, slowly repeated the magic words:

"Fifty livres tournoi!" and finally added in an awed whisper:

"I have not seen five livres tournoi for months."

"Fifty are yours, citizen, if you'll render me a service."

"What is it?"

"That friend of yours, to whom you spoke just now – outside the Café de la Lune – "

"Citizen Rémi?"

"He works in the Caristie House?"

"Yes."

"In what capacity?"

"Cleaner," the man replied laconically. "Rémi hung about for days trying to earn a bit of money. He hasn't a sou, you understand? Same as me. A few days ago one of the inside men fell sick. Rémi presented himself and got the work. I know him well."

"He has access to the prisoners?" Chauvelin asked.

"I suppose so."

"Then tell him that there will be fifty livres for him too if he will convey a written message to number 142 in room 12."

Again the man seemed to ponder: weighing the risks probably, and also the gain. Fifty livres tournoi! Immense. He had forgotten that there was such a sum of money left in the world: and then for him to have the handling of it! This led him once more to expectorate, which action apparently had the effect of stimulating his brain-power.

"It could be done," he murmured at last.

"It can be done," Chauvelin asserted emphatically, "but must be done quickly, or – "

"Rémi will be back at the Café de la Lune soon after eight o'clock. He always goes there for a sip of something after supper."

"Good! Then you can meet him at that hour and tell him to wait for you, then come at once and find me here, under this doorway. I'll have the letter ready – "

"The whole thing is very risky, citizen," the man demurred.

"If it were not," Chauvelin rejoined drily, "I would not spend one hundred livres tournoi in the attempt."

"Fifty livres is not overmuch, when one risks one's neck."

"You are not risking your neck," Chauvelin retorted, "as you well know. And you'll not get more from me than fifty livres each. Take it or leave it."

He knew how to deal with these mudlarks, apparently, for the man after he had spat once more once or twice, seemed satisfied.

"I'll be back here," he said laconically, "after I have seen Rémi again."

Then Chauvelin let him go. The darkness and the rain soon swallowed him up: but Chauvelin himself remained for quite a while standing motionless under the doorway. He had not yet burnt his boats, was still free, if he thought the risk too great, to fail in his appointment. The man did not know who he was, had not seen him in the darkness and under the wide brim of his hat: but there was the risk that this Rémi might be a spy, who would take the letter intended for Fleurette straightway to Pochart or Danou. The letter might thus betray him and so minimize his power of saving Fleurette. He had to safeguard himself against the merest breath of suspicion in order to keep his power. The more irreproachable, detached, incorruptible he appeared before the populace, the more Spartan in his attitude towards his own child until the day of her trial, the greater his chance of saving her at the last. But his desire to warn her against unconsidered words or any kind of admissions outweighed for the moment every other consideration. He hurried back to his lodgings through the rain, and at once sat down to pen his letter to the child.

"My beloved one," he began, "at last I am able to send a word to you, which I hope and trust will reach your darling little hands. Child of my heart, this is to entreat you to continue in your trust of me, for I swear to you by the memory of your dead mother, that while you trust me I can save you. I can save the man you love. Moreover, I entreat you, beloved child of my soul, do not make any admission when brought before the tribunal, as you must be shortly, alas! If witnesses testify against you, just hold your peace; if others question you, deny everything. This I entreat you to do for the sake of the love I bear you, for the sake of the tears I have shed these past weeks, ever since your folly hath brought you to this pass."

He signed the letter "Bibi." Thus he had mentioned no names and in addition taken the precaution of disguising his writing as far as he was able. After which he sealed the letter and slipped it in the inner pocket of his coat. Time was now hanging heavily. Like a beast in its cage, Chauvelin paced up and down the narrow room, his hands clenched behind his back, a world of soul agony expressed upon his wax-like face.

As soon as he heard the tower-clock of Notre Dame strike eight, he picked up his hat and cloak and once more sallied forth into the streets.

Thirty

A quarter of an hour later two out-at-elbows ragamuffins met inside the Café de la Lune. Outside the rain had not abated: both the men who were clad in what were little more than rags, appeared soaked through to the skin. At this hour the little café was almost deserted. Citizen Sabot, the proprietor, was sitting at one table with a couple of friends; at another a couple of road-menders were sipping their absinthe, when the scavenger from the prison-house came slouching in. He sat down on the bench against the wall in the darkest corner of the room and ordered a bottle of wine for himself and a friend. Presently the latter came and joined him, and for a while the two men sat drinking in silence. Soon an animated discussion arose between the proprietor and his friends on the respective merits of Vouvray and Beaujolais as a table wine.

This entailed much shouting and copious gesticulations. Sabot had a deep-booming voice which reverberated from end to end of the room and caused the window-panes to rattle in their frames.

The scavenger from the prison-house had apparently drunk more during the day than was good for him. His head leaned heavily on his hand, his elbow resting upon the table, his eyes had become bleary, his speech uncertain. His friend sat opposite to him with his back to the rest of the company, and when Sabot's voice roused the echoes in the small stuffy room, he leaned forward and whispered in the other's ear:

"You've had about as much as you ought to have, Citizen Rémi," he said drily, as he uncorked the bottle and set it on the table.

"That is none of your business, citizen," Rémi retorted with a bibulous laugh, "so long as I pay for what I drink."

He threw some coins on the table. Sabot picked them up with a shrug and then rejoined his friends, and resumed the discussion with them on the merits or demerits of Vouvray and Beaujolais. The other ruffian took the opportunity of shuffling out of the café, and the scavenger, sprawling over the table, composed himself to sleep.

Hugging the walls, the other slunk through the street till he came to the doorway, where effectively he had appointed to meet Chauvelin.

"Well!" the latter queried impatiently as soon as the other came in sight. "Have you seen your friend?"

"Yes."

"Does he agree?"

"Yes."

With a sigh of relief Chauvelin drew the sealed letter from his breast pocket.

"Fifty livres, remember," he said slowly, "for each of you, when you bring me back the answer."

"Oh!" the man exclaimed, visibly disappointed. "There's an answer then?"

"Yes! An answer. Your friend will see to it that you bring me back either an answer or some token which will satisfy me that the letter is in the right hands."

The man gave a short laugh.

"You do not trust me, citizen," he said.

"No," Chauvelin replied laconically. "I do not."

"I do not blame you," the other retorted. "I do not trust you altogether either. How do I know, when Rémi and I have risked our lives in your service, that the money will be forthcoming?"

"You do know that, citizen," Chauvelin rejoined drily, "and anyway you are bound to take that risk."

"Why should I?" the man retorted.

"Because you are more sorely in need of money than I of your services."

This argument appeared unanswerable. At any rate the ruffian now said with a light laugh:

"Have it your own way. Give me the letter, Number 142 in room 12 shall have it, you can wager your shirt on that."

Without another word Chauvelin handed him the letter. It was so dark under the doorway that it was only by groping that the other was able to get hold of it. He drew so near to Chauvelin that the latter, fearing that the man was trying to have a close look at him, pulled his hat lower down over his eyes. The other resorted to his habitual expression of indifference by spitting upon the floor; then he slipped the letter underneath his ragged blouse.

"Where do I find you," he asked, "after Rémi has done your errand?"

"You will go into the Rue Longue," Chauvelin replied, "to the house of Citizen Amouret, the chandler. Up the first flight of stairs, on the right-hand side, you will come to a door which is painted a slate-grey. Knock at that door and you will find me within."

"At what hour?"

"At any time tomorrow after the executions in the Place de la République," Chauvelin replied.

Thirty-one

To say that Fleurette had in the past few days become familiarized with the grim mummeries that went on in the common room, would be putting it rather strongly. But she certainly had no longer the same horror of them as she had had at first. The presentment of the mock guillotine still harrowed her, it is true, but she could not help laughing at the antics of the mock Satan and his satellites when they seized the President of the Tribunal and the Public Prosecutor by the feet and dragged them off to an imaginary hell. There was that one man in particular whom she had sometimes noticed before and who was aide to one of the warders, he was very diverting. She used to watch him turning and wriggling his huge body, which he had painted all over with soot and draped in bits of red rags. He made an ideal Satan with tail and horns complete, and sometimes it seemed to Fleurette as if he went through all his antics for the sole purpose of bringing a smile upon her lips. Moreover, in a vague kind of way, she associated him with that lovely letter from Amédé, which she had found inside the folds of her kerchief one evening.

The death of so many who had been her prison companions at first, especially that of Claire de Châtelard, had deeply affected her. The want of fresh air, of exercise, and above all of love and joy, had begun to affect her health: her cheeks had lost their freshness, her eyes their lustre, her lips their smile.

It was only in the recreation hour that she would smile sometimes. Always when the big, clumsy, hideous-looking fellow who was some kind of aide to one of the warders, set himself the task of fooling for her benefit. She came to look upon him as a friend, and remembering how mysteriously that letter from Amédé had come inside her kerchief, she would look up whenever he came near her, wondering if he had another such welcome message for her. And one evening – she really had not the least idea how it happened – she found a sealed letter inside her work-basket. And the letter was from chéri Bibi. Oh! the joy of it! The joy! She read, and re-read it, and kissed the paper whereon his dear hand had rested. How she had missed Bibi all these days! How she longed to reassure him that she was well and that she trusted and believed in him! As to obeying him in all things, of course she would do it. To begin with, she was not afraid, not the least bit in the world. He was watching over her, and he was so great and powerful that no danger could possibly assail her while he cared for her. She would indeed obey him in all things, hold her peace while that wicked Adèle tried to do her harm; she would hold her peace before the Tribunal just as *le bon Jésus* had done when he was questioned by his judges.

Oh! it was a dear, a comforting, an infinitely precious letter. And beside it Fleurette had found a tiny little slip of paper on which were scribbled the words:

"Let me have something to take back to the writer, to let him know that you are well. Leave it in your work-basket, and I will see to it that he gets it." And so Fleurette had written a few lines to chéri Bibi; told him that she was well, and assured him that she was not afraid and would obey his commands in all things. She would hold her peace and trust in him. This little note she had hidden that evening in her work-basket and by noon on the following day it had gone.

Thirty-two

"But me no buts, my dear Tony, I am sick of all these filthy rags. And if I am to see pretty Fleurette's papa then must I see him decently clad and in my right mind."

So spake Sir Percy Blakeney to his friend, late the following evening. It was in an attic under the roof of a half-derelict house in the Rue du Pont close to the river-bank. The owners of the house had long since disappeared, fled into the mountains or perished on the guillotine; no one knew or cared. Blakeney, and those members of his league who were with him, had hit upon it on their arrival in Orange, had made the attic their head-quarters, whilst most of the vagabonds of the city used the rest of the house as their lair. They too were outwardly vagabonds, dressed in rags, appeared unkempt, unshaven, and unwashed, when they sallied forth in the early mornings each on an errand of mercy to succour those in need of help or those who were in danger or distress.

It was only o' nights, sometimes, that an overwhelming desire for cleanliness and nice clothes caused these English gentlemen to cast aside their rags and to venture out into the open dressed in clothes that would have caused the ragamuffins of Orange to snarl at their heels like so many hungry curs.

They had been eight days in Orange now, and already Architect Caristie, with his wife and small son, the widow Colmars and her daughter, and poor old General Paulieu with his family owed their safety to this gallant League of the Scarlet Pimpernel. But there was still more to do.

"We must get that child Fleurette out of that hell," the chief had said, and since then brain and heart had been at work to find the means to that end.

Later on Lord Tony had remarked: "I wish we could find out about that father of hers; this man Armand. He seems to hold some kind of position under this government of assassins, but I for one have tried in vain to learn something more definite about him."

"I think," Sir Andrew Ffoulkes added, "that his position must be a high one, or the girl would have been brought to trial before now."

"Unless our amiable friend, M. Chauvelin, has got this Armand under lock and key somewhere else," was my Lord Stowmaries' comment upon the situation.

Sir Percy was silent. Frankly the position puzzled him. He would have liked to get into touch with the man Armand, but for once he and his friends were baffled by this anonymity which appeared so closely guarded. Great then had been the rejoicing in the attic of the derelict house in the Rue du Pont, when Lord Antony Dewhurst – a most perfect type of ruffian in rags and a thick coating of grime – related his adventure with the mysterious individual who, under cover of darkness and rain, had offered him and his friend Rémi fifty livres each for delivering a message to a prisoner, who was none other than little Fleurette.

"At last we'll get in touch with the mysterious Armand," they all declared eagerly. It was arranged that the chief would himself take Fleurette's reply to the house in the Rue Longue. But go on this errand in the filthy rags of a scavenger he would not.

"The night is pretty dark," he declared, "and I would rather the mysterious Armand saw me as I am. I may also have a chance," he added with his merriest laugh, "of coming across my good friend M. Chambertin. It is some weeks since last we met, and not to have had a pleasant chat with him all these days, while we were within a stone's throw of one another, has been a sore trial to me. I caught a glimpse of him a day or two ago, in the courtyard of the Caristie House. He looked to be sick and out of sorts. A sight of me might cheer him up."

"You won't take any risks, Blakeney," Sir Andrew Ffoulkes remarked.

"Any number, my dear fellow," Sir Percy replied laughing. "And you know you envy me, you dog. But I feel thoroughly selfish tonight. I mean to take the note to Armand myself, and I mean to take the privilege of having a little chat with my friend Chambertin. And both these things I am going to do as an English gentleman and not as a mudlark in stinking, filthy rags."

He had completed his toilet now, looked magnificent in clothes cut by the leading London tailor, which set off his splendid figure to perfection, with snow-white stock and speckless boots.

"If a single pair of eyes should see you," Sir Andrew insisted, with an anxious sigh.

"I should have a whole pack of wolves at my heels," Blakeney admitted. "But that wouldn't be the first time any of us have had to run for our lives, eh? nor the first time we gave an entire pack of them the slip."

He picked up his hat and took a last look at Fleurette's little note which he had to deliver at the house in the Rue Longue.

"This man Armand must be a very decent fellow," he mused, "his letter to the child was really fine in spirit as well as in affection. Yes! he must be a decent fellow and we must get the girl for his sake as much as for that of our friend Colombe. What?"

On that, of course, they were all agreed. The activities of the League, since the rescue of General Paulieu and his family, were centred now on Fleurette. There were still one or two minor points to discuss, arrangements of detail to complete, but the main project for the girl's rescue could not be determined until it was definitely known whether her father, Armand, was going to be a help or a hindrance.

"Anyway, I shall know more," Blakeney said finally, as he made for the door, "when I have sampled this man."

It was then nine o'clock in the evening. The night was dark and stormy. Gusts of wind alternated with sharp showers of rain – an altogether unusual state of weather for the time of year in these parts. The few passers-by of respectable appearance on their way home from business or work did no more than throw a cursory glance on the tall figure that passed hurriedly by. A few vagabonds clinging to their rags which the wind threatened to tear off their meagre bodies, did perhaps pause, cowering against a dark wall, murmuring a threat or a curse against the aristo, but an unexpected coin slipped into their grimy hands, quickly silenced both curse and threat.

Blakeney knew his way well through the streets of Orange. Having kept along the river-bank till he came to the bridge, he turned up the Rue de la République. Glancing up at a house on his right, a smile of pure joy lit up his anxious face. Three nights ago on this spot, he had carried Architect Caristie's small son in his arms, while Caristie and his wife followed him down the street to the market-cart which awaited them at the top of the bridge. Three hours later an officer of the revolutionary army was hammering at the door of Caristie's lodgings, only to find that the birds had flown. It had been a merry night, and merrier morning, while he, Blakeney, drove the market-cart out of the city with Caristie and his wife concealed amidst the sacks of haricots and peas, and the boy thrust into an empty oil jar.

Well! something equally daring would have to be devised for the girl Fleurette, and perhaps for her father, the mysterious Armand. Blakeney, throwing back his head in the teeth of rain and wind, drew a deep breath of delight. This was life in very truth. To plan, to scheme, to accomplish. Alternately hare and hound, to revel in this chase with human lives as the goal.

And if at times the thought of beautiful Marguerite, lonely and anxious in far-off England, caused a pang, like a knife – thrust to his heart, her soothing voice, her reassuring smile came to him as a swift vision from the spirit-land to encourage and console. In suffering and anxiety, as well as in the joy of reunion, Marguerite always understood.

Now he turned from the Place de la République into the Rue Longue, and the next couple of hundred yards brought him to the house of Lucien Amouret, corn-chandler. The outside door was on the latch. Pushing it open he found himself in a narrow hall, with an inner door leading into the shop on his left and a staircase in front of him. A lamp hung from the ceiling and shed a dim light on stair and hall. From the shop came the sound of voices in conversation, but though the stairs creaked under his tread, no one came out to see whose the step might be.

Sir Percy ran lightly up the stairs, and on the first landing came to the door, painted a slate grey. This part of the house appeared silent and deserted; the upper floors wrapped in dead gloom. A rusty bell-pull hung beside the door. Sir Percy gave it a pull, and a discordant clang roused the sleeping echoes of the chandler's house. A moment or two later he caught the sound of shuffling footsteps, the door was opened, an old woman in cap and shawl mutely inquired what the visitor desired.

"Is Citizen Armand within?" Blakeney asked.

The woman, he thought, looked at him rather curiously for a second or two, then shrugged her shoulders. Without wasting words she shuffled off down a dimly lighted passage, leaving him to enter or not, as he pleased. The next moment he heard a woman's voice – the same woman probably – say: "An aristo is asking to see Citizen Armand." Again a moment's silence, then the woman came shuffling back, signed to him to enter and closed the door behind him.

"In there," she said laconically, and nodded towards the end of the passage where a half-open door revealed a shaft of more brilliant light. Then she shuffled off again, presumably to her kitchen, leaving the visitor to his own devices.

Sir Percy took off his hat and coat and laid them down on a chair close by; he then walked the length of the passage to the half-open door, pushed it open and found himself in a small room, comfortably furnished, lighted by a lamp which stood upon a centre table. The table was littered with papers. Behind it sat a man writing. At sound of Sir Percy's footsteps he looked up. The eyes of the two men met, and it almost seemed to one of them at least that time for a few seconds stood still.

And then a pleasant laugh broke the silence, and a gentle lazy voice said slowly:

"Egad! if it is not my engaging friend M. Chambertin! The gods do indeed favour me, sir, for there's no man in the world I would sooner have seen at this hour than your amiable self."

After the first paralysing second, Chauvelin had jumped to his feet. He had thought that once again his feverish fancy was playing his senses a mocking trick, that the face which ever haunted his daydreams and his sleepless nights had only come to him on the wings of imagination. But the merry laugh, the lazy voice were all too real. His enemy was truly there, not a vision, but a cruel, mocking reality. Swiftly his claw-like hand shot out, fastened on an object that lay amidst a litter of papers, and would have lifted it, had not another slender and firm hand shot out likewise and fastened itself upon his wrist with a grasp like a vice of steel.

Chauvelin had the greatest difficulty in the world to smother a cry of pain. His fingers opened, spread out fan-wise, the pistol which he had seized fell back upon the litter of papers. With a soft laugh Sir Percy sat down on the edge of the table, picked up the pistol, withdrew the charge and swept it into the sand-box close to his hand, the while Chauvelin watched him greedily, hungrily, as a caged feline might watch a prey that was beyond its reach.

A white-faced clock on the wall struck the half-hour. Sir Percy laid the pistol down upon the table, and flicked his fine, well-shaped hands one against the other.

"There now, my dear M. Chambertin," he said gaily, "we can converse more comfortably together. Do you think it would have been wise to put a charge of powder through your humble servant? We should both of us have missed much of the zest of life."

"It is always your pleasure to mock, Sir Percy," Chauvelin said with an effort. "There are various popular sayings which I might recall to your mind, such as that the pitcher went once too often to the well."

"And Sir Percy once too often to visit his friend M. Chambertin, eh?"

"I think you will find that this is so," Chauvelin rejoined, trying, none too successfully, to ape his enemy's easy familiarity. "Orange is not a healthy place for English spies these days."

"Possibly not," Blakeney retorted lightly. "Nor for some unfortunate children of France, I am thinking."

"Traitors and spies, you are right there, Sir Percy. We have no use for them in Orange – or elsewhere."

"Or for honest men, eh, my friend? for chaste women and innocent children. That is why your humble servant and the league of which methinks you know a thing or two, propose to remove these from this polluted soil."

Chauvelin had rested his elbow on the table. His hand shading his face against the glare of the lamp, effectually concealed its varying expressions from the keen eyes of his enemy.

"You have not told me yet, Sir Percy," he said after a few seconds' silence, "what procures me the honour of your visit at this hour."

"Pure chance, my dear sir," Blakeney replied, "though the honour is entirely mine. As a matter of fact I came to find one Armand."

Twice did the pendulum of the white-faced clock tick the seconds before Chauvelin said quietly:

"My colleague? Have you business with him?"

"Yes," Blakeney replied slowly. "I have a message for him."

"I can deliver it."

"Why not!? since I came on purpose."

"My colleague is absent."

"I can wait."

"From whom then is the message?"

"From his daughter."

"Ah!"

Once more there was a pause. The white-faced clock ticked on but the two men were silent. Chauvelin's face was shaded by his hand, and it needed all the energy, all the strength of his will to keep that hand absolutely steady, not to allow a finger to tremble. In the other hand he held a long quill-pen and with it he traced a geometrical pattern upon a blank sheet of paper. Sir Percy Blakeney, still sitting on the edge of the table, watched him, motionless.

"Pretty drawing that," he said abruptly. And with slender finger pointed to the design that grew in intricate lines under Chauvelin's aimless pen.

The other gave a start, the pen spluttered, scattering the ink in spots all over the paper.

"There now, you have spoilt it," Sir Percy continued lightly. "I had no idea you were such a master draughtsman."

Chauvelin threw down his pen. He had his nerves under control at last, was able to drop his hand, to lean back in his chair, and with both hands buried in the pockets of his breeches, to throw back his head and look his enemy squarely in the face.

"About that message, Sir Percy," he said with well-feigned indifference.

"What about it, my dear M. Chambertin?" Blakeney rejoined lightly.

"My colleague, Citizen Armand, has been called away – to Lyons on State business."

"But how unfortunate!" Sir Percy exclaimed.

"I am sending a courier to Lyons this very night."

"Too late, my dear M. Chambertin! Too late, I fear!"

Chauvelin frowned. "What mean you by too late, Sir Percy?" he asked slowly.

"Armand's daughter is sick, my dear M. Chambertin," Blakeney rejoined, speaking very slowly, as if to weigh his every word. "Before your courier can possibly reach Lyons, she will be dead."

"My God – !"

It was the most heart-rending cry that had ever come from a man's throat. Chauvelin had jumped to his feet; his two hands, claw-like, as if carved in marble, gripped the arms of his chair; his knees were shaking, his pale eyes stared like those of a maniac, his cheeks were the colour of lead.

For the space of ten seconds he stood thus, with his whole body quivering, his senses reeling, his eyes fixed on those finely moulded lips that had dealt this appalling blow. Then slowly consciousness returned, a veil seemed to be lifted from before his eyes, knowledge had entered his brain. He knew that he had fallen into the trap set for him by this astute adventurer. He realized that he had betrayed the secret which he would have guarded with his life.

"So," Sir Percy said at last very slowly, " 'tis you are Citizen Armand, and the sweetest flower that ever bloomed in this putrid atmosphere has its roots in polluted soil?"

Still quite slowly and deliberately he drew Fleurette's note out of the breast-pocket of his coat; for a second or two he held it lightly between slender finger and thumb, then laid it on the table in front of Chauvelin.

"She is not sick," he said quietly, "nor yet dying. If you have not forgotten how to pray, man, pray to God now, pray with all your might, that the same power which enabled you to torture my wife and wellnigh to break her brave spirit, will aid you to save your daughter from those tigers whom you have called your friends."

Chauvelin had sunk back in the chair. His head was buried in his hands. Tumultuous thoughts rushed through his brain until he felt that his reason must be tottering. A haze was before his eyes. Perhaps it was caused by tears. Who knows? Only the recording angel mayhap. Even wild beasts cry in agony when deprived of their young.

Only after a few minutes did he become aware of the note penned by his little Fleurette and laid in front of him by his bitterest foe. The Scarlet Pimpernel! The only man in all the world who might perhaps have saved Fleurette, who would have saved Fleurette, if he, Chauvelin, had not betrayed the secret of his heart.

Like one waking from a dream, Chauvelin picked up the note, and looked fearfully about him, dreading to meet those mocking lazy eyes, which, no doubt, at this hour gleamed with malicious triumph.

But Sir Blakeney was no longer there.

Thirty-three

The stage was now set for the last act of the tragedy, which the chief actor himself knew could only end one way. He had schemed and planned until he felt that his reason would give way, until he feared that he would lose the nerve and the power of which he had such sore need. He had thought of everything, weighed every possibility from the bribing of prison warders, to the suppression – by murder if need be – of the two witnesses Godet and Adèle. He had thought of turning the tables on Pochart and Danou, by launching accusations against them. But all these plans had to be rejected one by one. Fleurette liberated today through the success of one or the other of these schemes would only be re-arrested on the morrow. The suppression of the witnesses, the arrest of his more powerful enemies, would only rouse more bitter antagonism against himself and, failing in the end to save his Fleurette, would end in precipitating her doom.

Driven by despair, he had at one time pinned his hopes of salvation for the child on the possible interference of the Scarlet Pimpernel, but even that fond and foolish hope had been shattered by his betrayal of his jealously guarded secret. What was there left to hope for? That his power was great enough at the Tribunal to force an acquittal in spite of the witnesses, in spite of Pochart and Danou and all the mob whom they had already gathered round them. The Public Prosecutor, a man of his own making, would not dare to side against him. But there was the populace, the rabble, the swinish multitude, who, now that even the worst type of venal and corrupt jury had been abolished, were judges and jury, advocate and prosecutor all in one. The last word always rested with them, and Pochart and Danou, egged on by envy and revenge, would know how to sway the rabble.

Chauvelin was not the man to indulge in illusions. He knew well enough – none better – that the passions of hatred and of spite which he himself had engendered and fostered in the hearts of his fellow-men, were turned against him, as they had been turned on all the makers of this bloody revolution, on your Brissots and your Carriers, your Philippe d'Orléans, and your great Danton. They would destroy his exquisite Fleurette as effectually as they had destroyed thousands of others, equally innocent.

And now the end had come. No longer could the day be put off. President Legrange and Public Prosecutor Isnard might be arriving in Paris any hour when the new aerial telegraph might be set in motion, or a courier sent down to Orange post-haste and burst the bubble of Chauvelin's machinations.

And then on that afternoon of the 15th of June two things occurred. To begin with when the Public Prosecutor placed before him the printed forms of accusation with the names left in blank, and with them a list of the names of those awaiting trial, Chauvelin with a hand that appeared quite steady, wrote in one of the blank spaces the name of Fleur Chauvelin, *nommée* Armand. Secondly when, an hour later, the captain of the guard stood in the courtyard of the Caristie House reading out the names of those who were to stand their trial on the morrow, Fleurette heard the sound of her own name.

She was not frightened, nor did she weep. Tears were a thing of the past for her. Twenty days had gone by since she had been happy, more than a fortnight since she had been brought into this house and deprived of air and sunlight and joy. One by one those who had been kind to her in this prison house had gone: Claire de Châtelard, Madame de Mornas, poor Eugénie Blanc, and kind M. de Bollène. Their names had been on the Roll-call. The next day they were gone, and Fleurette never saw them again. Lately she had been lonely too. No one had taken the place in her unsophisticated heart of Claire de Châtelard. The only friend she had left was the warder's aide, the rough scavenger who had brought her the two welcome letters. Amédé's and Bibi's. He still continued his antics, joined in the gruesome mummeries which still went on in the common room, and Fleurette somehow had a sense of reassurance when he was nigh. But this night of all nights, after she had heard the captain of the guard read her name upon the Roll-call, her grimy friend was not there. Fleurette missed him, and disappointment over his absence was the only sorrowful feeling of which she felt conscious, when she realized that her fate would be decided on the morrow.

She was not afraid. Had not Bibi enjoined her, begged her to trust him and not to be afraid? She wondered when she would be allowed to see Bibi, whether he would be there tomorrow, at her trial, encouraging her with his presence and with his glance when she was made to stand before the judge. She knew that in a sense she had done wrong. She had taken Madame's valuables and handed them over to Amédé. This she had no right to do, and since Adèle had seen her with M'sieu' Amédé that evening, and spoken ill of her because of that, she supposed that she would be punished. It was only vaguely that she marvelled what the punishment would be. But she was not afraid because she trusted Bibi. Nor did she regret her actions. If it had all to be done over again, she would act in precisely the same way. The mysterious voice often rang in her ear even now. She had obeyed the commands of *le bon Dieu*, and it was *le bon Dieu* who had chosen a still more mysterious way for saving M'sieu' Amédé from the consequences of her actions.

Thus did Fleurette envisage the day that was to come, with love and trust in her heart for Bibi, and the certainty after all these trials and tribulations of a happy reunion with him and old Louise at Lou Mas.

Not to mention the reunion with M'sieu' Amédé.

Thirty-four

The first thing that struck Fleurette's perceptions when she entered that huge room, was that up at the further end of it – upon a raised platform and behind a tall desk, sat Bibi chéri himself. Two other men sat there with him, but Fleurette hardly saw them. It was on Bibi that she looked. She had slept very little during the night. Excitement had kept her awake, as well as the tears and lamentations of two of her room-mates who were to appear with her this day before the Tribunal.

And it was Bibi who was to be her judge. Well then obviously she had nothing to fear. One of some fifteen of her fellow-prisoners, she was bustled with them across the room to a wooden bench where they were roughly ordered to sit down. As they crossed the room boos and hisses, and one or two louder cries of execration, greeted them. A few remarks, all of them malevolent, rose above the murmurs.

"That old man there, I knew him once. Old tyrant. He's getting his deserts at last."

"Do you see the woman next to him? Five free-born Frenchwomen she had at a time once, to wait on her and do her hair. Aristo, va! It won't take long to do thy hair tomorrow. One snick with the scissors, what?"

"That young wench too. Not much more than eighteen, I warrant."

"I hear she is a thief as well as a traitor."

"Pity they should have abolished the whipping-post. That would have done the young traitors a world of good."

"Me, I prefer the guillotine; quickest work, eh?"

Fleurette had blushed with shame to the roots of her hair. She tried not to look in the direction whence these voices, harsh and coarse, had come. She tried to think of all the prayers which M. le Curé had taught her long ago. She tried to think of M'sieu' Amédé and of the joy she would have when she saw him again. But she could not shut the gates of her consciousness against all these people who had gathered here for the sole purpose of seeing their fellow-creatures suffer. Men and women and even little children. The women for the most part had brought their knitting, for everyone was knitting socks these days for the brave soldiers who were fighting against the enemies of France, and through the murmur of voices, the monotonous click-click of the needles acted as an irritant upon the nerves.

All around there appeared to be a sea of faces. And eyes. Innumerable eyes that glared, and mouths that grinned and derided. And above the faces, a sea of red caps with tricolour cockades. Fleurette tried hard not to look. She closed her eyes and tried to murmur the prayers she and M'sieu' Amédé used to say together when M. le Curé prepared them for their first communion.

Bibi wore a hat with feathers. He had a bell in front of him, and this he often tinkled, when the noise from the crowd all around became too great. Once or twice he was addressed as "Citizen President." Fleurette had never seen him look so stern. The words which he spoke to the accused were not only bitter but terribly cruel. He seemed so unlike her real chéri Bibi, that she caught herself marvelling whether her fancy was not playing her aching eyes some strange and horrible trick.

One after the other the names of her fellow-prisoners were called, and one by one they were made to stand up and then walk to the centre of the room and up a couple of shallow steps to a small raised platform round which there was a wooden railing. In every instance as soon as the prisoner mounted this platform, and became as it were the centre of attraction for all these innumerable eyes, he or she would be greeted with groans and hisses and cat's calls, until Bibi tinkled his bell and loudly demanded silence.

A man in a red cap who sat just below Bibi's desk then stood up and read something out aloud, which Fleurette never understood, but which the crowd apparently did, for the reader was frequently interrupted by more boos and hisses and often cries of execration. After this reading Bibi, or one of the two men who sat beside him, asked the prisoner questions. These were sometimes replied to, but not always. The crowd invariably threw in loud comments on both questions and answers, and Bibi was then forced to tinkle his bell in order to demand silence. And through the noise, the cries and the hisses, the questions and answers, the one sound that was never drowned, and never was still, was the click-click of hundreds of knitting-needles.

The first batch of prisoners to face the Tribunal, were men and women almost unknown to Fleurette. They had not long been brought into the Caristie House, had replaced others who had been Fleurette's early companions in prison. She had seen them in the common room, acting in the grim farces that were the fashion there, but she had not made friends with them as she had done with Claire de Châtelard or Madame de Mornas. But when came the turn of a woman who had actually been her room-mate, who had sat next to her on the bench of the accused, and squeezed her hand ere she was led up to the raised platform with the wooden railing, then, Fleurette felt all her resolution of bravery and trust in Bibi giving way.

The heat in the room had become unbearable. The stench of dank and grimy clothes, of perspiring humanity, of hot breaths charged with hate, acted as a pungent soporific. Fleurette's head fell forward once or twice, her eyes involuntarily closed. For a time she lost consciousness. It was her own name spoken in a stentorian voice that brought her back to reality.

"Fleur Chauvelin, *nommée* Armand."

Someone nudged her elbow. An impatient voice rasped out a sharp: "Allons! allons!" and she found herself dragged to her feet and led by the arm to the raised platform, amidst a din which fortunately was too great to allow her ears to catch individual sounds.

She looked straight across to Bibi, who was as pale as a waxen image.

"Fleur Chauvelin, *nommée* Armand."

Thirty-five

There is no doubt that everything would have gone well, had it not been for Fleurette herself. Perhaps "well" is the wrong word: "differently" would be better. Nothing could have gone "well," because even though Chauvelin had succeeded in obtaining an acquittal, his enemies would have returned immediately to the charge, and forced on the girl's re-arrest even before she had left the Tribunal. There had been cases during the past few weeks, in Paris, in Lyons and so on, when prisoners were acquitted and re-arrested, re-tried, acquitted again, and again re-arrested. A regular cat-and-mouse game, at which Chauvelin himself was an adept. Nevertheless with a first acquittal there might have been some hope. And he practically had obtained that acquittal, when Fleurette herself ruined her chance, and caused her own condemnation. Chauvelin could have struck her for her folly. His love for her always pertained to that of a wild beast for its young; the instinct to devour in moments of peril. If she was destined to perish, then it should be by his own hand, not as a spectacle for the rabble to gloat on.

The *Moniteur* of the 22nd Messidor gives one or two interesting details concerning the trial of a country girl named Fleur Chauvelin, daughter of a Citizen Armand Chauvelin of the Central Committee of Public Safety, and member of the National Convention, and relates at full length the, extraordinary incidents which marked its close. Looking back upon that memorable day, and on the solemn hour which saw

the girl Fleur Chauvelin *nommée* Armand called to the bar
of the accused, we visualize Chauveun, the father, presiding
over that Tribunal of infamy, and having sent within the last
half-hour half a dozen fellow-creatures callously to death, now
seeing his own daughter, the only being in all the world whom
he had ever loved, standing there before him, accused,
condemned already in the eyes of the *canaille*.

There was no time wasted during the proceedings, wherein
the accused was allowed neither jury nor advocate. The State as
represented by its three nominees who sat as judges, was judge
and jury and prosecutor all in one. It was men like Chauvelin
who had invented this travesty of justice and eliminated all
procedure devised by civilization for the protection of the
accused.

The Public Prosecutor opened the proceedings by reading
the indictment in mechanical monotone; it was identically the
same as that framed against hundreds of others – guilty or
innocent alike – the printed formula invented by the odious
Foucquier-Tinville in which the words "Traitor," and "Enemy
of the Republic" were alone intelligible. All else was a jumble of
words. The crowd was not listening. Their attention was fixed
on the accused whose modest bearing and spotless attire
seemed to arouse their spite and their derision, more than the
rags and filth displayed by a previous prisoner had done.

When the reading of the indictment came to an end, Pochart
sitting beside the Presiding Judge asked the usual question:

"Is the prisoner accused publicly or in secret?"

And the Public Prosecutor replied: "Publicly."

Danou, the third judge then asked: "By whom?"

And again the Public Prosecutor gave reply:

"By one Adèle," he said, "of unknown parentage, and by
Citizen Lieutenant Godet of the revolutionary army."

"And to what will these persons testify?"

"To the treason committed against the State by the accused
and to her connection with the enemies of the Republic."

After which Adèle was called. Her small rat-like face looked wan and pinched; her hands trembled visibly, and she wiped them continually against the ragged apron which she wore. She was obviously very nervous and never looked once in the direction of the accused, but she spoke clearly enough in a shrill, high-pitched voice. Questioned at first by the Public Prosecutor, she presently embarked more glibly upon her story, relating the events which were intended to condemn Fleurette. Chauvelin already knew the tale by heart. The soldiers on the bridge. The raid on the château. Fleurette's halt that evening in the cottage of the widow Tronchet. Her assignation, through Adèle, with Amédé Colombe. The casket and wallet underneath her shawl, then transferred into young Colombe's keeping.

Ofttimes Chauvelin tried to break into the girl's narrative; he put stern questions to her, tried to intimidate her, to trip her into mis-statements of obvious contradictions. But Adèle held her ground. Informer, ingrate, wanton though she was, she was speaking the truth and was not to be shaken. Hisses and boos from the crowd oft greeted the President's cross-questionings, cries of approbation greeted Adèle's spirited rejoinders. In the wordy warfare between herself and Chauvelin, she scored nearly every time. Encouraged by the sympathy of the rabble, she lost her nervousness, whilst he gradually lost his self-control. He had so much at stake, and she nothing but the satisfaction of vanity and of spite.

"Be not intimidated, citizeness," Pochart put in forcefully at one moment, "let not powerful influences sway you from your duty."

"Vas-y Adèle of unknown parentage!" one of the women shouted from above. "'Twas some aristo doubtless who betrayed thy mother. Let this aristo at least pay for her kind."

Amidst thunderous applause Adèle stepped down from the bar. Chauvelin tried in vain to command silence, he was shouted down by the crowd.

"Thou'rt a true patriot, Citizen Chauvelin," one woman called out lustily. "To have a traitor for a daughter is a curse. Her death will not be for thee a sacrifice."

He waited in seeming patience, white to the lips, until the tumult had subsided, then calling all his reserves of strength, moral and mental, to his aid, he said in a calm firm voice:

"The witness has lied. The events which she has described could not have taken place in her presence seeing that on that day and at that hour she was in my house, at Lou Mas, half a league away."

This pronouncement was greeted with mighty uproar. Derisive laughter, cat's calls, whistling, strident shouts made riotous confusion. Only two persons in the crowded room appeared serene. One was the accused, the other her judge. The *Moniteur* says that throughout the whole proceedings the attitude of the accused was astonishingly calm: "d'unc sérénité étonnante." She looked straight before her, sometimes at the President, but more often her eyes appeared to be fixed on the tricolour flag draped over the wall above his head, and ornamented with a red cap and the words writ largely: "Liberté, Egalité, Fraternité ou la Mort."

And so too was the President equally serene. Outwardly. He stood upright whilst the turmoil continued, with head erect and hands held behind his back. Insults and jeers flew at him from every side. But he never winced. The rabble called him, "Traitor, Liar, Tyrant!" and various other names impossible to record. But he waited in seeming patience until the crowd, eager to hear more, fell to comparative stillness once more. Then Pochart's rasping voice cut through the silence, like the sound of a file against metal.

"You'll have to substantiate that statement, Citizen President," he said.

"My statements need no substantiation," Chauvelin retorted coolly. "The word of a representative of the people is sufficient against any witness."

And while Pochart was considering a suitable repartee, Danou put in smoothly.

"Should we not hear the next witness, Citizen Lieutenant Godet, before we discuss the matter?"

"Yes, yes!" the crowd yelled in response.

Scenting the unusual, the crowd was more excited than was its wont. Of late these hasty trials, six to the hour, with condemnation as a foregone conclusion, had become monotonous. One condemnation had been very much like another. But here was something novel. The rumour had already spread like wildfire that the accused was no less than the daughter of the President, Citizen Chauvelin, who was well known in the councils of State, a prominent member of many committees, and, some said, a personal friend of the great Robespierre. Here in truth was a test of supreme patriotism; a judge called upon to condemn his own daughter if she be guilty. And of course she was guilty, or she would not be here. There was no sympathy for either of them, only interest in the issue of this amazing trial. The crowd did not like the prisoner's attitude, what they called her aristocratic airs and disdainful ways; even the children pointed grimy little fingers at her and hurled the poisonous darts of loathsome epithets at the aristo.

Thus was the scene prepared for the entrance of Lieutenant Godet, who stepped up to the witness' platform with a display of self-assurance and a swagger that charmed the women. He was a man after their own heart, a real sansculotte in grimy rags, unkempt, unshaved, unwashed, the type of which the martyr Jean Paul Marat had been the most perfect exponent.

Conversations, objurgations, murmurs even were stilled; the click-click of knitting-needles alone made a soft accompaniment to Citizen Godet's replies to the Public Prosecutor's preliminary questions. It was indeed a remarkable, an amazing, an almost unbelievable tale, which he had to tell. And gradually as he unfolded the various details of this extraordinary adventure a hush fell over the crowded room, very like the calm which Nature assumes ere she sends forth the thunders of her wrath.

Godet, still with this air of self-assurance, related how he and the soldiers under his command, as well as the whole commune of Laragne had been tricked by a band of English spies whose actions proved them to have been in league with Amédé Colombe and with the accused. He told of the magnificently dressed soldiers. Their raid on the premises of Colombe the grocer of the Rue Haute. Their march through the village. Their captain's swagger. His orders to himself, Godet, and to the real soldiers of the revolutionary army.

Still the crowd gave no sign of approbation, or disapprobation. Only that ominous, expectant hush which presaged a storm. The accused, always serene, smiled – so the *Moniteur* avers – as she encountered the President's glance. Smiled cheerfully and trustfully. But the President's face was inscrutable, and the colour of wax.

And then Godet went on to relate the long, weary tramp along the mountain roads. The dust. The fatigue. The want of food. He told how ci-devant Frontenac and Amédé Colombe, wrested from the hands of justice, were presently taken to some unknown place of safety, while the soldiers of the Republic were left by the wayside, to perish of fatigue or inanition.

He had finished speaking, and still the click-click of the knitting-needles was the only sound that broke the silence. The witness, sensing this silence, feeling its menace, had lost something of his arrogance; the hand with which he stroked his shaggy moustache trembled perceptibly. The accused, overcome by the heat, wiped her forehead with the corner of her apron, then she smiled once more across at her father.

And suddenly through the solemn stillness a woman's shrill voice was raised.

"Those English spies did make a fool of thee, I am thinking, Citizen Godet!"

This suddenly relieved the tension. It was like a dam let loose. In a moment every kind of call and of cry, of laughter and of groan rang from end to end of the room.

"The English have made a fool of thee!"

Within a minute or two this became a general cry, accompanied by the stamping of feet, and loud and prolonged laughter, both malevolent and derisive. Godet, ludicrous in his bewilderment, rolled terror-filled eyes, whilst vainly trying to raise his voice above the din. The *Moniteur* says definitely that the accused put her hands to her ears. The uproar was in truth deafening.

A few moments of this confusion, and the next, Chauvelin was on his feet clanging his bell. His stentorian voice rose above the tumult, demanded silence, and in the lull that presently ensued, that same voice, now subdued to a lower, though no less impressive key, rang clear and calm.

"Is it not an insult, citizen patriots, to ask you to listen to the words of a fool, when the life of a French girl is at stake?"

The passionate earnestness with which he spoke, the burning indignation expressed in that calm, subdued voice, had the effect of awing the screaming rabble. They turned to gaze on him, as he stood there, facing them all, calm, proud, almost majestic, despite his small stature. Seizing this sudden advantage he began to speak. Without a gesture, hardly raising his voice, he began quietly, not choosing his words, or striving after eloquence, but only as a man speaking to his friends. And by one of those inexplicable reactions which will so often change the temper of a crowd, men, women and children ceased to curse and to deride. The innumerable eyes were fixed with more curiosity than malevolence upon him, the mouths, agape, uttered no further groan, and once more the click-click of knitting-needles was momentarily stilled.

"Citizens," he said, "you have heard two witnesses against the accused. One of these, the wench Adèle, I myself, representative of the people, have convicted of deliberate falsehood, spoken to the prejudice of a French patriot. The other your own words have condemned for a fool, and an easy tool in the hands of English spies. You called him a fool, citizens, but I call him a traitor. Lieutenant Godet was not a tool in the hands of the English spies, he was their confederate, their help. Can you bring yourselves to believe, citizens, that a loyal soldier of the Republic could be deceived by false uniforms, by French words spoken by alien lips? Can you believe this story of a forced march, of starvation by the wayside in the company of English spies whose every action, every word, every gesture almost, must have betrayed them as the foreigners they actually were. Citizens, I appeal to that reputation for clear thinking and for logic, for which French men and women are famous throughout the world. At this hour, when our beloved country is threatened on every side, is this the time, I say, for allowing yourselves to be duped by traitors who would sell you and your land, your dues and your liberty for English gold – ?"

"No! no!" came a lusty shout in response. And the crowd took up the cry. "No! We'll not sell our liberties for English gold."

"Say on, Citizen Representative."

Pochart had jumped to his feet; once or twice he had tried to break in on Chauvelin's peroration, with cries of: "Thou'rt slandering a soldier of the Republic!" or: "Traitor! thou'rt in league with thy daughter!"

But he was not listened to. There was something about Chauvelin which fascinated the mob. His white, calm face, his pale, piercing eyes, his voice, dull, even monotonous, but penetrating to the most distant corners of the room. And there was also that welcome element of novelty. This pleased the women. Trials and condemnations in incessant routine had begun to pall. Here was something new. Witnesses summoned, then discredited, and finally accused. Such a thing had never been witnessed before in Orange.

And so the crowd would not listen to Pochart or Danou, they wanted to hear Chauvelin; they did not particularly wish to see

Fleurette *nommée* Armand acquitted, but they did relish the prospect of the two witnesses being sent to the bench of the accused. That was novelty for them, and it was what they wanted for the moment. Moreover they did think that the citizen lieutenant with all his swagger had been such a consummate fool, if no worse, that it would be distinctly amusing to see that stupid head of his roll down into the basket of the guillotine.

Neither Pochart nor Danou, however, were men to give up the struggle quite so easily. In the fight against the representative on special mission, who had threatened them and lorded it over them for so long, they only contemplated one issue: victory. Victory! which would mean satisfaction of pride and of revenge. They had set out to win and did not consider themselves beaten. Not yet. Already Pochart was on his feet, and his rasping voice rose booming above the tumult. As soon as a slight lull gave him an opportunity he seized it, and cried in thunderous accents:

"Citizens! French men! French women! All of you!" And then again: "Citizens all! Let me put the same question to you, that the President asked you just now: will you allow yourselves to be duped? Will you go like sheep whithersoever traitors may lead you?"

The crowd murmured and shrugged shoulders, would have shouted Pochart down only that that rasping voice of his rose above the cry of: "À la lanterne, all traitors and fools!"

Pointing an accusing finger at Chauvelin, Pochart took up the cry.

"So say I," he roared in a terrific straining of his powerful lungs: "À la lanterne all the traitors who try to throw dust in your eyes. Have you forgotten that the Citizen President is the father of the accused? And that he knows well enough that if the child be guilty, then is the parent guilty too? To save himself he is trying to shield a traitor. Do not allow yourselves to be duped by him. Look on the Citizen President, my friends, and ask him how it comes about that he lavished all the treasures of his eloquence upon this one traitor, when yesterday, and the day before that, he sent to the guillotine every man, woman and child who came before the Tribunal, and on a mere suspicion of treason."

A dull murmur greeted this peroration. There had been something in Pochart's eloquence which caused the crowd not to veer round just yet, but at any rate to look on the President of the Tribunal with rather less awe, and something approaching suspicion.

"That is true," a woman said loudly. "The President showed no mercy to traitors yesterday. And it is treason now to be as much as suspected of treason, we've been told."

"It is my duty to protect the innocent," Chauvelin retorted firmly, "as well as to punish the guilty."

"Methinks," Danou now broke in, and his slow and suave tones came in strange contrast to the clamorous eloquence of his colleagues: "methinks that the traitor Danton made some such remark too, ere justice put her hand on him."

"Danton was a traitor, and thou too, Citizen Danou, art a traitor for speaking his name in this hall of justice."

"Justice!" Pochart cried, pallid with rage, for he had felt that the word "traitor" hurled at Danou was meant to strike him also. "Justice! hark at the traitor, who should be standing in the dock beside his brood."

"Vas-y, Citizen President," the women cried excitedly. "It is thy turn now."

They had cast aside their knitting, so palpitating had this duel become between these three men. Insensate, doltish as they were, they scented the tragedy that underlay this wordy warfare; they guessed that the man who presided over this infamous tribunal and who with a casual stroke of the pen had sent hundreds indiscriminately to death, had one soft corner in his callous heart, and that his colleagues, consumed with envy and hatred, were hitting at that vulnerable spot and had already succeeded in making him writhe in agony.

At the same time, such is the psychology of a multitude as against that of individuals, there was still a wave of sympathy tending in the direction of this father fighting so desperately for the life of his child, Strictly speaking, it was not sympathy, rather was it mere instinctive understanding of family ties. Five years of this awful revolution, during which every cruel lust in man or woman had been sedulously fostered, every softer mood repressed, had not yet succeeded in crushing altogether that feeling for family solidarity which is the most distinctive characteristic of the French nation. And this spectacle of a father sitting in judgment over his own child, and actually expected to pronounce the death-sentence over her, did undoubtedly for the time being sway the crowd in his favour. He was given a more respectful hearing than either of his colleagues or either of the witnesses, and when Godet's name recurred on the tapis, it was greeted with derisive cries of "Cet imbécile!" and when Adèle was mentioned, most of the women shouted spitefully: "Liar!"

Chauvelin, sensitive of course to the slightest wavering in the temper of the populace, felt his advantage and strained every nerve to press it home. The whole situation was of course terribly precarious. At any moment a look, a word, a false move on his part, might cause the crowd to veer right over against him. Even after an acquittal sometimes, the populace would suddenly demand that the accused be re-arrested: a second trial, more of a mockery and a travesty of justice than the first, would be insisted on, after which condemnation was a foregone conclusion. All this Chauvelin knew, none better, and there were moments when he felt as if madness or death were preferable to this terrible fight that in the end could have but one issue. And yet fight he must, fight for every inch of ground, fight with the last breath in his body, and with it silence the vituperations of those fiends who had raised their noisome voices against his Fleurette.

Even now Pochart was on his feet again, shouting, gesticulating, banging his fist upon the table.

"Citizens," he reiterated for the third time, "do not let yourselves be duped by men who are ruining your country by pandering to traitors. Look at the accused! I say she is nothing but a wanton, who should be tied to the whipping-post ere she be sent to the guillotine. Look at the aristocrat, I say, with the demure airs and the folded kerchief; she, forsooth, goes forth o' nights to meet her lover under the almond trees, there to concoct treason with her lover against the Republic. She was seen, remember, seen, I say, in spite of what interested parties may aver. You have heard the witness, a humble, simple girl, the victim of aristocratic lust and of tyranny. That witness spoke the truth. She saw the accused and her lover at dead of night whispering and embracing. I ask you, does a clean-minded, respectable woman, citizen of our glorious Republic, spend her nights in the company of her lover? Rather is it not the wanton, the traitor, who shuns the light of day and seeks the darkness, for the hatching of treasonable plots against the State? Look at the witness, citizens. Humbly and simply did she speak the truth – "

"She lied as well you know it, Citizen Pochart," Chauvelin broke in forcefully. "Liar, forger and thief, I decree her accused and command that she stand her trial for these offences against the Republic. Look at her, my friends, citizens all," he went on, and pointed an accusing finger at Adèle whose pinched little face had become the colour of lead, and who sat in a corner of the witness' bench, cowering within herself, her trembling hands, now and then, lifting a handkerchief to wipe the sweat of terror that had risen to her brow. "Look at her," Chauvelin continued, appealing to the sea of faces before him: "And now look at the accused. She is serene, because she is innocent, whilst the guilty trembles because she knows her treachery has come to light at last. Look at those two women, citizens, and yourselves pronounce which is the traitor and which is the stainless."

Of a truth all would have been well after that. Chauvelin passed a quivering hand across his brow. It was streaming with moisture. The strain had been immense. Mentally he felt broken by the effort. But he also felt that for the moment at least he had won the day. The *Moniteur* states definitely that: "ily eût tout lieu de croire qu'un acquittement eût été applaudi." At any rate the applause at the moment was deafening, and if Chauvelin' could have obtained a hearing for another sixty seconds he would have put the acquittal to the populace vote, and, as the *Moniteur* says, it would have been carried.

What would have happened afterwards nobody can say. The most fickle entity in the world is a multitude, and of all the multitudes, an audience watching the suffering of a fellow-creature is the most fickle and the most callous. For the next two or three minutes, at any rate, Chauvelin held the sympathy of the crowd. Fleurette did not count either way. For the spectators of this heartrending pageant she was just a thing, an insentient object placed there for their entertainment, the pivot round which circled their excitement. But Chauvelin, the father pleading for his daughter's life, had won their sympathy – the sympathy of tiger-cats, satiated for the moment and licking their chops in the intervals of snarling.

All then would have been well but for the action of one of the sympathizers who stood leaning up against the wall in the crowd; a giant he was, coated with grime – coal-heaver or scavenger probably, only half clad in ragged shirt and torn breeches, with dirty feet thrust stockingless into sabots, a red worsted cap over his unkempt hair, his face streaked with sweat and coal-dust. In one hand he held a large raw carrot which he was munching with loud snapping of the jaws and smacking of the lips. He was one of the noisiest in his approval of the President's peroration.

"Vas-y, Président," he shouted. "À la lanterne, the fools and traitors. Where is that trollop? Let her stand up. We want to look at her, eh, citizens?"

"Yes! Yes! we want to see her! Stand up, Adèle of unknown parentage! Let's look at you."

The women, of course, were the loudest in their demand for the unfortunate Adèle. Bred by misery, often out of degradation, trained by five years of an execrable revolution, the women of France were not *féministes* these days. The spectacle of one of their own sex on the guillotine gave them more satisfaction than that of a man. Now they wanted to see Adèle of the pinched, rat-like face, Adèle with the trembling hands and the shrinking shoulders, they wanted to see her squirm before their wrath, they wanted to see her wriggle like a worm prodded with a pin. Incidentally they had almost forgotten Fleurette.

Louder and even louder they clamoured for Adèle, and at an order from the President two soldiers of the National Guard did presently drag Adèle from the corner of the witness' bench where she was cowering like a frightened rodent, and dragged her – or rather carried her – to the bar of the accused. The crowd, seeing that its dictates were being obeyed, restrained its frenzy for an instant, and, through the comparative stillness that ensued, a piercing shriek rang out from the unfortunate Adèle.

"Mercy! Mercy!" she cried and struggled fiercely to free herself from the men's grasp. "I am innocent! I spoke the truth."

A thunderous shout of derisive laughter greeted her cry. The women, with their hands on their knees, were literally rocking with laughter. They thought that Adèle with a face like a rat, wisps of lank hair poking out from underneath her cap which sat all awry, with mouth wide open uttering shrieks which no one could hear through the deafening tumult, was supremely funny.

The President made no attempt to quell the disturbance. It was all to the good. The greater the hatred against Adèle, the

greater his chance, not only of forcing an acquittal now for
Fleurette, but also of keeping the wave of sympathy for himself
at full-tide, until he had the opportunity of getting Fleurette out
of Orange. He was striving with all his might to catch his
darling's eye. But Fleurette's glance was fixed on Adèle. She
seemed to him to be fascinated with horror, mute and paralysed.
She was looking on Adèle, and her dear little hand was fidgeting
the corner of her kerchief.

Through the ear-splitting uproar led by the women, Pochart
and Danou, their sympathizers, men of their own choosing,
vainly tried to get a hearing. As well try to shout down a
tempestuous sea as these hundreds of women gloating over the
spectacle of one of their own sex writhing in an agony of
terror.

"Hein !" came in a stentorian shout from the grimy giant in
the rear of the crowd; "thou wouldst slander the innocent girl
with lies. Take that for thy pains."

And he hurled the remnant of his raw carrot over the head
of the intervening crowd at the unfortunate Adèle. It missed her
by a hairbreadth, but the action delighted the crowd. They took
up the cry: "Take that for thy pains!" and sent various missiles
flying at the girl, who, crouching down on her knees, lay there
like a bundle of goods just below the bar of the accused where
Fleurette stood, gazing down at her, fascinated with horror.

Looking back later on that terrible moment, Chauvelin felt
that it was the action of the grimy coal-heaver – or scavenger,
whatever he was – that precipitated the catastrophe. He it was
who egged on the rabble to virulent hatred against Adèle. It
was he who by hurling that first missile at the girl brought in a
further, more immense element of cruelty and horror into the
situation. Certain it is that up to that moment Fleurette had
appeared more dazed than horrified. She must even in her own
gentle heart have felt a burning indignation against Adèle for
the treacherous part which she had played, and if the girl's
arrest had been effected outside the Tribunal, she would

perhaps never have actually realized what had brought it about. But with that shout of "Thou wouldst slander the innocent girl with thy lies," full consciousness returned to her, and with it the recollection of everything that had gone before. Chauvelin, who watched her with the devouring gaze of his love, saw as in a flash, through the quick glance which swept from Adèle to himself and thence over the sea of perspiring faces, the full workings of her mind.

He tried to keep the tumult going; he hoped that Fleurette would faint, so that she might be carried out of court. He prayed that the roof of the gigantic building would come crashing down and bury him and Fleurette and all that swinish multitude in its ruins ere she spoke the words which he saw hovering on her lips.

But none of these things happened. Rather by that perversity which is peculiar to Chance, a sudden lull broke in on the mighty uproar, a lull through which Fleurette's calm voice rang clear as water poured into a crystal glass.

"Adèle was not lying, nor did she slander me, I did give some valuable articles into the keeping of my beloved M'sieu' Amédé Colombe, at the hour spoken of by her, and I have no doubt that she did see me, as she says."

Thirty-six

One must of necessity turn once more to the *Moniteur* of the 22nd Messidor year II of the Republic One and Indivisible. There in the *Choix des Rapports XXV*. 516–17, despite its sobriety of language and paucity of detail, there is ample proof that throughout the proceedings it was the action of one unknown that precipitated the final catastrophe. "Un géant," we are told, "fût le premier à lancer l'accusation fausse contre le Président du Tribunal, et un tumulte irrépressible s'ensuivit."

"False," you observe. But on that 16th day of June, 1794, Chauvelin of the National Convention, member of commitees and confidant of Robespierre, did, we know, stand in danger of being dragged out into the open and hung on the nearest lamp-post. The crowd was in no mood even to wait for the paraphernalia of the guillotine. They wanted to see the arch-traitor, the perjurer, who had sworn false oaths and lied in order to save himself and his brood, hang then and there. The giant spoken of in the *Choix des Rapports* had, it seems, hardly waited till the words were out of Fleurette's mouth, before he pushed his way to the forefront of the crowd, with vigorous play of his powerful elbows. Down, he was now, in the body of the court. In the struggle, his ragged shirt had been half torn off his shoulders, and his broad chest and sinewy arms could he seen, nude and immense, and coated with grime. Out of one of the pockets of his tattered breeches he had produced another uncooked carrot, and into this he bit lustily, then with a wide sweep of the arm he launched one by one against the President of the Tribunal the damning invectives which the *Moniteur* has characterized as false. "Traitor!" he cried. "Liar and perjurer! Citizens all, have you in all your lives ever witnessed such infamy?"

The *Choix des Rapports* describes the tumult as irrepressible. Indeed at that moment it would have been easier to dam a raging torrent with one pair of hands, than to suppress the riotous confusion that ensued. Fleurette of a truth stood there forgotten, so did Adèle and Godet. All eyes were fixed on the President, every menacing gesture tended in his direction, all the strident cries, the insults, the varied and foul epithets were hurled against him. There were but few sober tempers in that crowded room at the moment. A dozen perhaps: no more. Older men, one or two women who watched rather than yelled. And what they saw interested and puzzled them, so much that, when the time came, when everybody else was shouting themselves hoarse to the verge of mania, they still kept cool and silent.

Like everybody else these few were gazing on the President. They saw him standing there on the bench like a figure carved in stone, and, like a stone, his face was of a grey, ashen colour. His eyes looked dim and colourless as if a hand had drawn a film over them; his lips were parted, his nostrils distended. The breath seemed to come with difficulty out of his lungs. A figure, in truth, of terror and despair. But calm and still. Motionless as a stone. The giant munching his carrot had waved his huge arms about and yelled himself hoarse until he had lashed all the spectators into a state of frenzy. Finally he strode across the room, and came to a halt close to the judges' bench facing the President.

The three judges had been watching him all along:

Pochart and Danou with undisguised glee, and President Chauvelin with that stony stare out of his colourless eyes. But even as the giant approached, Chauvelin, though apparently motionless, seemed inwardly to sink within himself, to crouch as a hunted beast in face of the menacing enemy. And suddenly, like that of an automaton, up went his arm. With finger outstretched he pointed at the giant and one word escaped his trembling, rigid lips.

"You!"

Those who were watching him could not understand the word, for it was spoken in an alien tongue. Nor could they understand what happened afterwards. But what actually did happen was that the grimy giant threw back his head and gave a quaint and altogether pleasant laugh.

"Why, yes!" he said in the same alien tongue, which no one present understood. "At your service, my dear M. Chambertin."

And Chauvelin murmured almost under his breath:

"You have your revenge at last, Sir Percy."

"Hitting back as you see, my friend."

It all passed unperceived in the midst of the irrepressible tumult, save by those few who sober-tempered chose to watch rather than to yell. It is doubtful whether even Pochart and Danou, who sat close by, saw anything of this brief, this mysterious scene.

The very next moment the grimy giant, this time with a hoarse and not at all pleasant laugh, had hurled his half-munched carrot straight into the President's face. Then facing the crowd once more he threw up his great arms high above his head.

"Why should we wait, citizens," he shouted louder than the rest of the yelling crowd. "À la lanterne, I say, the traitor and his brood. The guillotine is ready outside the Place. The executioner is to hand. Why wait?"

Nothing could have pleased the crowd better. They were all like tigers scenting blood, demanding it, licking their jaws in anticipation.

"Who is for a front place for the spectacle?" a man shouted from the rear of the crowd.

"À moi! the front place," a woman cried in response.

"À moi! À moi!" came from every side.

Then the general scramble began. A stampede down the gradients. The clatter of wooden sabots against the floor. The screams of women and children pushed and squeezed by the crowd. The grounding of arms, the click of bayonets, the words of command from the officer in charge of the guard, who were there to maintain order and who were quite powerless. They did of a truth try to stem the mob, to prevent the mad rush, the trampling, the stampede. But there were in reality too few of them for the task. All available fighting men being required for the army abroad, these were for the most part too inexperienced and too incompetent; raw recruits, half-trained for a wholly inadequate corps of *gendarmerie*. The officers did what they could, but the men themselves were soon caught in the vortex. Having no idea of discipline or duty, they soon became just a part of the mob, allowed themselves to be carried along by the crowd. They were just as excited, just as eager to see the President of a revolutionary tribunal sent summarily to the guillotine, as anyone else. Their lust for the spectacle was as keen as that of any ragamuffin in the place. They were but half-trained ragamuffins themselves, and as every man these days was at least as good as his officer and owed him neither obedience nor respect, it was small wonder that in emergencies like these the soldiers got out of hand, whilst the officers, shrugging their shoulders, viewed the scene with indifference.

In the meanwhile the grimy giant had effectually fought his way along the floor of the house as far as the bar of the accused, where Fleurette, wide-eyed, deathly pale, half crazy now with terror, had just fallen forward unconscious across the railing, drooping like a lily that is battered by the storm.

"And à moi the traitors," the giant shouted, and it was marvellous how his booming voice rang above the uproar and the confusion.

He dragged Fleurette's inanimate body from the bar and flung it over his shoulder, as if it were a bundle of goods. Then with two huge strides he was right in front of the judges' bench, and there turned back to face the crowd again.

"Take your places for the spectacle, citizens," he cried. "I'll bring the actors along."

He looked almost unreal as he stood there, dominating the crowd, grimy, unkempt, immense, with blackened face and huge bare chest, and the inanimate body of the girl across his massive shoulders. He seemed a being from another world, a Titan, a monster, a fiend-like fury, the embodiment of all the hates and the furies that animated the rest of the crowd. They glanced at him and trembled; some of them, who had not wholly forgotten their age and innocence, surreptitiously crossed themselves.

"Take your places for the spectacle, citizens," he went on lustily. "One actor I have ready for you. Who will bring the other?"

Three men in the forefront of the crowd were at that moment standing quite close to the judges' bench, where the President lay back in his chair, dead to everything about him, alive only through the intensity of his agony. In response to the Titan's suggestion, which was greeted with loud applause by the crowd, the three men scrambled over the desk, seized the inert person of the President between them. One of them flung a sack over his head. Thus adorned they hoisted him upon their shoulders while the crowd stamped and shouted with glee.

"Un tumulte irrépressible s'ensuivit" says the *Choix des Rapports* in the *Moniteur* of the 22nd Messidor. Tumult is but a poor word to express the actions of that multitude. Men and women and children had become blind, insentient with lust, mad with hatred and excitement.

"Take your places for the spectacle," the Titan shouted, "and I'll bring along the actors for you."

And so they rushed out in a compact, struggling mass, hurrying, scurrying, fighting and pushing and struggling. Out in the open, in the Place de la République, into the sunshine and under the blue vault of Heaven they rushed. The guillotine was set up there ready for its afternoon work, but, as the grimy giant had said, "Why wait?" Why indeed! No one was in a mood for waiting. The blackest traitor this town had ever seen had tried to save himself and his brood by slandering worthy citizens of the République. By the by, where were they? Adèle of unknown parentage and the swaggering Lieutenant Godet? Ah bah! they were forgotten. Lost in the crowd. Who cared? Time enough to cheer them when the traitors and slanderers were punished. Who cared indeed? For the moment the most important thing in the world was to secure a place of vantage for witnessing the wonderful spectacle. The President of a revolutionary tribunal, a representative of the people in the National Convention, was not often to be seen in Orange mounting the steps of the guillotine. That spectacle was reserved for the Parisians – lucky people ! – who saw the heads of ci-devant kings and queens, of generals and dukes and duchesses and of countless other aristos roll into the basket. Therefore everyone scrambled for a good seat. The houses all round the Place were invaded by the mob; windows and balconies were soon filled with eager faces; boys and men swarmed on the roofs, clung to the rain-pipes, the gargoyles on the Hôtel de Ville, the lamp-posts and lamp-brackets. Many were injured in the struggle. But that made no matter so long as one got a good seat. Fortunately the weather was glorious. The sun shone gaily on this scene which suggested a coming pageant.

In the centre of the Place, facing the steps of the Hôtel de Ville, the guillotine reared its gaunt arms, painted a vivid red. The officers of the *gendarmerie* had succeeded, by dint of threats, in restoring some semblance of order in the tenue of their men. They now stood at attention round the guillotine on the platform of which the executioner was busy with his grim task.

The crowd around was very still. Something oppressive, unconnected with the heat of midday sun, seemed to hang in the air. People were still pouring out of the Hôtel de Ville, though not in such compact numbers. Gradually these numbers too were thinned. Those that came out last appeared more sober, less excited than the mob that had spread itself all over the Place, shrieking and gesticulating in the manner habitual to these natives of the South.

Some of the last to come out were a group of men well known in Orange, one was the butcher from the Rue Longue, another the innkeeper of 'Les Trois Abeilles', a third kept the haberdashery shop over the bridge. Citizens Pochart and Danou were with them. They were all talking eagerly together as they came down the steps. A group of women were standing close by.

"Are they bringing the traitors?" they asked.

"Yes, Citizen Tartine," the butcher replied, "that fine patriot Rémi, one of the scavengers at the Caristie House, is close behind us, with some of his mates. They've got the traitors between them. We are to give the sign by firing this pistol when the executioner is ready."

He showed the women the pistol which he said Rémi himself had given him.

"The executioner is ready now," the women said, three of them speaking at once.

Citizens Pochart and Danou and the others then walked across the Place to the foot of the guillotine, one of them spoke a few words with the executioner. The crowd of spectators watched with feverish excitement. And presently Citizen Tartine, the butcher, raised his arm and fired a pistol in the air. A number of women shrieked. The excitement was so tense that the loud report sent the others into hysterics. Soon, however, the rumour went round that the pistol-shot was the signal that everything was ready for the spectacle and for the entrance of the chief actors in the play. After which every noise subsided.

The multitude held its breath; a thousand pairs of eyes were fixed on the wide-open portals of the Hôtel de Ville waiting for the grandiose appearance of Rémi the scavenger and his mates bearing the traitors upon their shoulders.

Up on the platform of the guillotine, the executioner was giving a last look to the pulleys. The soldiers stood at attention.

The huge crowd waited.

Thirty-seven

The *Moniteur* does not say much about what happened afterwards. "La foule attendit avec assez de patience," is all it says, "mais personne ne vint."

The portals of the Hôtel de Ville which should have been a frame for the entrance of the principal actors in the last act of the drama, showed nothing but the yawning black emptiness beyond. The crowd waited, says the *Moniteur*, with sufficient patience. They did wait quite happily for ten minutes, agitatedly for twenty. But nobody came. Citizens Pochart and Danou, also Citizen Tartine, the butcher, and three or four others, were seen to make their way back across the Place, to run quickly up the steps of the Hôtel de Ville and subsequently disappear inside its portals. Still the crowd waited, very much as a crowd will wait in a theatre when the entr'acte is too long; some of them hilariously, others with impatient yawns, others again with tapping of feet and presently with murmurs of, "La Lan-terne! La Lan-terne!"

The next thing that happened was the reverberating clang of the portals of the Hôtel de Ville being suddenly closed. Then only did the crowd realize that they were being cheated of the spectacle. Murmurs were loud, and there were some hisses and boos and cat's calls. But on the whole they took the event with extraordinary calm. There was no rioting as indeed might have been expected. A few hotheads tried to create a disturbance by loudly demanding that the executioner be given something to do. Madame la Guillotine should not be cheated of her dinner.

"She's hungry, give her something to eat," was the catchword these hotheads used in order to excite the rest of the crowd. Somehow it did not work. There certainly were a few bouts of fisticuffs, one or two broken heads, the soldiers round the guillotine and those on guard at the street corners did use their bayonets with some effect, but on the whole the crowd was strangely subdued, more inclined to whisper than to shout.

For quite a little while after the portals of the Hôtel de Ville had been closed, they still waited, thinking that perhaps something more was being devised for their entertainment. But as time went on and nothing happened, they thought they might as well get home. It was dinner-time. The children were hungry, and though there was little enough in the larders these days, one had to get home and give them what there was. The whole thing had been strange. Very strange. As men and women wended their way homeward, their thoughts reverted to that titanic figure with the grimy face and huge bare chest, one sinewy arm encircling the body of the wench Fleurette *nommée* Armand, which hung limp across his massive shoulder. He was no mere mortal, that was certain. And though the Government up in Paris had abolished *le bon Dieu*, and declared that it was Citizen Robespierre who was the "Etre Suprême," something of the old superstitions imbibed at their mothers' knees, still lingered in these untutored, undisciplined minds. That the Titan with the flashing eyes and grimy face should have vanished with the traitors whom he and his satellites had seized, was but the fitting ending to his meteoric appearance. The Government might forbid belief in God and the Devil, in Heaven and in hell, but here was proof positive that the Devil did exist. He was black and he was of abnormal stature, he had a great bare chest and strong muscular arms, and – clearest proof of all – he had before the very eyes of the citizens of Orange seized upon two traitors and carried them away with him to limbo.

SIR PERCY HITS BACK

Nothing would take that idea out of the people's mind, and long after these horrible days of the revolution had passed away and men and women had returned to sanity, those who were present on that day in June at the trial of one Fleur Chauvelin *nornmée* Armand, would recount the marvellous story of how the Devil had entered the court-house and spirited the accused away. Only a few knew the true facts of the case, and even so a great deal was left to surmise. Among those who knew was Citizen Tartine, the butcher. And this is what he told his friends when they pressed him with questions. It seems that when the crowd stampeded out of the Hôtel de Ville, he, Tartine, together with Citizens Pochart and Danou who had stepped down from the judges' bench, and three or four other notabilities of the city among whom was Motus, the chief warder of the Caristie House, put their heads together for a moment or two, wondering if something could not be done towards sending the wench Fleurette and her father by a back way to one or other of the prison-houses, with a view to bringing them up for formal trial on the morrow. They did feel, however, that given the present temper of the populace, such a move might prove dangerous to themselves. "The people will demand a victim, two victims, perhaps more," Danou said with a doubtful nod of the head. "They might vent their wrath on us."

That was sound logic, and the project was abandoned almost as soon as it was formulated.

Motus, it seems, then turned familiarly to the giant and said:

"Tiens, Rémi, is it thou?"

"Myself, citizen," the giant replied.

In response to inquiries from the others, Chief Warder Motus then explained that Rémi was a scavenger whom he himself had taken on in the Caristie House for extra work when the regular man fell sick. A splendid patriot, Motus averred. There was, therefore, not the faintest cause for suspicion.

"Come along, all of you," Pochart now said addressing Rémi and his mates. "Bring along the prisoners. The people are waiting."

"Give them time to settle down," Rémi replied with a shrug and laugh. "We are the chief comedians in this play. Do you all go and prepare everything for our entrance."

"You won't tarry?" Danou admonished.

"Not we," Rémi replied. "We're as eager as you for the spectacle, eh, citizens?" he added, turning to his mates who had the President of the Tribunal still between them.

Rémi then took a pistol out of his ragged breeches and handed it to Citizen Tartine.

"When the executioner is ready," he said, "and everything prepared for our entrance, just give us the signal by firing the pistol. We'll be with you a few minutes after that. We've yet another surprise for the spectators," he added with another laugh, "which will delight them and you."

Tartine vowed that not the slightest suspicion entered his head or that of his companions. How could one suspect a patriot vouched for by no less a person than Motus the chief warder? In the end, however, Pochart decided that two men of the *gendarmerie*, one of whom was a sergeant, who were still standing at attention below the judges' bench, should remain with Rémi and his mates and escort them when the time came, on to the Place.

After which the group of notabilities followed the rest of the crowd out into the open. When looking back upon what followed, they all agreed that some fifteen minutes must have gone from the time when they finally left the court-house and took their last look on Rémi and his mates, to that when they returned and found the place empty. They all said that even then, at first glance, no suspicion entered their minds and they stood about for a few minutes talking together, thinking that Rémi was preparing the surprise spectacle which he had promised them. Thinking too that every moment would bring the scavenger back with his mates and the prisoners. Tartine, the butcher, was the first to suspect that there might be something wrong. He crossed the floor of the room, and made his way to the private door which was at the back of the judges' bench and led to some corridors and private rooms, and also to the back of the premises of the Hôtel de Ville, and to a back door which gave on a narrow street that ran parallel with the façade.

The private door was locked, with no key to be seen. But even then, so remote was suspicion from their minds, that Tartine and the others hammered away on the door and called loudly to Rémi. The door was made of solid oak, but Pochart and Tartine were both of them powerful men. Receiving no answer to their call, they searched amidst the litter left pell-mell by the crowd upon the gradients, and found an axe and a leaded stick. Thus armed they attacked the panels of the door, whilst Danou and one of the others wisely thought of closing the portals of the Hôtel de Ville. The oak panels yielded after awhile. The door battered in, fell under the heavy blows dealt by Tartine the butcher with the axe. He and Pochart and two or three of the others striding over the debris, found themselves in a dark corridor. Some twenty paces down the corridor on the right, they came to another door. It was locked, but behind it came a vigorous sound of banging and the door shook now and again as if under heavy blows. Once more the axe was brought into play, the door was smashed in, and as it fell in with a crash it revealed the two men of the *gendarmerie*, with arms and legs securely pinioned, and their crimson caps stuffed into their mouths. One of them had succeeded in rolling along the floor, near enough to the door to kick against it with his otherwise helpless feet.

There could no longer be any doubt. The public had been hoaxed either by an impudent impostor, or by a traitor, bribed to aid the prisoners to escape. The words: "English spies," soon cropped up as did those of Amédé Colombe and Architect Caristie and a host of others. This too, no doubt, was their work.

At least this was the opinion of some, whilst others, headed by Danou, shook their heads dubiously. Citizen Chauvelin was known to be the sworn enemy of those English spies – weren't they called the League of the Scarlet Pimpernel? – and it was Citizen Chauveun and his daughter Fleur who had been so insolently spirited away.

Having hastily released the men of the *gendarmerie*, they all ran down the length of the corridor as swiftly as they could, chiefly because one of the soldiers said that this corridor led ultimately to a back entrance of the Hôtel de Ville. But the building itself was something of a maze, the passages were dark and narrow. It took them all some time to find that back door, and when at last they came upon it, they found it locked.

Once more the axe had to come into play, and time had in the meanwhile slipped by to the tune of some twenty minutes. Nor did the narrow back street reveal any of the secrets of this amazing adventure. Impostors, traitors or English spies, Rémi the scavenger and his mates had disappeared with the two prisoners and taken their secret with them. On the other side of the road there was a row of one-storied, tumbledown houses, inhabited by some of the poorest families in the city. Inquiries at each house in succession revealed but little. Nearly all the inmates had spent their morning as usual watching the trials in the Hôtel de Ville and were not yet home; but in one of the houses a sick woman had, it seems, been standing at the window when she saw four or five men come out of the building opposite. One of them, she said, was very tall and was carrying what she thought was a large bundle on his shoulder. The others were hustling a short, thin man who wore a blue coat and had on a tricolour sash round his waist. They turned sharply to their right and she soon lost sight of them. She thought nothing about the incident, one saw so many strange things these days.

In the meanwhile the crowd on the Place had begun to disperse, the first stragglers were wending their way to their homes. Pochart and Danou, holding high functions in the administration of justice, did not feel that it was incumbent upon them to go hunting for spies. That was the business of the *gendarmerie*, and they parted presently from their friends, declaring their intention of sending immediately for the Chief Commissary of Police. The others, feeling that it was not part of their duty either to run after escaped prisoners, found that they had pressing business to see to at home.

As far as Citizen Tartine, the butcher, was concerned, the incident had no further interest for him, save for the pleasure of recounting his share of the adventure to his numerous friends. A couple more traitors escaped from the clutches of justice, a few more English spies, when already the country swarmed with them, was nothing to worry one's head about.

Pochart and Danou did, on the other hand, worry their heads considerably about it all. They had a burning desire to know just what the English spies did ultimately do with their colleague Chauvelin. They hoped – oh! very ardently – that as soon as the much-vaunted Scarlet Pimpernel discovered that it was his inveterate enemy whom he had rescued from the guillotine, he would either hand him back straightway to the tender mercies of justice, or simply murder him in some convenient and out-of-the-way corner of the district. Pochart and Danou would have preferred the former alternative as being more satisfactory to their wounded vanity and their baffled spite.

Unlike Tartine, they seldom spoke of their experiences in connection with the affair. But their hopes did rise to their zenith when a week or so later President Legrange and Public Prosecutor Isnard returned from their fool's errand to Paris; there could be no doubt that even Robespierre, friend of Chauvelin though he be, would order the punishment of such a consummate liar and traitor.

Thirty-eight

An immense lassitude had held Fleurette in a kind of semi-consciousness, a dreamless sleep from which she woke at intervals, only to open her eyes for a moment, and immediately let the lids, heavy with sleep, fall over them again. It was the reaction insisted on by health and youth against the terrible nerve-strain of that awful day.

During the brief intervals while she had a certain consciousness of things about her, she found herself nestling against chéri Bibi's shoulder! and when, with half-dimmed eyes she looked up at him, and tried to smile between two yawns, she always saw his pale, grave face turned away in profile, gazing straight out before him into the dark recess of the post-chaise, in which apparently they were travelling. She called softly to him once or twice, but he never turned to look at her, only his hand, which felt cold and clammy, would gently stroke her hair.

How long all this lasted, what happened to her in the intervals of sleep, Fleurette never knew, but there came a time when the chaise rattled unpleasantly over the cobble-stones of a city, and lights darted to and fro through the darkness as the vehicle lumbered along through fitfully lighted streets. Fleurette sat up straight, all the sleep suddenly gone out of her eyes.

"Where are we going, chéri Bibi?" she asked. "Do you know?"

"No! I do not," Bibi replied, and his voice sounded hoarse and hollow. "Would to God I did."

Fleurette had never heard him invoke *le bon Dieu* before, and she tried through the gloom to peer into his face.

"But we are out of danger now, chéri?" she asked, wide-eyed, the old terror which had caused her to lose consciousness in that awful court-house once more clutching at her heart.

"I do not know," he murmured mechanically; "would to God I did."

And then, as if recalled to himself by the half-drawn sigh of terror from Fleurette, he seized hold of her, and pressed her head against his breast.

"No! No!" he said hastily, "they cannot harm you whilst I'm here to guard you."

Just then the coach came to a halt, and a moment later the door was thrown open and a gruff voice said:

"Will you descend, citizeness?"

Fleurette, frightened, clung to Bibi. She made no attempt to move. Whereupon the gruff voice resumed:

"If you don't come willingly I shall have to send someone to fetch you."

Fleurette buried her face against Bibi's coat. His arms held her tightly. A minute, perhaps less, went by, and then – suddenly – she heard a voice – a very gentle, very timid voice this time, saying:

"Mam'zelle Fleurette! Oh, Mam'zelle Fleurette, I pray you to turn to me. It is I – Amédé."

What had happened? Was she dreaming? Or had she died of fright and gone straight up to Heaven? Certain it is that she felt a timid hand upon her shoulder, whilst Bibi's hold upon her relaxed.

"Hold up the lantern, man," the gruff voice now broke in upon the delicious silence that ensued, "and let her see that she is not dreaming."

The light of a lantern flashed across Fleurette's eyes, she opened them and turned her head, and found herself gazing on M'sieu' Amédé's pink and moist face, into his kind eyes full of anxiety and of tenderness, upon his mouth which had taught her how to kiss. Gently, slowly, she extricated herself from Bibi's embrace. Gently, slowly, she seemed to glide into Amédé's arms.

He carried her whither she knew not. All she knew was that presently she found herself snuggling in a deep, cosy armchair, and that Amédé was kneeling beside her, with his eyes fixed ecstatically upon her as if she were *la sainte Vierge* herself.

"Where am I, dear M'sieu' Amédé?" she asked.

"At Ste. Césaire, Mam'zelle Fleurette," he replied.

"Where is that?"

"Just outside Nîmes. Your chaise passed through the streets of Nîmes."

"I dare say," she said with a tired little sigh. "I was so sleepy; I didn't know where we were."

"We are under the protection of the bravest men that ever lived," Amédé said slowly. "They saved me from death. They have saved you, Mam'zelle Fleurette."

A shudder went through her. She closed her eyes as if to try and shut away the awful visions which his words had conjured up. But his kind, strong arms encircled her closer, and she nestled against him and once again felt comforted and safe. He told her the entire odyssey of his rescue, from the hour when the mock soldiers entered his father's shop at Laragne, until when his brave rescuers took leave of him outside the derelict cottage by the banks of the Drôme, and he, seeing the pale crescent of the moon rise above the snow-capped crest of La Lance, had solemnly bowed nine times, praying for that joy which today was his at last.

He had spent a few very lonely days in the cottage after that, devoured with anxiety as to the fate of his beloved. He could not eat, he could not sleep. For hours he would watch the filmy crescent of the moon, whose pale light mayhap illumined the window behind which his own Fleurette would also be watching and praying. And three days ago he received the message which he was waiting for. It appeared mysteriously early one morning outside the cottage door. A missive, with a stone put upon it to prevent its being blown away by the wind. How it got there Amédé never knew. It came from the leader of that gallant little league of Englishmen who devoted their lives to helping those in distress. In it he, Amédé, was ordered to walk as far as Crest, to the house of Citizen Marcor the farrier, where he could hire a horse. And then to hie him straightway hither to Ste. Césaire, not sleeping in any wayside inn, but rather in the fields, under shelter of hedges or forest trees, getting food for himself and his horse as best he could. The missive further directed him, on arriving at Ste. Césaire, to seek out an empty house situated in the Rue Basse, and there to wait, for of a surety within two days he would hold his beloved Fleurette in his arms. Amédé had obeyed these commands to the letter. This very morning he had arrived at Ste. Césaire and found the house in the Rue Basse. It was neither empty nor uninhabited. There was furniture in the house, and what's more there were two friends, two fine English heroes, who had been expecting Amédé, and who made him welcome when he arrived. Oh! and didn't Mam'zelle Fleurette think that these Englishmen were the finest and bravest men that ever lived? As for their chief who was known amongst them as the Scarlet Pimpernel (*le mouron rouge*, M'sieu' Amédé called it), he surely was more like one of the mythological gods rather than a mere mortal.

M'sieu' Amédé seemed very anxious to know what Mam'zelle Fleurette thought about all these marvellous adventures, but how could she tell him, how could she talk at all when every time she raised her blue eyes to him, he broke off in the midst of a most exciting narrative in order to ask her in a voice vibrating with passion: "Tu m'aimes Fleurette?"

Thirty-nine

Chauvelin, after he had seen Fleurette safely carried away in her lover's arms, sat for awhile in the dark interior of the coach, staring into the gloom, his folded hands clasped between his knees. His thoughts were in such a whirl that it almost seemed as if he were unconscious. He certainly was insentient; he neither saw, nor heard, nor felt anything save the joy of knowing that his Fleurette was safe. It was only a few minutes – fifteen perhaps – later that a pleasant laugh broke in on his riotous thoughts, and that he became aware of a tall figure sitting beside him in the coach.

"You see, my dear M. Chambertin," the voice which he dreaded most in all the world said suddenly in his ear, "I would not forego the pleasure of bidding you au revoir."

Chauvelin half turned to his enemy, the man whom he had so persistently wronged, so persistently pursued with hatred and with spite. Through the gloom he could just see the outline of the massive figure, wrapped in a dark, caped coat, and of the proud head so nobly held above the firm, somewhat stiff neck.

Did all that this man stood for in the way of heroism and selflessness, strike a chord of shame in the heart of this callous, revolutionary tyrant? Who shall say? Certain it is that for the moment Chauvelin felt awed, and sat there in the gloom, silent, motionless, staring into the black vacancy. But after a second or two his lips uttered mechanically the name that was unpermost in his mind:

"Fleurette?"

"She is under my care," Blakeney said slowly. "Tomorrow at break of day she and her sweetheart will set sail for England with some of my friends. There she will be under the care of the noblest woman in the world, Lady Blakeney, who will take her revenge on you for all the wrong you did her, by lavishing the treasures of her sympathy upon your child."

"Then Fleurette will be happy?" Chauvelin murmured involuntarily.

"Happy, yes! she will soon forget."

"Then I am ready, Sir Percy."

"Ready? For what?"

"My life is at your service. My enemies are waiting for me over in Orange. You have but to send me back thither and your own vengeance will be complete."

For a second or two after that there was silence in the old post-chaise; only Chauvelin's laboured breathing broke the utter stillness of the gloom. Until suddenly a pleasant, mocking laugh struck upon his ear.

"Egad man, you are priceless," quoth Sir Percy gaily. "You must indeed credit me with a total lack of the saving grace, if you think it would amuse me to hand you over to your genial friends over in Orange."

"But I am at your mercy, sir."

"As I and my beloved wife have been once or twice, eh? Well! I am hitting back now. That's all."

"Hitting back?" Chauvelin exclaimed. "You have the power now. I admit it. I am in your hands. My life is at your command."

"La, man!" Sir Percy retorted lightly, "what should I do with your worthless life? For the moment all I want is to make that sweet child up there completely happy by telling her that you are safe and well. After that you may go to the devil for aught I care. You probably will."

"Then," Chauvelin murmured aghast, "you grant me my life, you – "

"I am sending you back safely as far as Nîmes. What happens to you after that I neither know nor care. You have tried to do me such an infinity of wrong at different times, you still hate me so cordially, you – "

He paused for a moment with firm lips tightly pressed together and slender hand clutched upon his knee.

"You are right there, Sir Percy," Chauvelin murmured between his teeth. "God knows how I still hate you, even after this. You have the power to hit back. Why the devil don't you do it?"

Whereupon Sir Percy threw back his head and his merry, infectious laugh woke the slumbering echoes of the sleepy little town.

"La, man," he said, "you're astonishing. Can't you see that this is my way of hitting back?"

BARONESS ORCZY

THE ELUSIVE PIMPERNEL

In this, the sequel to *The Scarlet Pimpernel*, French agent and chief spy-catcher Chauvelin is as crafty as ever, but Sir Percy Blakeney is more than a match for his arch-enemy. Meanwhile the beautiful Marguerite remains wholly devoted to Sir Percy, her husband. Cue more swashbuckling adventures as Sir Percy attempts to smuggle French aristocrats out of the country to safety.

THE LAUGHING CAVALIER

The year is 1623, the place Haarlem in the Netherlands. Diogenes – the first Sir Percy Blakeney, the Scarlet Pimpernel's ancestor – and his friends Pythagoras and Socrates defend justice and the royalist cause. The famous artist Frans Hals also makes an appearance in this historical adventure: Orczy maintains that Hals' celebrated portrait *The Laughing Cavalier* is actually a portrayal of the Scarlet Pimpernel's ancestor.

Baroness Orczy

The League of the Scarlet Pimpernel

More adventures amongst the terrors of revolutionary France. No one has uncovered the identity of the famous Scarlet Pimpernel – no one except his wife Marguerite and his arch-enemy, citizen Chauvelin. Sir Percy Blakeney is still at large, however, evading capture…

Leatherface

The Prince saw a 'figure of a man, clad in dark, shapeless woollen clothes wearing a hood of the same dark stuff over his head and a leather mask over his face'. The year is 1572 and the Prince of Orange is at Mons under night attack from the Spaniards. However Leatherface raises the alarm in the nick of time. The mysterious masked man has vowed to reappear – when his Highness' life is in danger. Who is Leatherface? And when will he next be needed?

BARONESS ORCZY

THE SCARLET PIMPERNEL

A group of titled Englishmen, under the leadership of a mysterious man, valiantly aid condemned aristocrats in their escape from Paris to England during the French Revolution. Their leader is the Scarlet Pimpernel – a man whose audacity and clever disguises foil the villainous agent Chauvelin. Who is he and can he keep one step ahead of the revolutionaries?

THE TRIUMPH OF THE SCARLET PIMPERNEL

It is Paris, 1794, and Robespierre's revolution is inflicting its reign of terror. The elusive Scarlet Pimpernel is still at large – so far. But the sinister agent Chauvelin has taken prisoner his darling Marguerite. Will she act as a decoy and draw the Scarlet Pimpernel to the enemy? And will our dashing hero evade capture and live to enjoy a day 'when tyranny was crushed and men dared to be men again'?

Made in the USA
Lexington, KY
21 April 2013